As the brute sprang she screamed and fell sideways. There was a snarling roar, a horrible choking gurgle and, as she tried to fling herself farther back upon the ground, she saw that the great cat was whirling round and round with her father underneath it. The fore-claws were buried in his shoulders and the hind ones tearing at his body.

She screamed again, half-mad with terror. The leopard suddenly stopped gyrating, then, seizing Henry's neck in its great teeth, it shook him like a rat. A rifle cracked, the leopard leaped sideways across her father's body and then Patricia fainted.

BY DENNIS WHEATLEY

NOVELS

The Launching of Roger Brook
The Shadow of Tyburn Tree
The Rising Storm
The Man Who Killed the King
The Dark Secret of Josephine
The Rape of Venice
The Sultan's Daughter
The Wanton Princess
Evil in a Mask
The Ravishing of Lady Mary
    Ware

The Scarlet Impostor
Faked Passports
The Black Baroness
V for Vengeance
Come into My Parlour
Traitors' Gate
They Used Dark Forces

The Prisoner in the Mask
The Second Seal
Vendetta in Spain
Three Inquisitive People
The Forbidden Territory
The Devil Rides Out
The Golden Spaniard
Strange Conflict
Codeword—Golden Fleece
Dangerous Inheritance

Gateway to Hell
The Quest of Julian Day
The Sword of Fate
Bill for the Use of a Body

Black August
Contraband
The Island Where Time Stands
    Still
The White Witch of the South
    Seas

To the Devil—a Daughter
The Satanist

The Eunuch of Stamboul
The Secret War
The Fabulous Valley
Sixty Days to Live
Such Power is Dangerous
Uncharted Seas
The Man Who Missed the War
The Haunting of Toby Jugg
Star of Ill-Omen
They Found Atlantis
The Ka of Gifford Hillary
Curtain of Fear
Mayhem in Greece
Unholy Crusade

SHORT STORIES

Mediterranean Nights   Gunmen, Gallants and Ghosts

HISTORICAL

A Private Life of Charles II (*Illustrated by Frank C. Papé*)
Red Eagle (*The Story of the Russian Revolution*)

AUTOBIOGRAPHICAL

Stranger than Fiction (*War Papers for the Joint Planning Staff*)
Saturdays with Bricks

IN PREPARATION

The Devil and all his Works (*Illustrated in colour*)

Dennis Wheatley

THE FABULOUS VALLEY

ARROW BOOKS

ARROW BOOKS LTD
3 Fitzroy Square, London W1

An imprint of the Hutchinson Publishing Group

London Melbourne Sydney Auckland
Wellington Johannesburg Cape Town
and agencies throughout the world

First published by
Hutchinson & Co. (Publishers) Ltd 1953
Arrow edition 1953
Sixth impression 1972
This edition 1975

Made and printed in Great Britain
by The Anchor Press Ltd
Tiptree, Essex

ISBN 0 09 905780 8

Contents

1

The Heirs Apparent of John Thomas Long

The rain ran in little trickles down the narrow panes of the window in the lawyer's waiting-room. The clerk stood in the doorway twisting his knobbly hands with a servile smirk.

'I am sorry, Mr. Long, but Mr. Bullett is busy on a Court case for to-morrow and says he can't see you until the others are here. He'll be pleased to give you a few minutes afterwards.'

Henry Long gave the bent old man a distrustful look from his shrewd grey eyes which were separated by a long, thin, knife-like nose, suggesting a certain closeness of character. Apart from that feature, however, his face was rather a fine one. His broad forehead was crowned with close-cropped grizzled hair, his cheek bones were high, but balanced by a firm mouth and determined chin. He nodded dismissal to the clerk and turned to his daughter who was seated near him.

'I might have known,' he muttered, 'that Bullett would find some excuse to avoid being pressed for any information before the reading of the Will.'

'Never mind,' she replied soothingly, 'we shall know all about it soon.' As she spoke the door opened to admit a woman in her early sixties, who bore a striking resemblance to Henry Long, and a dark, smartly dressed young man, whose eyes rested on the girl with quick interest.

'Well, Gertrude,' Henry Long offered a grudging hand to his elder sister whom he had not seen for many years. 'How are you?'

She smiled a little bleakly but her eyes held a gentleness which her brother's lacked. 'You haven't altered much. And this is your girl Patricia, I suppose? She does you credit, Henry!'

Patricia stared with envious admiration at this unknown aunt, the bad woman of the family, who had deserted her husband and children to elope with the rich landowner, Heron Kane-Swift. From her early childhood Aunt Gertrude had been painted for her as the Scarlet Woman of Babylon by her strictly religious parent.

'Of course, you haven't met my boy, have you?' Gertrude Kane-Swift went on; 'Michael, this is your Uncle Henry and your cousin Patricia.'

All that Michael had ever heard of his Uncle Henry had predisposed him to dislike the man and now that he met him he saw no cause to alter his feelings, but little cousin Patricia was quite a different matter. Unlike her father she had a Roman nose and a large pair of limpid hazel eyes. Her chin was strong and firm, and her thick, dark curls were cleverly arranged under a small hat.

As she took his hand she was studying him with equal interest. He too had the dark wavy hair of the family but his nose was almost snub, evidently a legacy from the late Heron Kane-Swift. He was a little under medium height but broad shouldered and well proportioned. Without being in any way good looking, his open and ingenuous face was full of charm. Their greetings were hardly over when the door opened once more, the clerk announcing in the low voice common to his profession, 'Mr. George and Mr. Ernest Bennett.'

'Hello, Mother!' The elder, a rotund and almost bald man of forty, advanced on Gertrude with a joviality that his acquaintances would have thought natural to him, but which in this particular instance was decidedly forced. He had not seen her since they had met seven years before in this same lawyer's waiting-room on family business. He and his brother had also been taught to regard her as a Scarlet Woman since their childhood and, although he was naturally of an easy disposition, he found such meetings awkward to a degree. He pecked her cheek in diffident haste and turned to the others.

'Hello, Henry!—Hope you're well,' he said abruptly. George Bennett found very few people in this world whom he cordially disliked but it did rankle with him that, when his father had committed suicide on their mother's desertion, his wealthy uncle had denied his brother and himself the benefits of an upper-class education, and allowed them to do as well as they could in a secondary school.

Ernest, a slimmer and slightly taller edition of George, differed from his brother principally in possessing his mother's nose developed to an unusual degree of fleshiness, and an underhung chin. His perpetually open mouth would have given him a stupid expression but for the quick dark sparrow-like eyes common to the two, inherited from their Bennett father.

He ignored his uncle altogether and, having kissed his mother with equal haste and embarrassment, shook hands with Patricia, then turned on the younger man. 'So this is half-brother Michael—Just to think of you being grown up now!'

'And a fine young fellow, too,' added the rubicund George. 'Put it there, my boy, I'm pleased to meet you—after all these years.'

Michael gave them both a friendly smile. When his mother had abandoned the middle-class Mr. Bennett for a higher social sphere, she had severed all connection with her family and, although Michael had suggested once or twice in recent years that he would like to meet his two half-brothers, she had been quite adamant about it. Perhaps it was partly a feeling of guilt at having deserted her two elder sons, but even more she had felt it her duty to protect her cherished Michael from any association with his socially dubious relatives.

'Well! well! here we are,' exclaimed George cheerfully, 'all come along to collect our share of Uncle John's spondulicks, eh?'

'I trust you're right,' agreed Henry sourly, 'and that he's done better by his family now that he is dead than he did when he was alive.'

'Oh, come,' George protested, 'his family didn't do much for *him* that I've ever heard of.'

'Speak of what you know,' the elder man's voice was sharp. 'Your Uncle John was a ne'er-do-well of the worst description. He was always in trouble and always writing home for assistance of some kind or other.'

It was on the tip of Ernest's tongue to say: 'Well, he didn't get much for you, I bet,' but he confined himself to a wink at his elder brother and said instead: 'He's been no trouble this last ten years any old how.'

'I wonder what he was worth,' Michael observed. 'I met a man two years ago who had known him in Hong Kong and said that he lived like a Merchant Prince. Kept open house for everybody—drinks galore—and apparently a sort of harem for the amusement of his friends.'

His uncle nodded. 'I can well believe it. That is just the evil course of life which John would have adopted directly he made money. We can only hope that he has not squandered it all, but set aside something for those to whom he caused so much trouble in his youth—but we are all here, so why does Bullett keep us waiting?'

'There is Susan's boy—Sandy,' Gertrude remarked, 'but it is hardly likely that he would come over from South Africa. Bullett will send him a copy of the Will.'

'Have any of you ever seen him?' George Bennett inquired.

They all shook their heads except Gertrude, who went on reminiscently: 'He must be about thirty-five now, I suppose, and I remember hearing somewhere that his father died shortly after Susan. Of course, she did quite well for herself because McDiamid owned a nice property at the Cape, so I suppose Sandy is still running the vineyards and the fruit . . .'

Before she could finish her sentence, the door opened and a tall, athletic-looking man was shown in. He, too, had the dark colouring of the Long family but his hair, parted at the side, lacked the usual curl and a long lock which swept across his forehead fell forward as he removed his hat.

He pushed it backwards with a quick movement of his hand, smiling a little uncertainly at this group of unknown relatives and striving to place them from the little his mother had told him of her dreary life in England with her brother Henry before she met and married the young South African wine-grower.

As a child he had often listened to his fiery father's diatribes against the mean and sanctimonious uncle who had made his mother's young life a burden and, in the chill, impassive man seated upright on a hard chair near the window, he had no difficulty in recognising his uncle.

Ernest Bennett broke the strained silence. 'Come in, my boy,' he cried, his prominent Adam's apple working overtime. 'This isn't exactly home, sweet home, but at least they've put "Welcome" on the mat.'

Sandy could not help laughing as he introduced himself to the rest of the party but before he could find a suitable reply the clerk reappeared with his smug little smirk and said:

'If you will please come this way, Mr. Bullett will see you now.'

2

The Will

Surrounded by the dusty litter of bygone legislation, Mr. Bullett, lean, parched and prim, regarded the group severely over his nickel-rimmed spectacles. Extra horse-hair covered chairs, the springs of which may possibly have been good when Queen Victoria gave birth to her first child, were imported from the outer office.

Sandy McDiamid looked round him with distaste. It was his first visit to England, for his fruit farm and vineyards tied him in most seasons. Moreover, a succession of bad years after his father's death had prevented the accumulation of sufficient funds to do the trip in real comfort, free of all anxiety as to expense.

Recalling the bright modern office of his own solicitor in Cape Town, it seemed strange to him that this London lawyer, presumably a member of a firm of good repute, should conduct his business in such gloomy surroundings.

The grey January light from an unbroken sky of lead filtered in through the grime on the rain-streaked window. A travesty of a fire consisting of three small lumps of coal, burned dully in a tiny old-fashioned, black-leaded grate. A few faded photographs, one of a severe-looking man with side whiskers, and others of cricket teams long since dispersed, hung on the dull, time-streaked walls. Bundles of dusty papers lay carelessly piled on every ledge and on top of four stacks of lustreless tin deed boxes.

Sandy was the only member of the party who felt no anxiety regarding the contents of the Will. With an independence of spirit, common among those whose parents have broken away from family ties to make their home overseas, he saw no reason why this uncle, whom he had hardly ever heard of, should leave him anything. If he were down for a hundred guineas—and he certainly did not expect more—it would be a useful contribution towards the cost of his holiday, but the lawyer would send him what was his due in any case. He had answered the summons in person only because, happening to be in England, he thought it would be amusing to have a look at any other members of the family who turned up, although he would never have bothered to hunt them out in ordinary circumstances.

When they had all shaken hands with Mr. Bullett and seated themselves round his desk, the lawyer observed blandly: 'You are, of course, aware of the business which has necessitated my asking you to call here to-day.' He gave a little dry cough and sat back in his chair, tapping his fingers softly together as he added: 'I have to read to you the Will of my late client, John Thomas Long.'

There was a little shuffling of feet as he selected a paper from one of the many be-ribboned bundles in front of him, opened it out carefully, and proceeded to read:

' "This is the last Will and Testament of me, John Thomas Long, gentleman, of Moon Gates, The Peak, Hong Kong, China, being of sound health and in my right mind.

' "I appoint William Yates Bullett of Messrs. Bullett, Bullett, Leggett and Bullett, solicitors, of No. 97, Gray's Inn, London, W.C.1., to be my sole executor, and ask him to accept the sum of one thousand guineas; in addition to any legal expenses to which his firm may be entitled, as a mark of appreciation of his trustworthy management of my affairs and the considerable trouble which I caused him when I was a younger man." '

Gertrude Kane-Swift nodded silently. Certainly John had caused the family lawyer trouble enough with the continual scrapes into which he used to get. A thousand guineas was a lot of money but surely it argued that, if he could afford so much to his lawyer, there was plenty more to come.

' "I direct that the aforesaid William Yates Bullet," ' went on the gentleman concerned, ' "should realise the whole of my Stocks, Shares, Property and Investments, with the exception of my house in Hong Kong, for cash, and that the following legacies shall be paid, from the sum realised, to the persons named below.

' "£20,000 to Lucy Benton, last heard of by me as living at 72, Mearton Mansions, Handel Street, Bloomsbury, London, in 1920." '

The family looked at one another silently, questioning if any of them knew the fortunate Lucy, but Mr. Bullett was reading on:

' "£20,000 to Aileen Orkney, wife of William Bishop Orkney, last heard of by me as living in Hilton Road, Sea Point, Cape Town, South Africa, in 1924." '

A sudden horrible fear crossed the mind of Henry Long. Was it possible that John's dreadful impish humour, which had made it so difficult for him to understand his brother, had induced him to make a mock of them by leaving his entire fortune to complete strangers? The others sat, tense and silent, hanging upon Mr. Bullett's words.

' "£20,000 to Violet Robins, *née* Twisdon, last heard of by me at 122, Cemetery Road, Norwood, London, S.E., in 1904.'

A sudden chuckle broke the stillness of the dusty room. It came from Sandy McDiamid, at the realisation that wicked Uncle John was parcelling out his splendid fortune to all his past mistresses. 'Anybody know these ladies?' he inquired, shaking back the dark lock of hair from his forehead again.

'I knew Violet,' Henry replied grimly. 'She was a slip of a girl that John was once in love with, but she turned him down for a man named Robins. This Will is a scandal and an insult.'

'Be patient, please,' Mr. Bullett reproved the interruption.

' "£20,000 to Judge Van Niekerk, of The Jacarandas, Church Street, Pretoria, South Africa." '

'Well, I know who he is,' murmured Sandy, 'but I thought the old boy was dead.'

Ignoring the remark, Mr. Bullet went on:

' "£20,000 to Mademoiselle Collette La Cloche, refugee from Armentiéres, last heard of by me as employed at the Estaminet of *Les Deux Frères* in the village of Bermicourt, near St. Pol, France, in 1917." '

A worried grin spread over George Bennett's plump face. 'Tribute to the part our gallant Allies played in the War, I reckon,' he said, with as much cheerfulness as he could muster.

'Old soldiers never die!' added his brother.

The spirits of the family had sunk to zero. Already £100,000 of that fortune which had occupied their every thought for the last few weeks had melted away.

Henry's lean fists were tightly clenched. His nails bit into the palms with indignation and anger. 'Go on, go on,' he muttered quickly, 'let's have this farce done with.'

The lawyer nodded.

' "£5,000 to Lieutenant Roger Philbeach, 461st Brigade R.F.A. (Territorial Force), last heard of by me as a traveller for Messrs., Rithen, Ruthern & Co,' Wine Merchants, London in 1923.

' "£5,000 to Joe-Jack Mahout, last heard of by me as barman at the Royal Hotel, Durban, South Africa, in 1923.

' "£5,000 to Israel Rubenstein, last heard of by me at 299, Old Montague Street, Whitechapel, London, in 1919." '

'Lord!' exclaimed George. 'It's like a draw in the Irish Sweep for all these people, isn't it?'

'Yes,' muttered Ernest, 'and we'll be lucky if we're listed in the hundreds.'

'There is only one more bequest,' went on Mr. Bullett, and that is:

' "£50,000 to the Mandarin Loo Hi Foo of Hang Chow, China, conditional upon his consenting to pardon and rehabilitate his daughter Almond-Tree-in-Blossom, who has filled the last years of my life with happiness. Should he refuse, this sum is to be paid to the aforesaid lady, together with, in any case, the residue of my Estate, including such sums as have been allocated to persons in this my Will should they pre-decease me.

' "To the above-named lady, Miss Almond-Tree-in-Blossom, I also leave my house in Hong Kong, together with all its fixtures, fittings etc. and my personal effects." '

The lawyer paused and regarded their disappointed faces for a moment over his spectacles.

'How much do you think this celestial beauty will come in for?' asked Michael curiously, his brown eyes twinkling.

'It is a little difficult to say. If her father accepts the £50,000 the bequests will amount to £166,000, but I learn that Van Niekerk and Violet Robins are both dead, so that reduces them to £126,000, but even after taxation has been paid the Estate should realise some £180,000 at a low estimate.'

With a grey face, Henry Long jerked himself to his feet. 'Come!' he snapped through clenched teeth to his daughter, 'I consider it is a disgrace that we should have been dragged here to listen to this wicked record of an ill-spent life. I shall consult another solicitor, Bullett, with a view to contesting the validity of this Will in the Courts.'

'One moment!' The lawyer held up a slim, dry hand. 'This Will is properly attested in due legal form and even a doctor's certificate as to the sanity of the testator at the time it was drawn up has been attached. You can consult any solicitor you like but I feel certain that he will bear me out in my opinion that its validity is quite unshakable. However, I did not ask you here to-day only to listen to the reading of a Will which benefits none of you—there is another matter.'

Henry sat down again, while the others stiffened to a new attention.

'You are, I think, all aware that up till about ten years ago the late John Thomas Long drifted about the world in what might almost be described as precarious circumstances. In fact, to the best of my knowledge, he never had a penny except the small sums which he earned from time to time as prospector and hunter or in casual employment as bond salesman, motor car agent—and temporary manager on various South African farms. Yet at a certain date we learn of his sudden and inexplicable rise to considerable riches. How his fortune, of which you have just learned the disposal, was acquired has always been a mystery, but in addition to his Will he left a letter giving particulars of the source from which it came. That is his sole legacy to his blood relations and I am about to read it to you now.'

3

If Blood is Thicker than Water?

Mr. Bullett coughed again, picked up another paper from his desk, adjusted his spectacles and proceeded:

'"Brothers, sisters, nephews and nieces. You will note that I do not address any of you as 'Dear' because you are not dear to me in any sense. You will by this time have heard the contents of my Will and have noted, with varying degrees of disappointment and anger, that I have left all my money to those who gave me pleasure in my lifetime, which none of you can ever claim to have done.

'"Old skin-flint Henry is listening to this, I have not a doubt, for he will cling to life just as he has always clung to his money bags, and it is one of my few regrets that I shall not be present to witness his discomfort. Gertrude, too, perhaps and, although I owe her nothing, in view of her consistent disregard of my letters asking for small sums which she could have well afforded during her later life, I take the opportunity to salute her as a kindred spirit at least, in having the courage to desert old Bennett and the ability to cajole Kane-Swift into making an honest woman of her. The Bennett boys will be there too possibly, if they escaped the War, and Susan, to whom I was tempted to leave a little money, since she was the best of a pretty miserable bunch. However, I see no reason why I should differentiate, as none of you have ever done a thing for me or given me one moment's thought.

' "Yet it is said, so often, when Wills such as mine are made public, that *blood is thicker than water* and that it is a wrong for a man to leave all his possessions away from his family, however indifferent to them he may be, so in the circumstances it is my pleasure to test that well-worn saying.

' "I could, if I choose, place each of you in a few months in possession of a fortune as great, or greater, than that which I have left; but I am not prepared to do so unless you can prove that the same blood which animated my brain to careful and laborious investigation, and strengthened my body to endure hardship, peril and distress runs also in your veins. I refer to the actual source of my great wealth, which could have been ten, twenty, fifty times as much had I desired a greater portion than I took for my modest enjoyment.

' "It was in Africa, years even before I returned to Europe to participate in the Great War, that I first heard of the fabulous valley which is known as 'The Place of the Great Glitter'. Certain prospectors were said to have visited it and come away with a fortune in their pockets. Many more have attempted to discover its whereabouts but died on their way thither, or failed in their undertaking. Every child in Africa knows this so-called legend, and anyone will tell you that it lies somewhere in the south of the Great Kalahari Desert.

' "The finding of it is, however, a very different matter. The whole of England, Scotland, Ireland and Wales could be set down in the Kalahari and their borders would not touch the fringe of civilisation by a hundred miles from any of their extremities. That vast area is almost entirely uninhabited— its rivers and mountain ranges still unmapped. Its wastes are trackless and desolate so that the very silence reacts with terrible force upon all people who are used to living in cities.

' "It was not until 1924 that I met a man who induced me to believe that the 'Place of the Great Glitter' was anything more than a legend, but after many months of sifting conflicting evidence as to its whereabouts I ventured out upon one of the most terrible journeys that any man can ever have undertaken. I found the Valley, and, having picked up, in a little under an hour, sufficient precious stones to ensure my comfort for the rest of my days, I succeeded in returning to civilisation in safety.

' "There are people still living who made the journey with me, and could lead you to this hidden source of fortune. Their names do not appear in my Will since they were amply rewarded for their services at the time and paid, in addition, a very considerable sum to keep the secret until I, or some person whom they would recognise by a a symbol, should seek them out.

' "These symbols, then, constitute my sole legacy to my family and should there be more than three of you, lots must be drawn as to who is to receive them. If you can interpret these tokens aright and have the courage, patience and endurance to undertake the investigations and the journey *Blood will have proved thicker than Water*, and you will indeed be heirs to whom I am happy to leave this great inheritance.

' "I go now to open a fresh consignment of old brandy which has just arrived from my wine merchants in Pall Mall. As I sample it, and Almond-Tree-in-Blossom sings one of her enchanting songs for me alone, I shall laugh a little over the thought of Brother Henry, whose avarice willl certainly induce him to accept the venture, as he lies down to sleep in the Valley of the Leopards.

' "JOHN THOMAS LONG." '

As the lawyer ceased reading a tense silence settled on the faded room. Each member of the family felt a secret thrill at the glamorous prospect of great wealth which had suddenly been extended to them.

Henry's eyes narrowed. It had always seemed a rank injustice to him that while he had had to slave for every penny of his modest fortune his spendthrift brother should have unaccountably stumbled upon great riches. John's cutting references to his avarice in the letter passed him by unmoved. That the legacy should have been flung to them in this contemptuous manner mattered nothing. It was there for those who had the courage to collect it. He must not involve himself with the others, of course. The Bennetts hated him, he knew, and would be certain to cheat him if they could—but he meant to get his share.

His daughter, her hazel eyes filled with sudden excitement, was thinking that it would be new life to be independent of him. Her own flat, a little car, and a glorious freedom from the dull routine of his narrow household.

To the Bennetts money meant more money. They saw themselves buying up the shares of the Company in which they had worked their way to directorships, and extending— new plant—new offices—a hundred travellers on the road— and at last a cessation of that constant nightmare—overheads.

Sandy McDiamid's face held a carefully guarded interest. The only South African present, he knew the snags as well as the possibilities of this legendary valley. The cautious brain which he had inherited from his Scottish father told him that a journey there was not a thing to be undertaken lightly, yet his mother's blood urged him to the gamble and he knew already within himself that he meant to try for it. Still—'If you must go, my boy, keep your own council and don't get mixed up with any of these unknown kinsmen.' As his glance shifted from the flushed faces of the Bennetts to the tight mouth of Henry Long he could almost hear his father speaking.

Gertrude was visualising her lovely home as she had first known it when Heron Kane-Swift took her there twenty-five years before. The carriages, the motors, the many servants, the hunt breakfasts beneath the cedars on the lawn, the ball to which all the county came each year; and Michael was seeing the other side of the picture . . . the empty stables . . . the neglected gardens . . . the beautiful old Jacobean house falling into disrepair.

He had been sitting with his elbows on his knees and his chin propped in his hands, now he sat up with a jerk. His broad, freckled face flushed with eagerness. He put an affectionate arm round his mother and said:

'This is too good to be true. I've got to go.'

She started as though brought back from a dream. 'But, Michael dear, the danger—I couldn't let you—besides . . .'

'I know,' he broke in with a swift whisper, 'you were going to speak about money for the journey, but think what this means to us.'

Gertrude Kane-Swift knew only too well. When her husband had been killed in the hunting field two years before, it had been discovered that, in order to keep up Harcourt Priory, he had been living almost entirely upon his capital. Gertrude had been struggling ever since with barely enough money, saved from the clutches of the mortgagees, to keep Michael and herself.

'I suppose I could sell the pearls.' she murmured, 'but it's your safety, my dear, that I am thinking of.'

Ernest Bennett leaned across to Sandy. 'I say, McDiamid, you know the country. Is it true about this Valley, or is it all my eye and Betty Martin?'

Sandy's full lips broke into a smile. 'Yes, I'm a South African, but it's a big country, and although I know the part round the Cape and the big towns like Johannesburg and Durban I've never been within five hundred miles of this place. The legend is well known, though, and as there's no other explanation for the old man suddenly securing all that money it looks as if the Valley really must exist.'

'What about it, Ernie?' George broke in.

'Nothing venture, nothing have,' replied the younger Bennett, fingering the enormous Adam's apple which stuck out like a walnut in his throat, 'but how about the bizz?'

'Oh, we'll fix that. What have we got partners for if we can't break away for a couple of months in a case like this?'

'Yes, and you were going for a trip anyway.'

George rubbed his hands and chuckled. 'This'll be more fun than going on a cruise with the stuffy sort of people you get these days—though it's a disappointment not to be able to use that fancy dress.' He swung quickly round on Henry, all his animosity evaporated in the excitement of the moment. 'How about you, Uncle?'

'I don't know,' Henry Long said, with quiet reserve. 'If I'd been a man to dash into things I shouldn't be where I am to-day.'

'But, Father, we must!' exclaimed Patricia suddenly.

'Surely you don't expect me to take you, even if I did decide to go?' He stared at her with incredulity. 'I couldn't possibly afford it.'

For a moment a cowed expression came into her slightly protruding eyes, then they brightened and she said hastily:

'All right, I'll pay for myself. I'm just as much Uncle John's heir as anyone else here, and I wouldn't miss this for the world.'

'Since when did you have any money that I didn't give you?'

Patricia's face grew stubborn. 'There is Aunt Mary's legacy, the five hundred pounds in War Loan that she left me. I can sell that out if I want to.'

Her father shrugged. 'All right, if you like to squander your money I can't stop you.'

'What about those clues?' Sandy asked the lawyer. 'Have you got them here?'

Bullett nodded and, rising from his chair, walked over to a long tin uniform case, which he unlocked and, removing the contents, carried them back to his desk.

The three articles displayed consisted of a fine knobkerrie of heavy, dark wood, the rounded top of which was curiously carved; a necklace some four feet long, consisting of tiny skulls, carefully graduated from a size not much larger than a thumb-nail up to that of a cricket ball; and a plain leopard-skin kaross, such as natives of the interior sometimes use as a body covering.

'Coo-er!' exclaimed Ernest, picking up the necklace. 'Enough to give anyone the willies, isn't it?'

Sandy took it from him and examined it curiously. 'It's a witch doctor's,' he said, 'and these are not human skulls from slaughtered children, only the heads of baby monkeys.'

Michael picked up the knobkerrie. 'By jove, what a weapon!'

'Weapon's the word, all right. It must have been this that started the song "Knock 'Em in the Old Kent Road",' Ernest agreed, chuckling at his own humour.

'If you please,' Mr. Bullet intervened. 'According to my client's instructions, since there *are* more than three of you, I am to distribute these by lot, and for that purpose I have this prepared.' He produced a small tin tobacco box in which there were seven carefully folded slips of paper of equal size. 'I suggest that you should draw them in order of age if you are agreeable.'

Gertrude took a slip, unfolded it quickly, and the words *Leopard Skin Kaross* were seen clearly printed in ink upon it.

Henry drew next, and to his obvious chagrin got a blank. George Bennett followed with a like result, then Ernest looked across at Sandy McDiamid.

'How do we run for age?' he inquired.

'I'm thirty-five,' volunteered Sandy.

'Well, it's age before honesty, then,' Ernest grinned, 'because I'm thirty-eight,' but, having taken his paper, he proved no more fortunate than his brother.

Sandy followed and landed the knobkerrie. Only the necklace of skulls now remained, with Michael and Patricia to draw.

'I'm twenty-four,' said Michael, 'but you can have first pick if you like.'

'No, go ahead,' she smiled. 'You beat me by a year.'

But although Michael drew first it was Patricia to whom the gruesome-looking necklace fell.

The interest in the draw having subsided, Mr. Bullett gave his dry little cough again. 'I should be glad if you would resume your seats for a moment,' he said, 'because there is one other thing that I wish to say to you.'

They fell silent at once, eager to hear if the lawyer had any other clues to offer. He regarded them steadily and then his parched face broke, for the first time, into the semblance of a smile.

'From the remarks which I have heard I feel that I am entitled to assume that certain of you are already contemplating a journey to Africa in search of this place which is mentioned in my late client's letter. In the circumstances, therefore, as your family solicitor, I think it is my duty to give you a very solemn warning.

'The dangers and difficulties set forth in the letter are, of ccurse, no part of my business, but there is a legal aspect to the matter, with which it is only right that I should acquaint you, before you incur any expense in regard to this undertaking. The fact that my late client discovered this exceptionally prolific diamond field gives him no legal right to dispose of it to anybody.

'His action in selling or exporting these diamonds without a licence, and his failure to report his discovery to the Government, rendered him liable to prosecution and very serious penalties. In fact, I have little doubt that he would have been sentenced to a long term of imprisonment if he had been caught. Should any of you, therefore, decide to go on this expedition your first duty will be to apply, in the proper quarter, for a prospector's licence, which I am given to understand can only be obtained in these days with considerable difficulty. Then, should your efforts to find the Valley prove successful you must report the matter immediately to the South African authorities, and under no circumstances should you remove any stones from it other than those necessary to prove your discovery.'

'Oh, come on now,' complained Ernest. 'Finding's keeping's—I always do say,' but Sandy shook his head.

'No, Mr. Bullett is perfectly right. I know enough about South African law to assure you of that.'

'Well, but what happens then?' inquired George. 'Surely the Government doesn't pinch the lot off us if we go to all the expense of finding the place.'

'Not quite,' Bullett replied gravely. 'From mines working in Cape Province they take forty per cent of the profits and from those on the Transvaal sixty per cent, but of course you would not be allowed to mine the entire Valley.'

'Why?' shot out Henry Long gruffly.

'Because the Law is, that when a new diamond field is discovered public notices of it must be given and a date fixed, some time in advance, for its official opening. Diggers from all parts of the country flock into the district, and on the day arranged each man lines up at a spot about a mile away with a peg in his hand. At a given signal the whole crowd, sometimes numbering several thousand people, moves off at a run, and races for the new ground; each one pegging his claim as near the place of the original discovery as possible.'

'That's right, and the big diamond interests hire all the crack runners in the Union to enter the race for them—so they get all the best claims,' Sandy added.

'Well, what happens to Poor Phil Garlic, I'd like to know?' inquired Ernest with a crestfallen look.

'I take it that you refer to the original discoverer?' the lawyer replied dryly. 'He does not go entirely unrewarded, for he is allowed a certain number of claims and those become his legal property.'

'Then we might not do so badly after all if the ground is thick with the stuff, like the letter says,' observed George.

'That is so if you can persuade the Government to declare the district open as a diamond field, but there you come up against the almost insurmountable difficulty which makes me stress this warning to you. Even if you can get your *prospector's* licence; even if, by patient investigation, you can find the persons to whom these strange clues, left by my late client, will have a meaning; even if you survive the journey through the wilderness and return with actual proof of your discovery, it is beyond the bounds of all reasonable probability that the South African Government will grant you a *digger's* licence and allow you to mine the place at all.'

'Why?' exclaimed Michael.

'Because the diamond industry in South Africa is very heavily protected. The price of diamonds has fallen in an alarming manner these last few years, and since the Government derive a considerable portion of their revenue from them, it is to their interest that prices should be maintained. I am quite certain that at the present time, and possibly for some years to come, they would not countenance the opening up of a new source which might cause the flooding of the diamond market.'

George mopped his semi-bald perspiring scalp. 'This doesn't seem too good to me,' he said ruefully to Ernest. 'It looks as though I'll be helping the passengers to have a jolly time on that cruise after all.'

But Michael grinned broadly. 'What's to stop us really following in Uncle John's footsteps?' he asked. 'Why shouldn't we find this place, fill our pockets with as much stuff as we can carry and chance getting out of the country just as he did?'

'Young man,' Bullett held up his shrivelled hand quickly, 'I must beg you not to make any such suggestions in this office. Moreover, I sincerely trust that you will put any such thought out of your mind. The difficulties of even locating this place on such slender evidence are apparent. The dangers and hardships of reaching it are fully set forth in your late uncle's letter. To add to these the risk of almost certain arrest and a long sentence of imprisonment would make the project absolute madness.'

'To Hell with that!' said Michael, standing up, 'I'm going to chance it.'

4

Certain Inquiries and an Unpleasant Surprise

'Michael!' Gertrude placed a restraining hand on his arm. 'You will do no such thing!'

'But why, Mother? If we can only find this place there's a fortune for us. It's the chance of a lifetime.'

'You seem to have forgotten that my brother's malicious humour caused him to leave us practically no evidence on which to find it,' cut in his uncle acidly, 'and after what Bullett has told us about the South African laws you'd be very stupid to waste your mother's money going out there on such a wild goose chase.'

Patricia's face dropped woefully at her father's words. 'Do you mean that you're not going out after all?' she murmured.

'Certainly not.' Henry Long's voice was decisive. 'Bullet is right. In the present state of the diamond market the Government would never allow us to open up a new mine and I have no intention of being sent to prison for I.D.B.'

'It would be Diamond Smuggling, not I.D.B.,' remarked Sandy quietly, 'but the penalties of both are much the same, and the South African police are hot as mustard, so it's a pretty nasty risk.'

Mr. Bullet coughed again. 'Really,' he protested, 'I must ask you to refrain from discussing the pros and cons of what amounts to a very serious breach of the law, in my office.'

'Fair's fair, I always do say,' agreed Ernest, 'and we ought not to wag our chins about it here. Can't we make a move to some place where we can "have one"—and talk it out?'

'Too late, old boy,' remarked George, after a quick look at a heavy gold watch, 'but why shouldn't we all meet to-night for a bite together somewhere? By then we'll have had time to think the whole thing over.'

'Fine,' cried Michael enthusiastically, while Sandy agreed with a casual nod.

'What about you, Henry?' The elder Bennett looked doubtfully at his uncle. 'Dinner's on me if you and your girl care to join us.'

The older man shook his head. 'Thank you—no. As we are not joining you on this wild goose chase, we should only interrupt your deliberations.'

George Bennett turned to the others: 'Let's make it Simpson's in the Strand, seven-thirty sharp, downstairs, eh?'

There was a murmur of agreement and, collecting their hats and mackintoshes, they all took leave of the lawyer, with the exception of Henry Long and his daughter.

'I shall want a copy of that Will, Bullett,' said Henry directly the door had closed upon the others.

'Certainly,' the lawyer nodded. 'Where is it, now? Young McDiamid had it in his hands only a moment ago. Ah! Here it is. Shall I post the copy on to you to-morrow?'

'Yes, but I'd like to have the names and addresses of the beneficiaries right away—their latest addresses of course, for I don't doubt most of them have moved since John last heard of them.'

'True, a number of them have, but I fear professional etiquette forbids my disclosing their present addresses. However, I should be happy to forward any letters from you, addressed to them care of myself at this office.'

'I see.' Henry did not seek to disguise his disappointment. 'Then let me have the old addresses to go on with.'

'Certainly. I will get my clerk to type them out for you.'

Ten minutes later Henry and his daughter had also taken leave of the lawyer and were hurrying out through the rain to his five-year-old Buick.

Unnoticed by them, Sandy McDiamid stood in the shadow of a nearby archway. Immediately he had watched them drive off, he ran swiftly back though the downpour, and up the stairs to the offices of Bullett, Bullett, Leggett and Bullett again.

Mr. Bullett's smile deepened a little as he listened to

Sandy's request, which was precisely similar to that which had just been made by Henry Long. He refused in the same terms and added dryly: 'I assume that *you* will not require the addresses given in the Will, since I fancy I saw you making some notes from it when the others were here.'

Sandy grinned. 'That's right, so if you can't give me any further information I won't trouble you any more for the moment.'

He had already studied his pencilled list and decided that Lucy Benton, of 72 Mearton Mansions, Handel Street, Bloomsbury, being the nearest, should be his first call. Hailing a passing taxi when he reached the entrance to Gray's Inn, he drove there at once.

A girl in a Japanese silk kimono received him in the narrow hallway of her flat. The colour of her corn-ripe curls obviously owed more to the efforts of her hairdresser than to nature.

'My!' she exclaimed. 'Who is this Lucy Benton, anyway? I've never heard of 'er.'

Sandy realised at once that the girl was one of those fleeting occupants common to small flats in certain quarters of London. The place had probably sheltered a hundred such, since the tenancy of Lucy Benton 'last heard of by Uncle John in 1920'.

'You poor dear! You *are* wet!' exclaimed the golden-headed lady with arch sympathy. 'Won't you come in for a moment and I'll get the maid to make you a nice cup o' tea.'

As she spoke she allowed the kimono to slip open, revealing a well-rounded length of silk-stockinged leg with a few inches of pink-fleshed thigh above it.

Sandy thanked her politely and declined the offer, but begged the use of her telephone. In a few moments he was through to Messrs. Burgoyne, the biggest importers of South African wines in London with whom, as a vineyard proprietor, he sometimes had dealings. They promptly supplied him with the address of Rithen, Ruthern and Co.

The tenant of 72 Mearton Mansions accepted his renewed

thanks and watched him go with regret, leaning from her doorway to call after him cheerfully: 'If you're ever lonely— come up an' see me some time,' as he ran down the narrow stone stairway of the block.

'320a Oxford Street,' Sandy called to the driver, as he jumped back into his waiting taxi. While it swished through the muddy London streets, grey with damp mist on this January afternoon, he heartily wished that he was back in his own Sunny South Africa where summer would be turning to autumn and the flowers a glory in the garden of his home.

On his way to Rithen, Ruthern's he considered his list again, as he thought it most important to learn all he could of Uncle John's past through the various beneficiaries in the Will. Such data might aid him considerably as to the right quarter in which to produce the knobkerrie. Sandy had already made up his mind to chance the danger of the journey into the Kalahari and if necessary arrest as well, in the hope of getting away with a fortune on his return to South Africa.

The taxi set him down at the Wine Merchants in Oxford Street, and the manager informed him at once that the fortunate Roger Philbeach had left their employment only a week before on receipt of an advance out of his legacy.

Sandy's face fell when he learned that the man lived out at Wembley, but apparently Philbeach had left a special request that if any South Africans or members of the Long family inquired for him, his firm should get in touch with him at once.

The manager obligingly put through a telephone call. Philbeach was in, and agreed to come up to his old firm's office in order to meet Sandy there at a little before six.

Out in the street once more, Sandy crossed the road to the Tube Station and procured a ticket for Whitechapel; the only other beneficiary who had a London address being Israel Rubenstein.

Arrived in the East End, he had some difficulty in finding 299 Old Montague Street. No taxis were available, the rain descended in a steady downpour and here, in the East End,

London seemed greyer and gloomier than ever with the early darkness of the winter night close at hand.

At last he found the number and discovered it to be a small pawnbroker's shop. To his joy he noted that the name of Rubenstein was still prominently displayed below three large golden balls smeared with dirt and grime.

Inside, a young Jew with eyes like a gazelle, set in a face pitted with smallpox, peered at him from a trap-hatch set in a high corner.

Sandy duly made his inquiry and the young man smiled, showing a row of perfect teeth. 'Yes, yes,' he nodded, 'it is my uncle that you want. Come in, please sir, come in,' and he swung open a door in the counter which led to a back office.

An elderly, bespectacled Jew rose from a desk as Sandy entered and drew forward a chair. 'Be seated, please. Vot can I do for you?'

'You have recently received a legacy, I believe, from my uncle, John Thomas Long,' Sandy opened frankly; 'five thousand pounds, I think, and I've called to ask you if you will be good enough to tell me what you can of your acquaintance with him.'

The Jew pursed his thick lips for a moment, then nodded solemnly. 'Your uncle vos a very unusual man. Vot can I tell you about him—I do not know. Only that like many others, in the ordinary course of my pusiness many years before the new laws came in, he came to me for a little accommodation. It vos for to make his furs' journey to South Africa, I think. I obliged him on not very good security, and later he repay me all that he owe me. Years pass; I see him again after the Var. Again he vants a little accommodation to go to South Africa. Vunce more I oblige him, and again in time I see my money back. He passes from my mind, for I have much pusiness which is always difficult. Then I hear quite suddenly from a lawyer that he has left me five thousand pound. Never before have I been so fortunate when I have made a little accommodation to a client. May his heirs do honour to him, and may his soul rest in the bosom of Abraham.'

Sandy nodded silently as the old Jew ceased on a note of deep religious feeling. Then he held out the knobkerrie which he had been carrying under his arm. 'You've never seen this thing before, I suppose?'

Mr. Rubenstein slowly shook his head.

There was obviously no information of importance to be gathered here. Uncle John's whimsical humour had led him, in the plenitude of his wealth, to remember the man who had financed him on dubious security for his journey to the country where he had eventually made his fortune.

Having thanked Mr. Israel Rubenstein for his courtesy, Sandy left the shop, and as it was now a quarter past five, he hurried through the dark and dreary streets back to the Underground station, a little nervous that he might be too late to catch Mr. Roger Philbeach, sometime lieutenant of the 461st Brigade, R.F.A., before Rithen, Ruthern's shut at six.

He was fortunate, however, and found Philbeach there when he arrived. He proved to be a big, hearty, red-faced fellow, getting on for fifty years of age. His expanse of face was so large that his little black eyes were almost buried in rolls of fat. Sandy stated his business and the wine merchant's traveller gave a sudden roar of laughter.

'Well, well, so you're old John's nephew, are you? I'm delighted to meet you, delighted! He was a great scout, was old John, and fancy his leaving me five thousand, too! The sportsman! I never knew anyone before to have such luck as that.'

'You knew him in the War, I suppose?' Sandy hazarded.

'Rather,' the other boomed. 'We shared a hut, we shared a dug-out, and we shared every bottle we could lay our hands on, too. But let's get out of this. Come along to some place where we can talk quietly and have a drink. Look here! you doing anything to-night? If not, come and dine with me. I'll give you the finest dinner we can buy in London and delighted to do it. We'll kill a magnum apiece to the memory of old John Thomas Long.'

'I'd love to any other evening but I'm afraid I'm fixed for to-night,' Sandy told him.

'Never mind.' With a cheerful 'good night' to his late manager, Philbeach led the way out of the shop and hailed a taxi.

'How are you off for time?' he asked as the cab drew up.

'I have to be at Simpson's in the Strand by seven-thirty, but I'm free until then.'

'Fine, we'll slip up to a little place I know, then. It's what I call a gentlemen's pub—if you take my meaning—and between you and me I'm thinking of buying it now I've got money—to run it myself, you know, if I can get the brewers to give me decent terms.' He gave an address to the driver and the cab moved off.

The dreary winter night had fallen, and hundreds of tired, rain-soaked wage-earners waited patiently for the crowded buses at Oxford Circus. As they turned north up Portland Place only a few pedestrians were hurrying with bent shoulders through the steady downpour, and when the taxi entered the Outer Circle of Regent's Park not a passer-by was to be seen on the glistening pavements.

Philbeach had taken the knobkerrie from Sandy in response to a question about it and was weighing it carefully in his hand.

'No, I've never seen this thing before—but what a weapon, eh?'

The dazzling headlights of a car loomed up, racing towards them out of the darkness. 'My!' exclaimed Philbeach, 'he's going it, isn't he—just look at him!'

As the car flashed past them Sandy leaned forward to peer out of his window, which was nearest to it. Mr. Roger Philbeach raised the knobkerrie in both hands. Sandy felt as though the whole of St. Paul's had suddenly descended on his head and pitched forward on to the floor of the taxi, unconscious.

5

Of Liars and Others

On the following afternoon Michael went down to Surbiton. He had telephoned to Patricia Long that afternoon to ask if he could see her and she had fixed the hour of four o'clock. As the Longs had not been at the family dinner at Simpson's the night before, he suggested she might like to know what had been settled there. Though he hardly realised it himself, he was very attracted by her and would have invented an excuse for meeting her again if such an excellent one had not lain ready to his hand. He had been desperately sorry for her pathetic disappointment when she had been compelled to forgo the fun of participating in the projected expedition, and judged that her life with her grim father was not at all a happy one.

Henry Long's father was a Noncomformist minister, and it nearly broke his heart when John Thomas—his baby and favourite—ran away from home at the age of sixteen.

Luckily. he did not survive the shock long enough to see his eldest daughter divorced or his younger elope with Sandy's father to South Africa.

Henry was his only comfort. Serious, bigoted, and upright, even as a boy he always managed to save a few pennies every week out of his meagre pocket money. These he would hoard, denying himself sweets or books, until he had sufficient to buy another coloured print to add to the collection on his bedroom wall.

His artistic taste developed rapidly—though it remained all his life a secret bone of contention between his aesthetic sense and his Lutheran conscience.

When his daughter Patricia was born he resolved to stamp out at an ealy age any sign of the family wildness. The girl, however, had her full share of the adventurous streak and all Henry Long's care had only served to repress it.

Both she and Michael were only children and yet they were a curious contrast. The boy had been brought up in luxurious surroundings, spoilt by his mother and adored by his father. His nature was fortunately too sweet to spoil and the hint of wilfulness he knew so well how to employ in cajoling his parents was rather attractive than otherwise. His round face, powdered with freckles, was plain enough but his eyes were always smiling under ridiculously long lashes. He had that subtle charm which is inborn, and with it cultivated manners which sat as easily on him as his loose tweed coat.

He found The Laurels, where the Longs lived, to be a large square house, fronted by a semi-circular drive and backed by quite a good-sized garden. As he rang the bell Michael prayed fervently that his Uncle Henry would not be at home. An elderly maid left him in the hall for a few moments and then showed him into a sitting-room, where Patricia was busy with some mending.

'Hello!' said Michael.

'Hello!' replied Patricia.

'It is nice of you to let me come and see you,' he said.

'On the contrary, it is nice of you to come!' she smiled quickly. 'Won't you sit down?'

'Thanks.' He looked round the room with some surprise. Michael did not know a great deal about paintings nor the one reason that would induce his Uncle Henry to loosen his purse-strings. He knew enough, however, to recognise an Henri Matisse when he saw one. There were three hanging on the cream-coloured walls, together with half a dozen other pictures that he felt had real distinction although he could not have named their painters. He turned quickly to Patricia, his merry face unusually solemn. 'I say, I'm most awfully sorry that you're not coming on this trip after all.'

'So am I.'

'Couldn't you possibly persuade your father to let you? We are cousins, aren't we? So it isn't going with strangers. Of course, we should have to leave you parked in an hotel in Cape Town while we went up country. We couldn't possibly let you take any risk—especially in the smuggling part of it

—but we should have tremendous fun on the boat going out.'

It was on the tip of Patricia's tongue to tell him that if she went at all she had no intention of being packed up in cotton wool, but she averted her eyes and said instead: 'I'm afraid it's quite impossible. Father would never let me go with you.'

'What a rotten shame.'

'Isn't it, but tell me,' she hurried on. 'Is Sandy McDiamid going, and what have you and the Bennetts decided to do?'

'I'd better tell you all that happened at Simpson's last night,' Michael answered. 'Sandy refuses to play, worse luck. I only wish he would though, because I like Sandy.'

'Yes. He's nice. But why is he called Sandy when he has dark hair?'

'I got stung on that last night,' Michael laughed, 'and he called me a silly Sassenach. For some obscure reason it seems that Sandy is short for Alexander.'

Patricia nodded. 'I see. Well, I like him much better than the Bennetts. I suppose they're awfully good-hearted people, but they really are rather—well—you know.'

'Of course I do! But they are enormous fun, particularly "Ernie", and both of them have guts. I've arranged to go out to Africa with them to-morrow, the 27th, on the Union Castle boat.'

'Does your mother mind you going?' asked Patricia.

'Naturally she is a bit upset,' he answered, 'but I persuaded her finally by putting it to her that finding these diamonds is the only chance of us being able to go on living at Harcourt.'

'Why?—were the death duties so bad '

'No, but my father had been living on his capital—like lots of other landlords—for years before he died. I had to give up my hunters and the place is practically shut up. We haven't even got enough money to keep it in good repair.'

Patricia's lovely hazel eyes gleamed. 'Won't it be wonderful,' she said softly, 'if you really do find a fortune? It must be dreadful to see that lovely old place, which has always been your home, going to rack and ruin.'

'It seems almost like a fairy story, doesn't it?' Michael agreed, 'but I must have a shot at it.'

'Yes, but if you do find any diamonds and get them out of the country how will you manage to dispose of them?' she asked thoughtfully.

'Oh, we're not worried about that,' he assured her. 'Ernest has a friend in Hatton Garden. Not a crook, you understand, but a legitimate diamond dealer. If this thing comes off we could well afford to offer him a handsome share of the profits to market the stones.'

'Won't he be taking a certain risk?'

'Perhaps, but Ernest says that if there's big money in it he is quite certain that his friend would come in with us.'

'I see. Did you have an awful bother raising your expenses for the trip?'

He shook his head. 'Not too bad. The Bennetts are putting up five hundred pounds apiece, and I could only manage three hundred, but as I contribute the leopard skin they are very generously counting that as the balance of my share. They are anxious to buy your necklace of monkey skulls, too—as you won't be using it yourself.'

'I know,' Patricia said slowly, her eyes on Michael's face. 'George rang me up about it this morning; but Daddy asked me to give it to him to keep as a curiosity, and when I gave him George Bennett's message he flatly refused to part with the thing.'

'What a pity!—so now that Sandy has lost the knobkerrie my kaross is the only clue we've got.'

'What do you mean about Sandy losing the knobkerrie?— What's happened, Michael?'

'Oh, of course you don't know—well, when he turned up at Simpson's last night he said he'd been in a taxi smash and had lost the knobkerrie in the confusion.' Michael looked at his pretty cousin, a little smile crinkling the corners of his eyes.

'Michael! I believe you're pulling my leg . . .' Patricia leaned forward and tapped his knee solemnly, her eyes twinkling. 'It's no good, my boy—you can't deceive the Wise

Woman of Surbiton!' She pulled such a comical face—imitating the nut-cracker jaws of an old toothless gipsy—that Michael burst out laughing. He began to feel that he had known this amusing new cousin for years.

'All right. I give in! The Wise Woman of Surbiton shall know everything; though,' he added with a mocking grin, 'I should have thought a really wise woman would not have needed a nit-wit like me to elucidate the mystery! However—here goes. Sandy didn't say much while the Bennetts were there except to tell us that he is sailing for Africa on the 29th—that is, a day later than the Union Castle boat—but he's travelling by the Italian Line from Marseilles, so he will be in Cape Town a day before us. He refused to join our party in the search—in fact, he says he knows so much about the dangers of illicit diamond smuggling that he wouldn't dream of embarking on the adventure at all. After my half-brothers had left he became much more forthcoming though, and just as we were leaving he asked me to lunch with him to-day.'

'Go on,' urged Patricia. 'You're getting me all excited—what really did happen?'

'It seems that he had had the idea of looking up all the people to whom old John left his money in the hope of getting some information out of them, although he says that he was doing it for the fun of the thing, not with any serious intention of following it up. He found that Lucy Benton had left her flat but he ran Rubenstein to earth somewhere down in Whitechapel. Then he got Roger Philbeach to meet him by appointment. Philbeach suggested taking him up to some pub that he was thinking of buying, for a drink, then as they were running through Regent's Park in the taxi the wine-wallah pointed to a car that was speeding a bit. When Sandy leaned forward to look out of the window, Philbeach picked up the knobkerrie and smashed him over the head.'

'Good gracious!'

'Pretty hot, wasn't it? When poor Sandy came to again the taxi man was shaking him and telling him that he had reached the address that his friend had given in Golders

Green. Of course, Philbeach had disappeared and the knob-kerrie with him.'

'But how extraordinary, didn't the taxi man or anyone in the street notice what was going on?'

'Apparently not. You know what a filthy night it was, and at that hour Regent's Park is practically deserted. Philbeach must have just propped Sandy up in a corner, got out when they reached the pub and told the taxi to drive to this place in Golders Green.'

'What have the police got to say about it?'

'Nothing. Sandy went out to Wembley this morning, where this chap Philbeach lives, and discovered that he packed up and cleared out last night. It was only a sort of boarding house and he hadn't been living there for long. After that Sandy got his previous address from the wine firm that the fellow worked for, which proved to be another place of much the same kind at Harrow. They couldn't tell him anything there either. He can't remember the name of the pub, so he says it is not worth the bother of going to Scotland Yard. I think he's right, too; after all he wasn't sufficiently badly hurt for the police to take it up as a case of attempted murder and one can hardly expect them to excite themselves about the recovery of an old knobkerrie.'

'I wonder what this man Philbeach is up to? It looks as though he means to do a bit of treasure-seeking, too.'

'That's about the only explanation there is for it and as a matter of fact that's why, on second thoughts, Sandy decided to tell me what had really happened. He seems to think Philbeach may have a go at trying to get the leopard skin from me.'

'How could he know that you've got it?'

'I don't know that he does, but if he's sufficiently interested in this thing to risk cracking Sandy's skull he may know the whole family history and even have been watching us yesterday when we walked out of old Bullett's office with our various bits of native gear.'

Patricia nodded. 'Yes, I suppose that is a possibility, but

why should Sandy take the trouble to invent this silly story about having had a taxi smash?'

'Oh! that was awfully funny.' Michael sat back with a sudden chuckle. 'It seems that he dislikes the Bennetts so much that he couldn't bear the thought of confessing to having been fooled in front of them.'

'Quite a reasonable little bit of human vanity, I suppose,' Patricia smiled. 'Anyhow, it was nice of him to give you the tip.'

'He gave me something else as well, which I thought was jolly decent of him, and that's a book about the place. Look! I've got it here.'

'But how thrilling.' Patricia took the book and read out the title: ' "The Seven Lost Trails of Africa. A record of sundry expeditions, new and old, in search of buried treasure, by Hedley A. Chilvers." Have you had a chance to read it?'

'Yes, and jolly interesting it is. Unfortunately, it only gives about ten pages on our Lost Valley of Precious Stones, that the natives call the "Place of the Great Glitter", so I was able to run through them on the way out here. It definitely says, though, that early prospectors reached it, and that a number of attempts had been made to locate it since. Of course, Uncle John must have been there about six years before it was written, but naturally the author wouldn't know anything about that. Anyhow, he confirms all we've heard about the difficulty and danger of getting there, and it sounds a most gruesome place from his description.'

For a few moments Patricia sat silent, quickly skimming through the account of her illegal inheritance that was given in the book.

Michael meanwhile picked up a little statuette of a prancing horse from a nearby table. 'This is jolly nice,' he remarked. 'The action is so natural.'

'Do you like it?' She looked up with a quick smile. 'I think that's one of the best things I've ever done.'

'What! You don't mean to say you did this?'

'Yes, I sculpt a bit, you know.'

'Do you—really! I say, that makes me feel awful small

fry. I only just scraped through the engineering exams that my father was so anxious I should take, and I can't do anything out of the ordinary except speak Portuguese.'

'That seems a strange accomplishment. Why did you learn it?'

'Oh, one of my aunts on Father's side married a Portugoose. She's a darling and I've stayed out there dozens of times ever since I was a kid. The only other thing I'm any good at is handling horses. Do you like horses too?'

'Yes, I adore them. My one regret is that I can't live in the country—I have to cheat myself by modelling horses instead of riding them—which I only get the chance to now and then.'

'You must come down to Harcourt,' he enthused. 'We get some damn good hunting. Of course, it's not quite the same since my father died, but the people round about are most awfully good—and I'm sure I could fix you for a mount.'

'I should love to. I don't get much practice but I'm pretty good because horses like me, and I'm game to try any mount you care to put me up on.' She turned back to the book and when she looked up once more her eyes were grave and a little unhappy. 'Michael,' she said suddenly, 'do you often tell lies to people?'

'Well—no,' he smiled, 'not about serious things. It makes me feel so darned uncomfortable.'

She nodded. 'Yes, so it does me. That's why I want to tell you something.'

'What?' he asked quietly.

'Father would be furious if he knew that I had let the cat out of the bag, but we *are* going to Africa—too.'

6

A Thief in the Night

Once Patricia had made her confession she felt easier in her mind, despite the fact that her father had impressed upon her the necessity of secrecy. Michael's frankness had made her feel uncomfortable and she felt that as he had kept nothing back from her it was only fair to let him know the true situation.

The knowledge that she was going to Africa after all increased Michael's disappointment that they could not make the journey together. He could think of no reason for his uncle's secrecy even if he was determined to travel alone. Patricia could not enlighten him in the least. In exchange for the warning he had given her about Philbeach however, she told him that they had also inquired at Lucy Benton's late address and Israel Rubenstein's in Whitechapel the previous afternoon—and added that her father had intended to trace Philbeach through his old firm, if possible that morning.

Over tea he begged her not to go further than the Cape, and at all costs not to allow herself to become involved in any smuggling activities that her father might devise.

She was a little touched by his solicitude but could not help laughing at his romantic desire to treat her as a storybook princess instead of a modern girl.

When they had finished tea they talked for a time about their everyday lives. Then she took him to a small room at the back of the house and showed him her other efforts at sculpture. Patricia felt very mature beside this new cousin who seemed to bring such zest into the ordinary business of living. She heard herself laughing and joking in a way which would have surprised and shocked her father.

She had been reared in a hard school and learnt to control her emotions when she was still an infant. Her mother died

44

when she was twelve and her father was embarrassed and awkward if she attempted any familiarities.

Michael's demonstrative affection for his mother—the caressing way in which he slipped his hand through her own arm as they stood in front of her models—gave her a feeling of mental liberty and well-being for which her repressed nature was hungry. Suddenly she caught sight of the clock. Astonished that the time had gone so quickly she became suddenly apprehensive that her father would arrive before Michael was out of the house.

There was no reason why Henry Long should object to Michael calling, yet she knew quite well that if he came upon them laughing together he would manifest one of those solemn disapproving silences during the rest of the evening which always made her feel so miserable and uncomfortable. Sometimes she thought that she was unjust to him and only imagined that his moods had any connection with her own doings. That did not affect the fact however, that they often made her feel a quite unreasonable sense of guilt for having indulged in some perfectly innocent pleasure.

In nervous haste she promised to make one last effort to induce her father to alter his mind and join the others on the African expedition instead of them going alone. Then, having assured Michael that whatever happened she would take good care of herself, she hurried him out of the house.

Henry Long did not actually make his appearance until an hour and a half later. He had no regular business but owned several considerable blocks of flat property which he managed himself to the distress, irritation, and sometimes fury of his numerous tenants.

No landlord in London possessed, to quite the same degree, the art of postponing small but necessary repairs, for which he was liable, until the occupants of his flats were driven by continual discomfort into doing them at their own expense. Now that he had made up his mind to leave England for a period, which might extend to several months, he had a multitude of instructions to impress upon the miserable underdog who earned a pittance in his office. In addition he had spent a good portion of his day in a fruitless search for Roger Philbeach.

As they sat down to dinner he told Patricia of his visits to the wine merchant's office and the boarding house at Wembley from which, to his disgust, he had learned of Philbeach's sudden departure the night before. In return, although she would have preferred not to mention Michael's visit, she felt bound to tell her father the reason for Philbeach's flight.

Rather to her surprise he seemed more amused than annoyed that Michael should have called, and questioned her eagerly as to all that he had said regarding the plans of the Bennett party.

After dinner they had just finished listening to the News Bulletin over the wireless when a telegram arrived and having read it Henry looked across at his daughter.

'Listen to this! *"Mother knocked down by taxicab this afternoon and seriously injured, taken to St. George's hospital, come at once. Michael."* '

'Oh, that poor boy, how terrible for him!'

Henry gave her a sharp glance from his shrewd eyes. 'Do you know where this young man and his mother are staying?'

Patricia shook her head. 'No, he never mentioned it.'

'That's a pity, and it's too late to get their address from Bullett, because his office will be shut.'

'But the wire says they have taken her to St. George's Hospital.'

'I wonder.' Henry refolded the telegram carefully and put it in his pocket. 'I am by no means convinced that Gertrude has been run over at all.'

'You think . . .'

'That this is nothing but a plan to get me out of the house for a couple of hours to-night while Philbeach tries his hand at breaking in—in the hope of getting the necklace.'

Patricia nodded. 'Seeing what happened to Sandy I shouldn't be at all surprised, but how can you be certain? It would be a terrible thing if Aunt Gertrude is dying and you didn't go.'

46

'I should certainly go in the ordinary way if she sent for me, but this telegram is supposed to come from Michael, not his mother. Since your aunt has never displayed anything but a most unreasonable bitterness towards me I hardly think it likely that she would wish to see me at her deathbed.'

'What do you mean to do then?'

'Stay here. Or rather I shall leave the house in about ten minutes and return through the garden gate at the back of the orchard. Then I shall be here if Mr. Philbeach does attempt anything.'

'What do you wish me to do?'

'It would be best if you stay here and continue your sewing for about half an hour. Then put the lights out and go up to bed in a perfectly normal manner. Don't read in bed though, or not for more than ten minutes, because your light should be out too, in order to give him the impression that he has a clear field. If this is a plant it would take me about an hour and a half to get up to St. George's—discover I had been tricked—and get back again, so he will have to make his attempt some time before half past eleven. It is a quarter to ten now. If you do as I have told you the coast will be clear for him apparently by about half past, and he'll think that he has got a good hour in which to search for the necklace before I get back.'

'I see.' Patricia stood up. 'What about the servants?'

'We needn't worry about them. They always go up about ten.'

'But, Daddy, remember what he did to Sandy—say he went for you—isn't it awfully risky?' Patricia looked at her father with an anxious look in her hazel eyes.

'Don't worry, my dear, I shall have the whip hand of him all right. I want you to keep your ears open and, directly you hear me stamp on the floor three times, or if you hear any sound of a struggle, run down into the hall and telephone for the police.'

As the clock on the mantelpiece chimed ten Henry Long left his house, and going round to the garage at the side, got out his ancient Buick. Carefully locking the garage doors he drove slowly down the short drive and took the road for London. When he had gone about three quarters of a mile he pulled up at a filling station and handed over his car to the man in charge. Then, with swift steps he hastened down a few byways which led to the back of his house and let himself in to the garden by the orchard gate.

He stood there for a moment scrutinising the dark shadows and listening intently in case the expected intruder had already secreted himself among the trees. No sound broke the stillness except that of an occasional car going down the main road in front of the house. He tiptoed carefully across the grass under the deep shadow of a hedge and, noting that the servants had already gone up, slipped into the house through the scullery door. When he had passed through the dark kitchen he found the light still on in the hall and not wishing to be seen through one of the lighted windows flattened himself against the wall until he reached the door of his study.

There was just enough light filtering in through the curtains for him to discern vaguely the more bulky pieces of furniture. Walking softly over to his desk, he took a service revolver from one of the drawers; then arranging an armchair behind a screen which stood near the door, so that he would only need to stretch out his hand to switch on the light, he settled down with his revolver on his knees to wait.

Some ten minutes later, although it seemed considerably longer to him as he sat intent and watchful in the darkness, he heard Patricia go up to bed. For a while faint sounds reached him of her movements overhead, then complete silence settled upon the house. The time seemed interminable as the minutes dragged by and he began to believe, after a period which he calculated to be at least an hour, that the telegram must have been genuine after all; yet it was not in Henry Long's nature to give up once he had set his mind to a thing. He was determined to sit it out until he heard the clock in the church down the road strike midnight, by which time he would certainly have got back to his house from London if the telegram was a fake.

Just as he had made up his mind as to the time limit he would set upon his watch, the clock began to chime. Surely it could not be midnight yet he thought, and having counted the strokes suddenly realised that it was only eleven. At that moment he heard a faint creaking at the window.

With the greatest care to make no sound he rose to his feet and peered round the edge of the screen. In the faint light he could see the curtain moving and the dark shadow of a man stealthily climbing in over the sill. He waited for a moment until the intruder had produced a small electric torch and, flashing it round until it rested on the desk, tip-toed over towards it. Henry switched on the light and pointing his revolver said gruffly:

'Hands up!'

The stranger dropped his torch and swung round with a muttered oath. He was standing at the far side of the room from the window. In the face of Henry's revolver, he saw that he would stand no chance if he made a dash for it so with a rueful grin, he raised two leg of mutton hands above his head.

'Mr. Roger Philbeach, I believe?' said Henry quietly.

'That's me.' The big man lowered his hands again. 'You're pretty smart, aren't you, driving out in your old tin can of a car like that and then sneaking back?'

'I thought that was the best way of making certain of being able to hand you over to the police.'

'I don't think somehow you're going to be such a fool as to do that.'

'Why? I've caught you red-handed breaking into my house with felonious intent.'

'Oh, it's a fair cop all right but what good would it do you if you did?'

'None, except the satisfaction of having put a stop to your game whatever it may be and, after that blackguardly attack you made on my nephew last night, I imagine they would put you away for quite a little time.'

'So you know about that eh?' Philbeach's big, coarse face broke into a grin. 'Well that's all to the good because you must have heard that I managed to get possession of the knobkerrie.'

Henry, scowling by the door, still held the big man covered with his gun. 'That does not interest me in the least.'

A worried frown suddenly creased Philbeach's broad, low forehead. 'Go on! you don't mean that,' he said huskily. 'These things your brother left mean a fortune if only anyone can show them in the right quarter.'

'What do you know about it?' Henry asked, his interest skilfully concealed by the brusqueness of his tone.

'What do I know?' The other leaned forward eagerly. 'Why, wasn't I you brother's best friend? No one knew him better than I did. That's why the moment I got the lawyer's letter about his having left me the money in the Will, I said to myself, "Now here's a chance, a real chance, five thousand's very nice, but old John's left something of far more value I'll be bound to one or other of his relatives, and if I play my cards right there's a million in this thing for me."'

'So you set about it by cracking young McDiamid over the head?' said Henry dryly.

'Oh, I was on the game long before that,' Philbeach assured him. 'I made a pal of a young fellow in the lawyer's office and paid him a pretty tidy sum to get me a copy of the Will and that letter while old Bullett was making his inquiries about how the diamond laws might affect you. Then yesterday afternoon he tipped me off as to which of you had drawn the knobkerrie, the necklace and the skin. After that, all I had to do was to sit pretty and wait events. It was a cinch that one or other of you would try to get in touch with all the beneficiaries in the hope of digging up the low-down on where old John got the stuff. McDiamid was the first to fall for it and I was lucky enough to be able to deal with him.'

'And to-night, I suppose, you thought you would collect the necklace? Instead of which you're going to prison for several months.'

'Now look here, for the Lord's sake talk reasonable. I don't know if you meant to take a trip to Africa or not. Maybe, having only one of the clues and no other information, you thought the chances against finding this place too great, but between us now we've got two out of three of them and if we work together we'll have the other before long . . .'

'I thought one was sufficient in any case,' interrupted Henry.

'Not a bit of it,' Philbeach hastened on, 'one clue leads to the proper use of another. Your necklace may be absolutely useless without my knobkerrie, but if we could get the three, with my special knowledge of old John's doings, there's a million in this thing for us both.'

For the first time Henry allowed his face to relax and lowered his gun. Patricia, lying awake in the darkness upstairs, waited in vain for the pre-arranged signal. It never came and thinking of Michael she at last dropped off to sleep.

7

The Quickest Way to Africa

Immediately Patricia woke the following morning the events of the previous night came back to her and, with a sudden sickening feeling that something terrible might have happened to her father after she had fallen asleep, she leapt out of bed and rushed into his room.

To her relief Henry was there, safe and well. In answer to her hurried inquiries he told her blandly that Philbeach had not put in an appearance the night before after all and so he had come up to bed a little after twelve.

She began to worry then on Michael's account, assuming that the telegram must have been genuine and his mother possibly dying. Directly after breakfast she rang up Mr. Bullett in the hope of getting his address. The lawyer could only give her Harcourt Priory and had no idea where the

Kane-Swifts were staying in London. She then tried St. George's Hospital and was puzzled to learn that they had no one of that name in the wards. Having no other means of ascertaining his whereabouts, she had to abandon her inquiry.

That afternoon her father telephoned to say that he was bringing a friend home to dinner and when they arrived just after seven, Patricia did not know quite what to make of this new acquaintance—introduced as Mr. Philip Wisdon. He was a big, blustering man of about fifty with a booming voice who talked incessantly in a kind of cheerful, racy slang. His small, pig-like eyes looked even more minute in his big, heavy face, calculating and unsmiling even when he laughed heartily, devoid of the merriment his voice conveyed. Instinctively Patricia came to the conclusion that he was not to be trusted —not even with a hairpin!

She would have been even more convinced of this if she had known that Henry had insisted on Philbeach taking another name to avoid explaining his sudden *volte face* towards the raider of the night before.

He stood talking for some time after he arrived. At frequent intervals he looked hopefully—first at the clock and then at the door. Finally with boisterous joviality he said:

'Now, what about a little drink? Something with gin in it for preference—or a glass of sherry would do. Don't mind my asking, do you? The sun's been over the yard arm and gone down the other side again by now.'

On being informed that he was at present in a teetotal household he displayed a set of ill-fitting false teeth in a comically rueful grin and asked: Would they mind if he sent round the corner to buy a bottle of whisky and a couple of siphons for he couldn't talk business half the night dry like that.

Patricia began to wonder more and more the reason for her father having invited this stranger to the house. A man whose ways were so ill-assorted with his own; whose grossness so flagrantly contrasted with his cold austerity. Mr. Wisdon's request having been complied with, they sat down to dinner. Noting her wondering look Henry Long gave Patricia a brief explanation of Wisdon's presence.

He was, it appeared, not actually a South African but had lived there for many years and, curiously enough, had known Uncle John. He had been concerned in some small transaction between the two brothers a number of years before and, his name having occurred to Henry that morning, he had gone along to Wisdon's old address. The ensuing conversation had resulted in Mr. Wisdon being engaged as their courier, guide, and general assistant on the trip.

Wisdon knew all about niggers. Oh yes! and ox-spans, and biltong. He could inform you, very definitely, that Plus Four Whisky was the best to be had in the Union, although you might not know it well over here. He could talk by the hour about Assays and I.D.B. and diamondiferous ground, and if you preferred he could do it equally fluently in Basuto or Afrikaans.

After dinner they adjourned to the study where Henry outlined the whole of the situation, as he and Patricia knew it, for Mr. Wisdon's benefit.

'Trouble!' said Wisdon gravely when Henry had finished telling him what he knew of Michael and the Bennett's plans. 'Bad trouble! We've got to fly—that's all there is for it.'

'Fly!' exclaimed Henry. 'I don't think I'd care to do that.'

'Think again, old friend, think again,' boomed Mr. Wisdon. 'If we don't get there first we're sunk. I know the country so I can fix things up all right for us, but if there are a lot of innocents floating around Koranna Land on the same lay, they'll go and give the whole game away and like as not we'll get pinched too.'

'You think our only chance is to get there first and get away again before the others arrive then?' asked Patricia.

'That's the ticket,' he agreed, 'though I doubt if we could do the journey into the Kalahari and get back to Upington before they're on the spot, but the great thing is to get a few days' good start. Then, if necessary, we can break back by a different route, west perhaps across the Molopo River into Great Namaqualand. Of course we may run up against the

South African—Sandy what's-his-name—if he goes by air too, but we've got to chance that.'

'My daughter tells me that McDiamid has definitely decided not to make the attempt,' remarked Henry.

'Don't you believe it.' Mr. Wisdon closed one of his small dark eyes in a heavy wink. 'He *says* so, perhaps, because he doesn't want those inexperienced Londoners slung round his neck, but I'll bet a case of "cham" with anyone that he means to have a cut at it on the sly.'

'He is returning to South Africa on the Italian Line,' added Patricia; 'Michael told me so yesterday and I think he said that the ship sails from Marseilles the day after to-morrow.'

Wisdon nodded. 'Then he starts from London to-morrow morning. Those "Iti" boats beat the Union by a couple of days so he'll be in Cape Town on—let's see now—yes, the 12th February. There's an Air Liner leaving on the 1st. I looked it up before I came along this evening. It's an eight day trip so if we take that we'll be in Jo'burg by the 8th, and inside the Union four clear days ahead of him.'

Henry nodded unhappily. 'You feel then it is absolutely essential to fly?'

'I'm dead certain of it. If we can put our inquiries through quick, then get down to Upington on the Orange River, not much comment is going to be caused by one party buying an out-span and setting off up country if they give out they're going on a bit of a hunt. If another party turns up, like these Bennetts, who've never handled a gun in their lives, and then perhaps a third, all sorts of people are going to sit up and take notice, so it's up to us to strain every nerve to get there—*and* two or three days' march clear of the town —before the balloon goes up.'

'All right,' Henry agreed, 'since you consider it essential. At all events we shall be ahead of the Bennetts. The Union Castle boat does not get into Cape Town until the 13th.'

In consequence, five days later Patricia found herself boarding an Air Liner with her father and the boisterous, capable Mr. Wisdon, who seemed to have taken command of

54

the party. Her feelings were extremely mixed. Apart from a few visits to the Continent she had never been out of England before and she was thrilled at the thought that she was now going to see something of a more spacious world. She was a little anxious that she might be air sick, but that was compensated for by the knowledge that she would be stopping in such exciting places as Egypt, The Soudan, Uganda and on the border of the Great Lakes. She was, however, by no means happy in the society of Mr. Wisdon, who seemed to have taken an embarrassing fancy to her in the last few days. After her father's reticence it was pleasant to have her opinion asked about the smallest details of their plans, but there was a suggestion of a desire for something more than mere friendliness in the way he presented her with a large box of chocolates on his second visit to Surbiton, flowers on the third, and now more flowers, more chocolates and a sheaf of illustrated papers for the journey. He was, within a few years, as old as her father although, from the difference in their behaviour, they might have been generations apart. Her great difficulty lay in concealing her strong dislike for his personality and the way in which his bumptious joviality got on her nerves.

Before sailing Michael had written her a charming letter which was at present reposing in her bag, saying that he had hoped to find her name on the passenger list, but failing to do so he assumed that she was travelling by a later boat. He wished her every possible good luck and hoped very much that they would meet in South Africa, but he said no word of any serious accident to his mother, which seemed extraordinary. If there had been an accident she thought it odd that he should gaily set off for Africa, leaving his mother in such a state, yet how otherwise was the telegram to be accounted for, since Philbeach had never attempted to enter the house after all. Her woman's curiosity still demanded an explanation of this seeming mystery. She revolved these problems from every angle in her mind but was at last compelled to give them up.

The journey was uneventful and, after the first two days, boring in the extreme. Hour after hour the plane roared on while brown, green, grey, and yellow stretches of land seemed to be ripped away from underneath them. The height was too great for them to distinguish much detail and, despite the swiftly changing latitude, the scenery proved incredibly monotonous; but the nights were a joy. Each evening they landed many hundred miles farther to the south and the varying costumes of the native servants, the strange new foods which were served at the Air Port Hotels, and the tropic nights with their countless stars and croaking tree frogs, kept Patricia in a glow of happy excitement. Even the heat on the Equator and the unwelcome attentions of Mr. Wisdon were not sufficient to mar her enjoyment seriously.

On the eighth day after leaving London they landed, in accordance with schedule, at Germiston, outside Johannesburg, and, driving into the town, put up at the Carlton Hotel. Their plans had already been completed before leaving England. Wisdon had a vague acquaintance with old Van Niekerk who was mentioned in the Will, and described him as 'one of those damned Dutchmen, who think they're the Salt of the Earth because their families happen to have lived out in South Africa for a couple of hundred years.'

'There's a whole bunch of them,' he had gone on to explain. 'The Cloetes, the Marais, the De Villiers and the Van der Buls and a few more such who form a sort of aristocracy on their own. They're not altogether Dutch either but have quite a good bit of French blood in them from the Huguenots who settled out here in seventeen something, and of course a bit of British too, because all the families have intermarried quite a lot, but they think of themselves only as South Africans, and they run the whole place from first to last. Some of them fought against us in the Boer War too but for all the good our winning that war did us we might just as well have stayed at home. All the lower-class farmers support these S.A. blokes at the elections. They get nearly all the seats in Parliament and in consequence collar every Government job that's any good.'

'Well, plenty of them fought *with* us in the last war and

after all it is their country,' Patricia had protested, which closed the conversation.

They knew, of course, from Bullett, that old Van Niekerk was dead, but being a member of such a prominent family they felt that it should be easy to trace his relatives, as they had the address at which he had lived in Pretoria.

Accordingly, on the morning following their arrival Wisdon, who had hired a car, drove them over to Pretoria. As they ran out through the fine suburbs of Johannesburg towards the north, Patricia and her father were astonished at the size of the town. Both had always thought of it as still a mining town with probably one or two streets of good shops and a few hotels and theatres. Neither had visualised it as the second largest city in Africa. To their surprise thousands and thousands of fine houses, each with its lovely garden, tennis court, and swimming pool—reminiscent, with their white fronts and red-tiled roofs in the Spanish or Dutch Colonial style, of pictures that they had seen of Hollywood —stretched for miles round the outskirts of the city.

The thirty miles of good road were soon eaten up and by eleven o'clock they entered the smaller, old world town of Pretoria, all exclaiming, as they ran up Church Street, at the beauty of the wonderful Union building dominating the town from its position on a hill-side to the north. The brown stone of its pillared porticos and long surfaces radiated the brilliant sunshine. In its setting of cypress trees and lovely gardens, it looked like a fairy palace.

Henry would not allow Patricia to drive up to it as she wished, insisting that business must come first. Having found the right number in the long street, which cuts through both town and suburb, they pulled up outside the Van Nierke. ks' house.

Their inquiry from a native boy, dressed in white with a red sash like a foreign order running from his shoulders to its tasselled end on the hip, elicited the information that the house was now occupied by Mr. Cornelius Van Niekerk, the old man's son.

On asking to see him they were shown into a wide, low,

airy room giving on to a broad veranda. Masses of brightly coloured flowers were set about it in black, curiously designed pots of native ware, and Patricia was enchanted with the bright, cheerful colourfulness of the room.

After a few moments a tall, fair young man, dressed in a smart grey lounge suit, came in to them. With a pleasant smile and a quick wave of the hand he asked them to sit down and tell him what he could do for them.

Henry stated their business and asked if he had ever known his brother John. But young Van Niekerk shook his head.

'No, I never met him,' he said in rather a high-pitched but very cultured voice. 'But, of course, I've heard lots about him.'

'Then I should be much obliged if you can tell me anything of his life out here that you may know,' said Henry.

The little wrinkles round Van Niekerk's bright blue eyes suddenly crinkled into a smile as he sprang up from his armchair and whipped a cablegram off the mantelpiece. 'I'm sorry,' he laughed. 'I can't tell you a single thing, and if you read that you will see why.'

Henry took it from him and as he scanned it his brows drew down into an angry frown. It read:

Van Niekerk, Jacaradas, Church Street, Pretoria, S.A. Was at Cape University with your cousin Paul. He will give you particulars of me. Regret by your father's death you will not benefit under Will of late John Thomas Long. Inquiries may be made from you concerning source of Long's wealth. In your own interests give no information until my arrival. Sailing January 29th. Proceeding Pretoria immediately. Sandy McDiamid.

8

The Knobkerrie of the Zulu Induna

After his production of the telegram Mr. Van Niekerk insisted that they should join him at morning tea, inquired politely as to their journey out, and mentioned a number of interesting things that they should certainly see while they were in South Africa. But he remained absolutely firm in his decision to give them no information whatsoever with regard to the late John Thomas Long.

When they left his house Patricia had her way, and they drove up to the Unigebouw, after which they spent a couple of hours in the town and, having lunched at Turkestra's, returned to Johannesburg. Patricia would have liked to stay longer in Pretoria but Wisdon was feeling the heat, for the town, ringed in by hills on every side, was sultry to such a degree that he was anxious to get back to the higher altitude of Johannesburg. Van Niekerk having refused them his assistance, they were a little worried now that Sandy might have cabled the other beneficiaries and that they would meet with similiar opposition from them. Henry pointed out, however that Van Niekerk had probably been influenced by the fact that McDiamid was a friend of his cousin's, whereas it was not likely that he would have any pull of that kind with Mrs. Aileen Orkney or Joe-Jack Mahout.

It was decided that, Durban being so much nearer than Cape Town, they should endeavour to trace the Indian barman before attending to Mrs. Orkney and so the following morning they set off to motor to the coast.

The first part of their journey lay through the heart of the Gold Fields which have brought the great Metropolis into being. Vast, flat-topped heaps of sand like miniature mountains loomed up a mile or so distant from each other in every direction. In colour they varied from the palest silver to a deep brown gold, having a peculiar beauty of their own in the strong sunshine. Wisdon told the others that the giant dumps composed the residue of the millions of tons of rock which had been hewn and pounded from the great Witwatersrand, or Ridge of the White Waters that ran beneath them, in the forty years since its first discovery.

When they had passed through the mining area the country became dull and uninteresting. Long stretches of coarse grass, baked brown by the relentless sun, alternated with patches of mealies and Kaffir corn. Patricia, who had expected to see tropical vegetation and strange animal life, was horribly disappointed. Hardly a tree was to be seen, and except for a funny little bird called, she learned, a Sakabula which could hardly fly more than a dozen yards owing to the weight of a tail at least eight times the length of its body, no living thing, other than a few cattle and an occasional native, was to be seen. The dreary landscape reminded her rather of Salisbury Plain as she had seen it after a year of exceptional drought. Wisdon, however, told her that Johannesburg was situated on the high veldt, nearly six thousand feet above sea level, but that when they got down to the coast by Durban she would see plenty of real sub-tropical scenery.

At the little town of Volksrust which they reached about twelve o'clock, they passed out of the Transvaal, entered the Province of Natal, and pushed on as far as Newcastle for luncheon. In the afternoon the driving became much more difficult, since the road had no sort of resemblance to the fine Johannesburg-Pretoria highway upon which they had been the day before. It was little better than a sandy track with deep ruts and occasional patches of loose stones. When they reached the Glencoe district they found that it had been raining in the morning, and every now and again they encountered stretches where the moisture had turned the surface of the track into red slime. Henry was scandalised that any civilised people could allow a main road between two such important cities to remain in such a shocking state and Wisdon said gruffly:

'Scandal's the word all right! The Government own the

railways here so they deliberately neglect the roads in the hope of forcing people to travel by train. All I hope is that we're able to get through at all.'

As they passed Majuba they were not averaging more than ten miles an hour and in places the car skidded from side to side in a most alarming fashion. Fortunately Wisdon had had the forethought to put chains on his tyres before leaving Newcastle and so they got through all right. It was not until half-past six that they managed to reach Ladysmith, where he insisted on stopping for a couple of large whiskies which he very badly needed.

Patricia and her father, meanwhile, took a stroll up the main street of the little town and were interested to find a photographer's shop which had in its window a number of faded photographs of young men with long moustaches and broad-brimmed hats, grouped in various postures about old-fashioned guns and redoubts, taken at the time of the famous Siege.

At seven o'clock they set out again. A slight drizzle began as the short twilight deepened into darkness. After half an hour they passed the Tugela River at Colenso and an hour later pulled up at Estcourt where they decided to stay the night.

They were all thoroughly glad of the warmth and cheerfulness in the Plough Hotel after their long day, and Patricia was enchanted, when she entered the dining-room, to see on every table tall bunches of the long-stemmed cosmos flowers, white, mauve and purple, which she had noticed on their journey growing in great patches, a weed among the mealie fields.

Wisdon made for the bar directly after dinner but Henry and his daughter decided on an early night, as they were to set off again at nine the following morning.

They woke to a day of drizzling rain and the Longs found the scenery even more depressing than on the previous day. As they entered the uplands of Natal large banks of white mist obscured all but an occasional view, and often encompassed them entirely. But when they reached Howick

Falls it lifted a little and, running down the long gradients into Pietermaritzburg, they at last saw something of the desolate grandeur of the valley of a Thousand Hills.

Owing to the mist their going had been slow again in the morning, so they had an early lunch in the capital of Natal and pressed on to Durban, then in the last fifty miles of their journey Patricia was able to see palm trees and pawpaws, and banana and mango plantations, with the blue sea of the Indian Ocean stretching away in the far distance.

They drove at once to the Royal and having booked their rooms inquired at the office for Joe-Jack Mahout. They learned that he had left the hotel several years previously. Owing to recent inquiries made by a London lawyer, however, the hotel people were able to furnish them with his present address—a house in the Indian quarter on the shores of the land-locked bay beyond Albert Park; so they drove out there immediately.

The way lay through the wharfs and factories in the commercial quarter of the town and then along low-lying marsh ground round the curve of the Bay which looked like a great lake. In one place the Longs noted a white Indian Temple decorated with elephant heads and ornate carving in the true Hindu style. It seemed queerly incongruous in this country of whites and negroes, lying apparently unattended on the waste ground below the level of the road, but a mile farther on they saw the reason for its presence. Long lines of ramshackle tumbledown bungalows and shacks, in the last stage of disrepair and squalor, seethed with a multitude of white-veiled women, turbaned men and screaming, quarrelling Indian children.

No names or numbers appeared on any of these crowded properties and it was only after prolonged inquiries at various tin-roofed stores, all displaying the same strange assortment of goods from calico knickers to mouldy lemons, that they discovered Mahout's dwelling. A fat, oily-looking woman, from whose ears dangled a couple of gold ornaments like chair springs, waddled out to meet them, accompanied by a horde of noisy, lank-haired children. To Wisdon's questioning she answered that Joe-Jack was no longer there, great fortune had descended on him in his old age and no more than a week before he had moved to more spacious quarters. It seemed that Joe-Jack Mahout was now the envy and admiration of the entire Asiatic population of Durban, numbering some fifty thousand souls, and their informant assured them that had they asked for him by name, instead of inquiring for his old address, the first child in the street could have led them to his new residence. She gabbled quick directions and, ten minutes later, they pulled up outside a long bungalow which was in the process of receiving a new coat of paint. Here disappointment awaited them.

Joe-Jack Mahout's seventh son received them in a room crammed with gaudy carpets, beaten brasses, shawls, filigree silver-ware and other Eastern finery; all obviously quite recently acquired. He smirked and bowed and smirked again washing his yellow hands with invisible soap, but informed them that his altogether admirable parent was not at home. Joe-Jack's first purchase on receiving the five thousand pounds had been a motor car, and in it he had gone off that day to visit his miserable poverty-stricken brother. He would however, his son thought, have returned by the following afternoon.

The Longs had to return to Durban and possess themselves in patience, but Patricia was not unhappy about the respite from further journeying, for although it was four days since their arrival at Johannesburg she seemed to have done nothing yet but travel all the time. Now she would have a few hours at least in which to see something of one of South Africa's finest cities.

The wide streets and open spaces impressed her greatly when they drove round Durban on the following morning and particularly the fine houses on the Berea above the town with their magnificent view of the great land-locked bay.

Before lunch they drove out to the ocean beach, and the two men sat watching the great white rollers, while Patricia went in for a swim. Her father was a little nervous because Wisdon said that there were plenty of man-eating sharks off the Durban beaches, but the bathing attendant assured him that she would be perfectly safe as long as she kept inside the line of breakers and that he had already warned her. She came out glowing with health from the buffeting of the surf and lay for as long as she dared afterwards in the grilling sunshine. Then they all lunched at the Hotel Edward and afterwards drove out to Joe-Jack's once more.

The Indian was at home this time and rose with some difficulty, owing to his enormous bulk, from a couch which seemed little wider than an arm-chair when he occupied it. Like the Van Niekerks he had received a telegram asking him to give no information about his benefactor before Sandy McDiamid's arrival, but the ex-barman saw no reason why he should pay the least attention to it. He proved to be a simple jolly creature who delighted in the chance to talk about his late patron. On one point only he preseved a careful silence, skilfully turning aside Wisdon's leading questions, and that was the nature of the service he had rendered to John Thomas Long which had resulted in that gentleman remembering him in his Will. For more than an an hour he gave rambling garrulous descriptions of the feckless white man's scandalous way of life and open-handed generosity when he had money in his pockets, while his enormous paunch shook like a jelly with rumbling laughter as he described some more than usually drunken party at which he had been in charge of the liquid refreshment.

Of leopard skin karosses, knobkerries, or witch doctors' necklaces he could tell them nothing, but one important fact came to light in the conversation. A Zulu Induna named N'hluzili had been John's head boy on a number of his prospecting expeditions, and Joe-Jack was certain that he had been with him when he had last set out. Moreover, the native in question was still living a year before, a rich and influential petty chieftain, in his kraal near a place called Sezela about fifty miles down the coast.

In high feather at this real success the Wisdon party took leave of the gargantuan Hindoo and, at dinner that night, Wisdon insisted upon Patricia sharing a bottle of champagne with him, suggesting also that she should call him 'Phil'.

The next morning they set out for Sezela and passing round the land-locked bay of Natal to the rising ground on its far side caught glimpses of the town and harbour, spread out like a map below them, through gaps which occurred here and there in the dense jungle-like woods, where tiny monkeys chattered among the thick impenetrable creepers.

Unlike the day before the weather was magnificent and the road wound through valley after valley, some areas of which were planted with broad fields of sugar-cane, and the barrenness of others relieved by cactus, aloes, century plants and aged tattered banana palms. In the whole fifty-mile journey only two villages were passed, and a sugar factory where the stench of the rotting cane was abominable, but the country was abundant with life. On almost every hill-side little clusters of round bee-hive huts marked a native kraal. The cattle near them seemed plentiful and well tended and many Zulus were to be seen on the roads. The women were invariably carrying some article, which would vary in size from a small milk jug to an entire bed, upon their heads. The further they advanced the more picturesque the inhabitants became. The dirty dungarees and cloth caps of the men gave place to worked leather aprons and curious head-dresses—the cheap cottons of the women to a splendid nudity except for a bead-embroidered loin cloth and necklace. Patricia could now appreciate why the Zulus have been described as the finest physical race in the world. A little before midday they pulled up at a small village in a well wooded area called Umboni Park, and secured directions to N'hluzili's kraal.

Having taken a side road for a few miles through another valley Wisdon halted the car at a bend in the road below a steep slope. Some three hundred yards up the rise an unusually large collection of beehive huts showed a good-sized native village. Getting out, Wisdon produced a suit-case and a parcel from the luggage box at the back of the car, then seeing that Patricia had got out too he said to her quickly:

' 'Fraid we can't take you with us to see this chap.'

'Oh! Why?' she protested.

'Well, the nigs are a bit touchy about white women, you know. They don't mind men, but it wouldn't be exactly etiquette to take you up to this old boy's hut. In fact he'd probably be so annoyed that it would queer the whole pitch, so you'd best wait here.'

Concealing her disappointment as well as she could Patricia climbed back into the car, while her father and Wisdon started off together up the hill.

When they reached the kraal, Wisdon asked one of the little naked native children if the Induna N'hluzili was still alive, and learned to his great satisfaction that he was. The woolly-headed brat scampered off, and a few moments later a tall, skinny old man with a circle of leather about the top of his bald head came, with a slow, dignified step, towards them.

Wisdon offered greetings in fluent Zulu and, unpacking the parcel, displayed two bottles of Scotch whisky which he presented with a jovial flourish. The old man signed to one of the numerous women who stood in a group behind him gazing curiously at the strangers, and she carried the bottles away. Then he led his visitors to his own hut, a complete bee-hive, with only a hole big enough to crawl through for an entrance but considerably larger than the rest and, motioning them to be seated in front of it, sank down himself on his lean haunches.

Kaffir beer was set before them, a white frothy mixture in clay pots, which Wisdon assured Henry was non-alcoholic, rather than have to explain his reason for not accepting the Induna's hospitality. While emaciated old women and plump-breasted young ones, children of both sexes and all ages, goats, chickens and kaffir dogs crowded round, Wisdon explained their business and the old chief nodded gravely, making a sign of reverence when he heard mentioned the name of John Thomas Long.

Wisdon then produced the necklace of monkey skulls from the suit-case and handed it to N'hluzili who looked at it curiously for a moment.

'This is not of my people,' he said fingering the sparse

grey beard that decorated his bony chin. 'Such are worn by the miserable Bushmen in whose blood my nation washed their spears in the days that are gone. It may be that this thing has been handed from father to son as a memory of the time when Dingaan's Impis made the earth thunder with the stamping of their feet. It may belong to some survivor of this Slave Race who live now on the edge of the "Great Thirst" which is all of Africa that your people and my people have left to them between us, but I have never seen this thing before.'

With a nod of understanding Wisdon translated the Zulu's speech to Henry, adding that by the 'Great Thirst' N'hluzili meant the Kalahari Desert. He then produced the knob-kerrie.

At the sight of the weapon the old native's dark eyes brightened and taking it with loving care into his skinny hands he weighed it carefully.

'This I know well,' he said at once. 'It was my own when I was a young warrior and with it I have sent many men to join the Spirits of their Fathers.'

Wisdon gave a sudden chuckle of joy and slapped Henry on the back.

'Got it, my boy!' he cried excitedly. 'Now we shan't be long!' and he rushed into a quick spate of Zulu, asking N'hluzili how soon he could be ready to guide them upon the same journey as the last which he had undertaken with his old master.

'I have many wives,' said N'hluzili slowly. 'Much cattle, strong sons, and all things that I could desire—but few years left me in which to enjoy them.'

'Now don't you be stupid,' Wisdon urged with an angry look. 'We'll pay you well—much money—many head of cattle!' But he knew that the law would prevent his forcing the Zulu should he refuse to go and he was filled with bitter helpless rage when N'hluzili replied with slightly contemptuous finality:

'Nothing that any man can offer would ever tempt me to enter the "Land of the Great Thirst" again.'

9

Sandy Makes an Alliance in Pretoria

On the morning of the Longs' interview with Joe-Jack Mahout, while Patricia was sampling the delights of pawpaw served with orange juice as a breakfast dish, Sandy McDiamid was passing his baggage through the Customs at Cape Town.

He was the only one among the relatives of the late John Thomas Long who fully realised the dangers and difficulties of the task they were attempting, and it was for that reason he had declined to go in with Michael and the Bennetts.

As a South African he considered that he stood a sporting chance of reaching the place and getting away with the spoil; but he was quite convinced that the odds were heavily against any of the others succeeding. These Englishmen knew nothing of the country, the natives, the preventative measures of the South African police against illicit prospecting and a hundred other pitfalls which they would have to face. Far from being a help, he felt that they would be a perpetual embarrassment to him and, being such obvious town dwellers, draw most unwelcome attention to themselves directly they prepared to set off into the desert.

His overseer met him with his car outside the Customs shed and as they drove to the Grand Hotel he questioned him about a hundred details concerning the well-being of his property, and learned that there was every prospect of a good vintage.

They breakfasted at the Grand, an old-fashioned hotel in the centre of the town, occupying three floors above a block of shops. For years Sandy had made it his headquarters whenever it was necessary for him to spend a night in the capital—preferring it to the more modern and expensive places overlooking the ocean out at Sea Point because he considered the food and the service better. The manager, a man of his own age and an old friend, personally supervised the ordering of his breakfast and, immediately the white-clad, turbaned Malay waiters had served him with tea and a big slice of Sponsbeck melon, Sandy broke the news to his overseer that he would have to leave him to handle the vintage, stating that important business necessitated his going north and that he might be detained upon it for some weeks to come.

It was only after mature consideration on the voyage out that Sandy had reached this decision. To be absent from his property during the latter part of February and early March was a serious step. There was not only the wine making but all the packing of his fine Hanepoot grapes, peaches, nectarines for export to be seen to. Every hand was needed —but Sandy felt the absolute necessity of being first on the spot if he meant to go through with his bid for fortune. Michael and the Bennetts were attempting the venture in any case and would arrive in the Union Castle boat on the following day. If they succeeded in handling their clues aright, the mere presence of such an unusual trio buying ox-wagons on the edge of the Kalahari was certain to arouse suspicion, and although old Henry Long had so firmly declared at the lawyer's that he would not risk it, Sandy placed little weight upon his statement. In fact he would have been prepared to take a bet for a reasonable amount that old Henry and his daughter were either on the Castle boat as well or, if they wished to avoid the Bennetts, on their way to Africa in another. Their presence in the neighbourhood of Upington would be equally embarrassing. Speed was essential if he was to keep his lead of the other parties and get clear away before the authorities took an interest in their activities.

Dismissing his overseer to make certain purchases in the town immediately they had finished breakfast, he collected his car and drove straight out to Hilton Road, Sea Point.

The name or number of Mrs. Aileen Orkney's house had not been stated in the Will. In consequence he had to make a laborious door to door investigation. At last, in a house on the left near the top end furthest from the seashore, he found an elderly woman who informed him that her husband had bought the house from a Mrs. Aileen Orkney about three years previously. She thought that Mrs. Orkney had gone to live in Salisbury, Rhodesia, but after a time letters which had been forwarded to her had been returned from there marked 'Not Known' and she could not give Sandy the name of anyone through whom he might trace her predecessor.

This was a disappointment. Had he possessed one of the three clues he would have made straight for the dorps lying on the southern fringe of the Kalahari and sought out the various local native chiefs, since that was the obvious line of investigation. Without them he was almost entirely dependent on picking up old John's trail from one of the three South African addresses mentioned in his Will. However, even if number one had proved a dead end he was not seriously perturbed because his principal hope lay in the Van Niekerks at Pretoria.

Having driven back to the town he picked up his overseer in Adderley Street and drove out again up the steep gradient towards Constantia. The day was still young but gave promise of great heat, no tablecloth of cloud fringed the flat top of Table Mountain, rising steeply to his right against a sky of brilliant blue. Below him on the other side, Cape Town flats spread out, vanishing into a misty distance at the right horn of the bay, and merged to the left into the harbour and the town. The aromatic smell of the pine woods came fresh and strong to his nostrils and he drove with a great elation at being back in his own lovely country once more.

His home was a fine example of the seventeenth century Dutch farm-house—white-plastered walls and tall rounded gables, upon which the monogram of the original owner was prominently displayed.

The front of the house formed one side of a quadrangle. Two lines of ancient oaks and the long bodega where the wines were made and stored completed the others; in one corner could still be seen the decaying stump of an old oak tree against which the slaves had once been chained and beaten.

Inside, the central room was lofty as a barn, made so for coolness' sake. At each end hung heavy wooden doors opening in two sections like those of a stable, a relic of the days when wild animals still roamed the Cape peninsula; the upper half could be opened to admit the air while the lower remained closed to serve as a precautionary barrier against unwelcome intruders. The windows, composed of a number of medium sized square panes, were broad and lofty. Round the walls huge highly-polished kists of stinkwood with ornamental clasps and locks of shining brass, together with two fine old walnut china cupboards, gave the place the comfortable air of having long been lived in.

To his delight he found everything as he had left it. After his long absence he had expected that there would be a thousand urgent matters for hm to attend to, but the work seemed to have gone on in uninterrupted good order and, having made a tour of his property he had to confess to himself that his presence was by no means so important as he had thought it. In fact by three o'clock he found that, apart from the new arrangements necessitated by his journey up to Pretoria, there was nothing for him to do; so he got out the car again and drove over to Muizenberg for a dip and a laze on the sands at False Bay.

By six he was driving back across the beautiful valley of the Peninsula. In the far distance, fifty miles away, behind him the blue mountains of Hottentot Holland showed clear against the evening sky, and stretching towards him lay mile upon mile of green, well-wooded country, speckled with white houses and red-tiled roofs.

He had already booked his sleeper on the Union Limited by telephone, thinking at the time how fortunate it was that the best train of the week ran on the following day, but his pleasure was off-set by the knowledge that it ran from the docks in connection with the Union Castle Boat. Michael and the Bennetts would be on it too, unless they decided to stay in Cape Town to try to find Mrs. Orkney before proceeding to the Van Niekerks at Pretoria, and Sandy was extremely anxious not to run into them.

He could not bear the Bennetts and had already been tempted into telling Michael perhaps a little more than was altogether wise, by his liking for him. Sandy knew his own shortcomings and one of them was a foolish weakness for making confidants of people whom he liked. If he met Michael again he could visualise himself being seduced, against his better judgment, into acting as adviser to the boy and possibly even being drawn into the same party. At the price of having to put up with the Bennetts, Sandy thought that the prospect was very far from being good enough.

On Monday therefore, at just about the time that the Longs were setting out in search of N'hluzili, Sandy boarded the Johannesburg express at the last moment. To his relief he found that the other party were, at all events, not in the same coach as himself. Drawing down the blinds of the windows onto the corridor, he settled himself as comfortably as possible since he inteneded to remain in his compartment for the next thirty-three hours. He had brought with him a good supply of food and a couple of bottles of his own wine so that he could avoid the risk of running into the Bennetts in the restaurant car. Dressed in his oldest clothes, he prepared to face the heat, dust, and general discomfort of the tedious journey with as much stoicism as he could muster. A silent young Dutchman shared the same compartment with him but, apparently having friends farther along the train, he relieved Sandy of his morose society for most of the day and that which followed.

At Johannesburg the Dutchman collected his bags and Sandy, peering cautiously out of the window, caught sight of the younger Bennett, who had evidently just alighted, on the platform. He was a little puzzled as to why the rival party should be getting out at Johannesburg, but pleased that he had succeeded in avoiding them, and that the trouble he had taken to that end had not been in vain. The last thirty miles of his journey was made in solitude and just before seven he arrived in Pretoria.

72

Having secured a room at Polley's Hotel he had a much needed bath then, despite the hour, hastened out again.

At the Jacarandas he was shown into the same room that Patricia had admired five days before. Van Niekerk, tall, slim and tanned, was there, and with him a fair-haired, blue-eyed girl whom he introduced as his sister Sarie.

'We were expecting you,' Cornelius said at once. 'I'm so glad you didn't put off your call until to-morrow. Sarie was certain that you would come in on the Union Limited so we've taken it for granted that you'll dine with us.'

'How very nice of you both.' Sandy smiled from one to the other. 'I was afraid you would think me a lunatic when you got my telegram, but I sent it on the off-chance that it would stop you saying anything to various other people—if I happened to be delayed in Cape Town.'

'It was just as well you did.' Van Niekerk smiled back at him. 'They were here the other day. A sour-faced looking old chap, a girl who was not unlike my sister here in a way only darker, and a most awful blackguard. Will you have sherry or gin and French?'

'Gin and French, thanks.' Sandy moved over to the table where his host was pouring drinks and added hastily: 'I know who the old man and the girl are, I suppose they must have come down by air, but tell me about this other chap.'

'Ach now! let's see. He was a good six foot tall and broad with it. Rather a puffy face with dark eyes that I didn't much like the look of and he had that sort of beastly insincere heartiness that always makes me want to scream.'

'By Jove! that sounds like Philbeach, the murderous devil who darned nearly did me in three weeks ago.'

'You don't seem much the worse for it,' the girl observed and Sandy turned to look at her again. She was tall and slim like her brother with a healthy colouring which spoke of open air and exercise and, as he caught her smiling eyes, he thought again how good it was to be back, once more, in his own country.

'Luckily I've got a pretty solid skull,' he assured her. 'Most Scotsmen have.'

73

'You're not a South African then?' she asked in surprise. 'We naturally assumed you were—as you were at Cape University with our cousin Paul.'

'Oh yes I am,' he said with a quick laugh. 'One hundred per cent South African. I was born here and although my mother was British my father's people have lived in the Cape for three generations—I was only talking of my Scottish ancestry.'

The black house-boy, in his white livery and red sash, appeared in the doorway. 'Dinner is ready, Missis,' he announced in almost a whisper.

'Do you mind if we go in at once?' said Sarie, looking at her guest. 'Bring your drink with you.'

Over dinner Sandy laid the whole position before his new friends. It took most of the time that they were occupied with the meal, and except for a few casual references to things which he had heard his father say about old John Thomas Long, Van Niekerk remained practically silent, playing the part together with his sister, of interested listeners.

When they had returned to the lounge, Cornelius looked at Sandy and said gravely: 'You know the diamond laws. Do you really think that the risk is justified?'

'I do,' Sandy nodded. 'I should certainly not have left my property at the Cape, with the fruit picking in full swing, to chance a term of imprisonment if I didn't.'

'And you're not worried by any moral scruples?'

'Not in the least. This is our country, isn't it? And if there is natural wealth in it to be had for the taking, surely we are as much entitled to it as the Diamond Kings who've had these laws passed to protect their own interests?'

'I suppose that is so.'

'Well, that's how I look at it.' Sandy hurried on. 'A generation back such a situation could never have occurred. Everybody who had the guts to endure the hardship was entitled to help themselves, and these laws have nothing to do with the preservation of general security and happiness. They have only been pushed through for the benefit of half a dozen wealthy men and a few thousand shareholders in London and the other European Capitals.'

'That's true—and you are starting out for this place on your own?'

Sandy nodded vigorously, his unruly lock of hair falling over his dark eyes which were shining with excitement. 'I am—except for such guides and native servants as are absolutely necessary.'

'I see,' said the Dutchman thoughtfully. As he moved over to the window Sandy noticed that he limped slightly.

'The Bennetts wanted me to join them but I would rather go on my own than have to play the part of nurse to inexperienced people in a difficult country, still . . .' Sandy paused suddenly.

'What?'

'Oh, nothing.'

'Go on.'

'Well, if you must know, it just occurred to me that you should also have benefited under my uncle's Will but your father's death has deprived you of £20,000.'

'Yes, I've been chewing that over ever since I received your telegram.'

'D'you mean that you might . . .?'

'Why not? Luckily Sarie and I are by no means hard up. The family has had property in Pretoria ever since Pretorious put it on the map, and it is growing in value every year, but I must confess that a real adventure of this sort intrigues me enormously and a hundred thousand if one can make it is a hundred thousand after all.'

'By Jove!' Sandy's face was beaming. 'This is a different proposition altogether from going in with the Bennetts, and if we ever get to this place there's a fortune in it for us both.'

'All right, that's settled then.' Cornelius smiled as he handed his guest a little glass of Vanderhum. 'As you say, there's plenty in it for both of us if we can only pull it off. Personally I don't think we need worry ourselves unduly about the police who interest themselves in the Diamond

Fields. Most of them must be occupied on the mines that are already working.'

Sarie uncrossed her slim legs and sat forward suddenly. 'You'll need a horse-holder while you tackle the leopards and one who is not going to give you away,' she said quickly.

'Now, that is quite enough,' her brother shook his finger at her. 'This is not the sort of game on which one requires stupid creatures like you.'

'Stupid be damned,' she cried hotly, much to Sandy's amusement. 'I matriculated when I was a year younger than you. I can ride a horse that would throw you on your bottom inside two minutes and I'm by no means convinced that I'm not a better shot.'

Cornelius shook his fair, curly head ruefully. 'Don't rub it in, darling. One of the most serious problems in the whole of my young life was to convince our late lamented parent that I wasn't necessarily a complete fool because you happened to be a brilliant child, but all the same I won't have you mixed up in this.'

'Now be sensible.' Her blue eyes smiled at him from beneath lowered lids. 'It isn't as though you are used to really roughing it, Cornelius, you know you can't with a game leg. The sort of thing we do out at the farm over week-ends is only fun and Mr. McDiamid doesn't look as if he'd be any more capable of looking after himself than you. If you employ native boys each one you take on will add to the risk of betrayal and arrest. We know we can trust old Willem but he can't look after the oxen and do the cooking and everything. You'd far better let me come, and between the four of us we shall be able to dispense with outside help except for the actual guide—if we can find one.'

'All that you say about not trusting a soul more than necessary is absolutely sound.' Sandy agreed. 'And although I can do my whack in providing for the pot, you are right about my never having really roughed it. If I had gone on my own I'd have had to employ a native cook, or face the additional hardship of almost uneatable food cooked by myself.'

76

'Exactly, and on a journey like this, which is going to be difficult enough anyhow, it may make all the difference between failure and success if the strength of the party is kept up by well-cooked, nourishing food.'

'Yes, but all the same I don't think you ought to be mixed up in this, because there is a risk of our being sent to prison, you know.'

Cornelius nodded, 'I quite agree. If this thing were all open and above board I'd love to have you with us, Sarie. As it is, it is quite out of the question.'

'All right!' she shrugged her shoulders. 'But if you don't agree to take me you don't get my share of information.' She stuck out her pointed chin stubbornly.

'What do you know about it anyhow—that I don't?' laughed her brother.

'Something that may be very useful indeed. You see you never actually met the old man at all, because you were at school when he was here on his last visit. I was only about thirteen myself at the time but I saw quite a lot of him. He often used to sit out there in the garden and talk to me in the way that grown-ups will sometimes to a child. Really that sort of thing is more ruminating to themselves aloud for the purpose of getting their own affairs straight in their minds, without actually confiding their secrets to anyone, and quite honestly I didn't understand more than a quarter of what he said. Only that he was going to a place where no fruit trees grew, where there were no chocolates, ices, or anything at all to drink, but that there were leopards and snakes and wild cats and hyenas. There was a cave too and he ussed to make funny little models out of the earth to show me what he thought it looked like. He'd ask me, with a sort of funny seriousness, if I would take a chance on swimming down an underground river that went into the face of a mountain, with no sort of certainty as to if one would ever come out on the other side. Bits of those strange monologues have been coming back to me ever since Mr. McDiamid's telegram arrived, and there's one thing that I have been trying to remember for days. It is the name of a place which he mentioned quite a number of times and I am certain that it was the village where he was going to secure his guides and porters before setting off into the unknown. Now it's only ten years since he made the journey, so some of the natives who went with him must still be alive. If you knew it you could go straight there and start making inquiries at once—couldn't you?' Her smile deepened, mocking them: 'Well, the name of that place came back to me last night.'

For a few moments the two men argued with her, trying to persuade her to give them the name but she was adamant, and at length a compromise was reached. She should come on the journey but, if they succeeded in their quest, she was to come straight back to Pretoria immediately they reached the fringe of civilisation again, in order that she should not be involved with the illegal business of getting diamonds out of the country.

This decision having been made they went into details of their journey and discussed the prospects of the other parties, but it was not until about an hour later that Cornelius Van Niekerk suddenly stood up and cried:

'Stop everything! We're tackling this thing from the wrong angle altogether.' Then, waving his arms as he limped rapidly up and down the room, he outlined a completely new plan.

'By Jove!' cried Sandy. 'You're right! And that's the way it's got to be done.'

10

From the Cape through the Karroo to First-hand Information

The Bennett party's decision to come north on the Union Limited directly the Castle Boat docked at Cape Town had been governed by a piece of good fortune on the ship. No sooner had the liner left Southampton than Michael secured a passenger list from the second purser. Their arrangements were, at that time, to stay in Cape Town first of all to get in touch with Mrs. Orkney, then proceed to the Van Niekerks at Pretoria, and lastly go down to Joe-Jack Mahout's at Durban. But Michael pointed out to his half-brothers that it was quite on the cards that one or all of these people had changed their address since the dates mentioned in his uncle's Will. There were a considerable number of South Africans travelling on the ship and he suggested that, if they made it their business to question every one of these, it was just possible that they might pick up some later information regarding the people with whom they wished to get in touch.

If he had had to do the job of introducing himself to the several hundred passengers he would have found it an unpleasant and almost impossible task, because, although he was not shy with people whom he liked, he was always reluctant to force himself upon strangers. Fortunately, however, George did not suffer from this squeamishness. In his opinion it was the sacred duty of every person on the ship to know everybody else if the trip was to be anything like a success.

How it was done Michael never quite understood. It may have been that George was the first person to offer the ship's doctor a drink immediately the hatch in the bar went up on their leaving port, or it may have been his arrangement that they should sit at the Chief Purser's table, but the fact remains that, elected by nobody quite knew who, George became chairman of the Entertainment and Sports Committee for the voyage. After that Michael's task was easy. From eight o'clock in the morning until the passengers were sent to bed George was to be seen puffing up and down the ladders from one deck to another, a constant stream of jovial badinage floating from his lips and with lists of every description in his hands. With equal enthusiasm he arranged the shuffle board, ping-pong, deck tennis and bridge tournaments. He bullied reluctant people into making an asinine display of themselves on the night of the fancy dress dance in crepe paper, coloured cottons, and horse-hair procured from the barber's shop. He sucked money from them for sweepstakes, seamen's charities and for a woman in the third class who had given birth to twins.

In the course of these activities he very soon became acquainted with all his fellow passengers and while a certain number regarded him as a perfect pest the majority looked on him as a jolly good fellow, who undertook the extensive labour of arranging all the amusements which they enjoyed. Before they were four days out, he knew their ailments, businesses, addresses in South Africa or England, personal idiosyncrasies and capacity for drink, so it was easy enough for him to introduce Michael to any of those returning to their own country who might possibly be able to give him the information which they sought.

He did not learn anything of interest however, until George, mopping his bald head with a brightly-coloured handkerchief as he arranged the ceremonies for crossing the line, caught sight of an elderly lady in a deck-chair and, seeing Michael standing near her, introduced them.

Mrs. Witney's name appeared in only one of George Bennett's many lists, that of the Bridge Tournament; and it was for this reason that he had not thought of introducing Michael to her before. While he dashed off in frantic haste to hunt for Neptune's crown which had been mislaid by the elderly bachelor who was taking the sea king's part, Michael settled down beside the slim, grey-haired lady with the kind, humorous eyes. He liked her immediately and saw quite a lot of her during the remainder of the voyage, but on the first afternoon he discovered that, although she was not a South African, she knew Aileen Orkney well. She was even aware of the wonderful legacy which had fallen to her friend only a few weeks before, and told him at once that Mrs. Orkney had left Cape Town at least a couple of years before, had lived for some time in Rhodesia, and was now settled in Johannesburg. Further Mrs. Witney told him that he would find Aileen a charming person and provided him with a letter of introduction which would facilitate his inquiries.

In the days which followed Michael talked with many other people until, when they at last reached Cape Town, he had questioned practically everybody upon the ship. The only other information which he secured was that Van Niekerk had left two children, Cornelius and Sarie, who were still believed to be living at Pretoria; also a statement from a planter who lived near Durban that he vaguely remembered Joe-Jack Mahout as barman at the Royal Hotel some seven years before.

By the time they reached Cape Town the Bennetts and Michael were glad that the voyage was over. At first it had been a pleasant rest, free from anxiety and the petty worries of everyday life; but as they neared their destination they began to tire of the routine and suffered from the loss of appetite common to travellers who have been living for more than a fortnight upon foods, the original flavours of which have lost their individuality through refrigeration. They felt compensated to some extent by their gradually browning skins acquired with infinite pain by sunbathing.

On February 13th they were roused, quite unnecessarily, by the stewards several hours before there was even a possibility of the emigration authorities coming on board, but their reward was to see Table Bay in the first flush of the dawn as the ship slowly steamed past Robin Island.

Unlike the previous day when Sandy had seen it at its greatest beauty the top of Table Mountain was overhung by billowing white cloud, the fringe of which seemed always about to roll down the precipitous sides, yet evaporated in curling wisps before obscuring the greater portion of the mountain.

By ten o'clock the formalities of landing were over and the three were taking a second breakfast in the restaurant car of the Union Limited. By half past they were clear of the city and running swiftly through the fertile valley with its lovely old Dutch houses and carefully tended vineyards. An hour and a half later they began the great climb from sea level to two thousand feet up in the mountains and while they lunched the glorious panorama of the Hex River, winding its way between giant cliffs a quarter of a mile below, was spread out before them in the brilliant sunshine.

By the early afternoon they had entered the Karroo and were surprised to find that it was not completely flat as they had assumed from what the South Africans on the boat had told them. On the horizon steep kopjes, the tops of which had been sliced off flat as a table by the glaciers of the last ice age, rose from the barren, rocky, uneven ground; the desolation of this great upland plateau had not been exaggerated. Many miles separated each wayside half from its neighbour and apart from these not a solitary house was to be seen in that parched, inhospitable country. No trees or crops broke the monotony of the reddish boulder-strewn ground, only one variety of stunted shrub—the karroo bush, which exists miraculously even after years of drought, and is sufficient for the great flocks of sheep to feed on that constitute the only industry possible in that great trackless area.

After a further hour's progress they began to appreciate the warning which they had received about the journey up to Johannesburg. The train was comfortable enough, but the dust became a serious inconvenience. Every few miles a dust devil would rise from the rocky soil and come sweeping towards the train, a whirling column of infinitesimal red particles which penetrated every cranny of the compartments even if the windows were whipped up at its approach. It was impossible to keep them closed for any length of time owing to the stifling heat.

For hours they watched the unchanging scene roll past while the dust coated their faces and hands and got into their eyes and hair. The monotony was broken by a glorious sunset but the dust seemed to have coated every morsel of food which they put in their mouths at dinner. Sleep was a welcome respite from the torment, but all the following day they were compelled to sit in their shirt sleeves mopping their perspiring faces, and growing ever dirtier as they gradually climbed another four thousand feet to the level of Johannesburg.

At a little after six they arrived at their destination and drove straight to the Carlton, rejoicing in the immediate prospect of hot baths. Then, feeling that they could not very well call on Mrs. Orkney that night, they dined and did a cinema together.

On Wednesday Michael made inquiries from the hall porter as to the whereabouts of Park Town, where Mrs. Orkney lived. On being informed that it was one of the most fashionable suburbs, some way outside the town, he decided that it would be best to telephone before driving out there in case she was away from home.

Mrs. Orkney was there however and said she would be very pleased to see them if they would come out and join her for morning tea at eleven o'clock, so they hired a taxi and admiring, as Patricia had seven days before, the great modern office buildings in Eloff Street and the fine private houses and blocks of flats which lay beyond the station, they drove out to see her.

She turned out to be a small, elderly lady whose white hair, sweeping back from her forehead, clear eyes and regular features betrayed the fact that she must have been very lovely when she was a younger woman.

The Bennetts obviously amused her greatly but she took an immediate fancy to Michael and, for his sake rather than the others, told them what she knew of their uncle, while they sat on the stoep above her garden, gay with cannas, gladiolas, dahlias, fairy daisies, and golden shower.

'He was a reprobate of course, but he had charm, oh,

great charm,' the old eyes twinkled kindly as she looked at Michael. 'You have something of his looks yourself, but not his wonderful physique. I knew him first in 1908 and I fear my poor husband objected rather to our friendship because John had quite a reputation even then. He went away of course and for a long time it made me most unhappy. You will think it very wicked of me I suppose, seeing that I had a husband already, but life so seldom turns out to be exactly as we expect it. John came back, just as the bad pennies of this world always do, and after that—well, we became very friendly. I never left my husband, but I had no children to think of and by that time I had found out that he was no better than he should have been, so he couldn't very well prevent me doing as I liked.'

'What's sauce for the goose is sauce for the gander, eh?' Ernest interjected cheerfully.

She nodded and went on: 'From time to time John would stay with us in Cape Town and then disappear again, often for months at a stretch. After the War he was just the same as before and I began to despair of his ever settling down to marry or earn an honest living, so I took no particular notice when in 1923 he stayed with us for a few days before going on one of his expeditions, and said that if he ever saw me again it would be as a man who had at last made his fortune. John had told me that sort of thing so often before, you see, and there was no special reason why I should believe him on this occasion.'

Michael quickly swallowed a piece of melon *comfyt* and asked eagerly: 'Did you ever see him again?'

'Yes,' the old lady smiled at his keenness, 'I saw him about two months afterwards and he looked a changed man. He was lean—haggard—and could hardly stand for the fever that was on him. I put him to bed and it was from his delirium in the days that followed that I learnt something of John's last journey. Hostile Bushmen had attacked his outspan, murdering two of his native boys before he could drive them off. Then one night when he was in a part of the desert where no fuel of any kind was available, he was unable to light fires and so the leopards killed and carried away his oxen. Yet despite everything he had managed to reach his objective and return from it with a fortune in uncut diamonds. I saw them, although he never knew it, for they were round his waist in a thick pouch-belt. When he was well again he left us and I never saw or heard of him again until I learned that he had remembered me in his Will.'

'That's very interesting, Mrs. Orkney, George remarked, unwrapping a brown paper parcel which he had picked up from beside Michael's chair. 'Now could you tell us if you've ever see this thing before?'

'I hardly know,' she murmured taking the leopard skin from him. 'This is just an ordinary kaross, I have seen hundreds such in the last fifty years.'

'We were hoping you might be able to give us the name of its original owner,' Ernest commented. 'You see Uncle John left this thing to us and it's the only clue we've got.'

'Yes, I remember now,' she nodded slowly as she drew her wrinkled fingers over the coarse hair of the skin. 'John had one with him in his baggage that last time when I unpacked for him when he was so ill. There was a necklace of monkey's skulls and a knobkerrie with it if my memory serves me. Except for a few pairs of shorts and an extra pair of boots, I think that was all the luggage that poor John possessed; although of course he had a fortune on him at the time. Perhaps those things belonged to one of the native boys who made the journey with him.'

'That's it—that's it,' urged Michael. 'Can you possibly remember his mentioning the name of any of his guides?'

She thought for a moment and then said slowly: 'There was one name that he often mentioned in his delirium and that was Kieviet and there was another—let me think now—yes, N'hluzili—"Quick, N'hluzili, quick, your assegai!" I can hear him shouting now as he tossed about the tumbled bed.'

Michael jotted the two names down on a piece of paper while George refolded the leopard skin kaross but although they talked for a further hour with the delightful old lady they could obtain no other information from her which promised additional help.

Having returned to Johannesburg they congratulated themselves on learning so much from their first inquiry, and George suggested that they should press on to the Van Niekerks at Pretoria that afternoon.

After lunch they walked through the crowded streets, where the colourful frocks of the white women relieved the dull background of shoddily-clad negroes and long lines of cars parked in herring-bone formation along either pavement—to the station. The journey of thirty miles seemed little more than a tram ride after the long hours spent in the train the day before and by five o'clock the three of them were entering the garden gate of the Jacarandas.

Cornelius Van Niekerk received them courteously, studying each in turn with concealed interest which he masked by an air of apparent surprise when they stated the reason of their visit.

They showed him the leopard skin but he shook his head and assured them that he had never seen that particular skin before, as far as he knew. He was, however, happy and willing to give then any information about their late uncle which he possessed.

They questioned him at some length and particularly as to if he could remember anything which their uncle might have let drop about two natives called Kieviet and N'hluzili.

Cornelius made a careful mental note of the two names and regretted that in this too he was unable to help them. To their further inquiries be let it slip out, quite casually, that he was certain beyond question that John Thomas Long had started on his journey from a place called Zwart Modder about sixty-miles north-west of the town of Upington, because his father had told him so on a number of occasions.

The delighted Bennetts promptly exchanged a hearty handshake while Michael smiled with quiet satisfaction. Their quest seemed to be far easier than any of then had imagined. In half a dozen hours they had not only secured the names of two men who were most probably their late uncle's guides, but also the village from which he started out. It was reasonable to assume that tidings of the guides might be picked up there, as the chances were all in favour of them being local men.

Van Niekerk provided the Bennetts with whiskies-and-sodas and Michael with a gin-and-french, after which they thanked him for his kindness and left his house hoping to be back in Johannesburg for dinner.

No sooner were they outside the railings of the garden than Sandy, with Sarie beside him, came hurrying in to Cornelius from the room beyond, where they had been concealed.

'How did it go?' they asked in one breath.

'Marvellously!' Cornelius helped himself to another drink. 'They positively leapt for joy when I gave them the name of Zwart Modder and, not suspecting that I was an interested party, gave me the names of two of the old man's guides, Kieviet and N'hluzili, which they must have fished up from somewhere—better jot them down while they are still fresh in our minds.'

'Splendid! that's a real bit of luck,' agreed Sandy; 'yet all the same I'm devilish nervous of that crowd. By sending them on ahead of us like this we're trebling the risk of the authorities getting wind of the fact that people are out prospecting in the neighbourhood.'

'My dear fellow, if you'd managed to keep possession of that knobkerrie it would have been quite another matter. Without it or one of the other clues what chance should we have had of getting the guides to talk, even if we could find them. As it is they have the leopard skin and now that we have given them the district they'll be off on to-morrow's train to do all the dirty work of hunting up some wretched nigger and persuading him to risk another journey into the "Great Thirst".' Cornelius, with a happy grin, set down his glass.

'That's right, darling,' Sarie flung a slim brown arm round his neck, 'and all we'll have to do, once they set off, puffing and blowing across that filthy desert in their wretched out-span, is to follow them in your plane.'

11

The Return from Durban to the Rand

As Wisdon had forseen, his every effort to tempt N'hluzili into acting as their guide failed completely. At length they were compelled to drop the matter and content themselves with such information as they could secure from the old Induana about his last journey with John Thomas Long.

He told them that oxen and a wagon had been secured at Upington and that thence they had travelled by road to a tiny dorp, the name of which he could not remember. After that they had journeyed for a day and a half to the north-westward by a rough trail to a place where there existed a great pan or lake. There they had entered the trackless waste to the north and, after a further day's journey, had rested at another much larger pan, where they were attacked by one of the miserable remnants of the almost extinct bushmen tribe, the enemy of white and Zulu alike. They turned then a little and trekked for seven days, bearing to the north-eastward across seemingly endless rolling slopes of coarse grass until they finally entered a sandy waste beyond which lay a great range of mountains; during all that time no sign of human habitation was ever seen. On the eighth day they reached the foothills and at the hour when they would normally have re-started their journey after the midday rest, his master had ordered him to remain with the out-span while he went forward with his Hottentot guide into those desolate spirit-haunted gorges. It had been two days and a night before he rejoined them and N'hluzili could tell them nothing of the white man's doings during that period. Having regained his camp, old John had been about to turn south once more but that night was overtaken by a great misfortune. They had already used all the wood and scrub which could be found and, their fires dying down, the leopards had attacked them. Only by barricading themselves in the wagon had they escaped with their lives, and in the morning they found that not a single one of their oxen remained to them. The days that followed had been a veritable nightmare of which even the old Zulu, with the poetry of his race, could give no adequate description. Of the party of seven that had set out, three only had survived: the white man, himself, and the young bushman tracker who, being a native of that particular territory, had more easily withstood the rigours of the journey.

Immediately the Induna finished his story Wisdon asked him what the bushman had been called, but he shrugged disdainfully and answered that he doubted even if he had ever heard the tracker's name; it was for the men of his great nation to mix with a tribe whose nearest cousins were the larger apes. It was obvious that nothing more could be got out of him, so Wisdon and Henry retraced their steps down the hill to Patricia, who was waiting in the car.

They had a late lunch at Sezela and then returned to Durban. Over tea on the wide balcony of the Royal, they held a fresh council of war, while below them motors, pedestrians, and gaily decorated rickshaw boys, moving at a slow jogtrot between the hotel and the palm trees in the garden of the square, made an animated scene.

N'hluzuli had confirmed Wisdon's view that Upington was the place to secure an out-span. From the railway map it seemed that the easiest way to reach it was by train via Bethlehem and Bloemfontein to Kimberley, where they would change on to the Johannesburg-Cape main line—go scuth as far as De Aar Junction—and, changing again, take the direct line from there.

Wisdon, however, pointed out that they had either to take the hired car back to Johannesburg, or else make some arrangement about it; and that it would probably be quicker in the long run to take the express from Johannesburg to De Aar than go by local train across country via Kimberley in any case.

In consequence, after tea they set out for Pietermaritzberg which was fifty-six miles away. If they slept there they should be able, by hard driving, to accomplish the other four hundred odd miles despite the bad roads on the following day and reach Johannesburg on Tuesday night.

At Pietermaritzburg they put up at the Imperial, took their coffee in its restful old-fashioned central courtyard, strolled round the town and went early to bed in preparation for the long day before them.

They made a very early start but the weather had changed for the better, and in the forenoon the Longs were able to enjoy the magnificent vistas which opened up before them as the car climbed the twisting road back towards the grassy uplands. The lunched at Newcastle, after which the passing scene became dull and tedious once more. By the time they passed the dump of the Village Deep Mine—strangely beautiful in the bright moonlight—on the outskirts of Johannesburg, Patricia was utterly weary. Fifteen minutes later she was throwing off her clothes in a bedroom at the Carlton preparatory to tumbling into bed.

Next morning they assembled in the so-called palm lounge. The place was innocent of any greenery and contained nothing but long rows of glass-topped tables surrounded by creaky wicker-work chairs. Wisdon, making his breakfast of a whisky-and-soda, then sprang it upon the Longs that at least two other white men would be necessary as assistants for the next stage of their journey. He pointed out that both Patricia and her father were incapable of playing any part but that of passengers upon the expedition. Since they were to venture into the Great Thirst, water was their principal consideration, and their wagon should be loaded almost entirely with this vital necessity. For food they must depend upon such game as they could shoot and if an accident happened to him when they were a few days out from Zwart Modder they would be utterly helpless, as neither of them could handle a rifle. It was essential, then, that they should have companions who understood the natives and were capable of providing supplies for the pot.

Henry protested that an accident was most unlikely but Wisdon reminded him of the Valley of the Leopards, through which they had to pass, and the dangers of the journey which N'hluzili had so graphically described. Their assistants would have to receive a handsome remuneration, of course, but owing to the many years that he had spent in Africa, he felt certain he could produce a couple of reliable, hard-bitten fellows, who were prepared to undertake any sort of journey. He then proposed to set about the business of looking up his old friends at once with a view to securing two who had the necessary qualifications.

Henry was reluctant to trust others with their secret for fear he would be subjected afterwards to blackmail if they succeeded in their quest. Wisdon, however, argued that the place of the Great Glitter held such an abundance of wealth that anyone's claim could be amply satisfied; so, realising how helpless he and Patricia might be should some misfortune overtake their ally, Henry agreed to the proposal.

It amazed Patricia more each day to see how her unwelcome admirer had succeeded in gaining her father's confidence. The former personified all that the latter hated in the normal way yet some strange bond seemed to link the two and Henry, like some clever but fascinated bird, was now completely under the influence of the python-like Philbeach, whom she knew as Philip Wisdon.

Actually Henry despised the man, but had fallen a victim to his own conceit. His narrow outlook led him to suppose that mental weakness always accompanied moral laxity, and, while he considered that he had made a shrewd move in securing the assistance of this adventurer, so experienced in the ways of a country strange to him, he believed that he would be able to bend him to his will and sever his connection with him directly his objective had been achieved. In the meantime, until they secured that fortune which coloured every thought in his money-ridden mind, Henry deliberately shut his eyes to Philbeach's shortcomings on account of his very obvious usefulness.

After Wisdon had left them Patricia produced a letter which she had already mentioned to her father. It was an introduction from one of her most intimate friends to a big stockbroker called Masterton. Patricia suggested that since they might have to spend a day or two in Johannesburg while Wisdon made his arrangements, it was the obvious, as well as the courteous thing, to make use of it.

Henry agreed, so they left the Carlton and, although they lost their way at first among the innumerable blocks of large stone buildings, all so similiar in appearance, they eventually discovered Mr. Masterton's office in Pritchard Street.

Masterton proved to be a fair-haired, middle-aged man who gave them a hearty welcome, and telephoned to his wife at once to join them. Since the Longs were only in Johannesburg for a very short visit he suggested taking Henry to see the Stock Exchange and then on to lunch while his wife entertained Patricia at the Country Club. He asked their impressions of the country and protested that, now they had arrived in the Union, they should certainly not leave it without having spent at least a fortnight in Johannesburg—visited the National Game Reserve in the Northern Transvaal and motored down to Cape Town via the Wilderness, which he glowingly described as one of the most beautiful places in the world. Then his wife, a small, fair, pretty woman arrived and rushed Patricia away from her father.

Mrs. Masterton had her car below. With a hundred questions as to Patricia's plans which were difficult to answer, she whirled her through the outskirts of the city. A quarter of an hour later Patricia was trying to extricate herself from a most hospitable entanglement—a party to be given in her honour a few days hence, when she might quite well be setting out into the Kalahari—while her hostess pressed her to another cocktail.

They lunched on the long stoep of the Country Club. Between its tall white pillars Patricia viewed the lovely gardens sloping to a lake where palms, weeping willows, and an abundance of semi-tropical verdure made her feel for the moment that she was still in Durban, rather than in this naked country, which before the discovery of the Reef, had been treeless and almost uninhabited.

Mrs. Masterton introduced her for the first time to the

Avocado Pear, a queer almost tasteless fruit of a custard-like consistency which had a subtle individual flavour.

The newness of everything—the country, the people, the food—appealed to Patricia intensely. This adventure held far more than she had ever anticipated.

As coffee and liqueurs were being served she leaned a little to the left side of the table for her bag, and suddenly saw Michael lunching not a dozen tables away along the terrace.

He had spotted her a quarter of an hour earlier and when he saw Patricia and her hostess leave the stoep—a waiter following with their cups and glasses—and ensconce themselves in a swing hammock with a small table before it on the sloping lawn near the lake, he excused himself from his host, a medical man whom he had known at Cambridge, and walked quickly across to them. She introduced him as her cousin to Mrs. Masterton.

After a little desultory conversation her hostess, seeing Michael's obvious desire to be alone with Patricia, excused herself—a carefully guarded twinkle in her eye—by saying that she was anxious to telephone to one or two people about some golf fixtures, and the two were left together.

'So you've arrived,' he said.

'Rather obvious—isn't it?' she smiled quizzically.

'Yes, by Jove!—so it is. Now I'm going to say that I like your hat, but perhaps that remark is obvious too?'

'I hope so, but none the less it's most acceptable.'

'It's a bit surprising to see you here so soon. How long have you been in Johannesburg?'

'It's just over a week since we arrived here first,' she said airily, 'because we had the sense to fly; but as a matter of fact we only got back last night from Durban where we have been doing a little of the Sherlock Holmes business with Joe-Jack Mahout.'

'Did you have any luck with him, Holmes?' he asked casually.

'I don't know that I ought to tell you, my dear Watson,' she smiled up at him from beneath the gay striped awning of the swing hammock, 'since you're in the opposition camp.'

'Is there any reason that we shouldn't agree to a private armistice while we are in Johannesburg?' he asked. 'It would be fun if you would let me take you out to dinner and a movie afterwards—what about to-night?'

'I should love that,' she agreed, knowing full well that she would incur her father's disapproval but determined to discount it against the pleasure of an evening with Michael. 'Where are you staying?'

'The Carlton. Where are you?'

'We are there too, so I suppose we should have run into each other anyway, but what do you suggest about to-night?'

'I shall be in the place they call the palm court at 7.30. If you'll come down to me there we'll find out what the town has to offer by way of amusement.'

'All right,' she rose, as she saw her hostess approaching from the club-house. 'Father will be livid but he can't reasonably object since we are cousins!'

At a quarter past seven Michael was discussing a cocktail in the place that he had named, distinctly thrilled at the thought of the evening which lay before him.

Upstairs Patricia was humming a little tune to herself as she combed her brown curls round her fingers. Only after seeing him again at the Country Club that morning had she fully realised how much of her thoughts had been devoted to her charming, freckle-faced cousin during these days of journeying since she left England. 'Oh, how good it is.' she thought, 'to be young and attractive, and going out to dinner with someone one really likes.' She felt full of vitality in this great throbbing city where the height accelerated her heart beats and sent the blood coursing through the veins of a healthy body. Her feet itched to dance and, her eyes shining with excitement, she scorned the lift and ran lightly down the stairs to join him.

After a cocktail he inquired from the hall porter the best restaurant in the town and they set off to dine at the Criterion.

In one of the white wooden alcoves round the walls of the restaurant they enjoyed an excellent dinner washed down by a bottle of Alphen Burgundy. They then saw the latest screen

94

success at the Metro Theatre, which had only had its *première* in London three weeks before.

When they came out into the brightly lighted streets the crystal air of the City of Gold, set at its great altitude so many thousand feet above sea level, made them feel that it would be a sin to go straight home to bed, and Michael suggested that they might see if they could find a place at which they could dance.

A friendly commissionaire informed them that, if they had not already been there, Aasvogelskop was undoubtedly a place that they should visit. Hiring a taxi they drove up into the hills beyond the city, and secured a table at the famous night resort.

The place was crowded with youngish people and to the strains of a jazz band which played all the latest tunes, Michael soon discovered that his cousin was a good mover. After supper and a few more dances, he suggested that they should take a stroll outside in the darkness and see the view from the terrace below the restaurant.

Nothing loath Patricia readily agreed and, with the murmur of the band coming faintly to them from the wide windows of the night club, they stood beside a giant cactus looking out over the dark valley, where a million lights, twinkling like stars, showed the great sleeping city below them in the distance.

With a sudden jerk he pulled her round towards him and taking her face between his hands kissed her passionately on the mouth.

12

Love and Conspiracy in Johannesburg

'Michael!' Patricia looked across at him with shining eyes as they sat down again at their table on the edge of the dance floor. 'Let's turn this armistice into a peace treaty. I can't bear the thought of you running all over Africa and spending your money to no purpose, when we've done it all for you in the last week. Father wouldn't come in with you in the first place because he had some private grouse against George Bennett, but it isn't as if this treasure was one single thing that we were all anxious to grab before the others could get hold of it. If the letter Uncle John left us is accurate, there are diamonds galore in this place and enough to provide a fortune for us all. Anyhow I'm going to tell you the result of our inquiries so far.'

'That's sweet of you,' he said with an affectionate smile. 'But I was just going to say the same thing, for, although we haven't been here for anything like as long as you, we've managed to find out quite a good bit. Let's swop our stories.'

He told her then of his good fortune in tracing Mrs. Orkney and ascertaining important particulars of their uncle's journey from the Van Niekerks.

On hearing of the latter she raised her eyebrows in grave surprise. 'How extraordinary. Mr. Van Niekerk would not tell us a single thing. He had had a telegram from Sandy asking him not to give anything away until his arrival.'

'Perhaps, but Sandy's boat docked at Cape Town a day before mine, and if you remember he took rather a fancy to me in London, so possibly he has seen the Van Niekerks already and told them to let me have any information that they could.'

'That may be the explanation,' she nodded. 'Anyhow I can tell you that N'hluzili is a dead end. We managed to hunt him out at his kraal in Natal and although he told us all about the last journey that he made with Uncle John he flatly refused to come out of his retirement and act as guide for us.' She gave him then an account of all that they had learnt from Joe-Jack Mahout and the Zulu Iduna. In return he gave her the name of Kieviet to help the inquiries of her party and of the jumping-off place—Zwart Modder.

Both felt a tinge of joyous guilt in giving away the secrets of their rival expeditions to each other, and considerable pleasure in thinking that there was now a chance of their meeting when they reached Zwart Modder. But although Patricia made little mention of Wisdon in her story, Michael sensed her strong antagonism to this stranger whom her father had taken on to accompany them as a sort of courier and guide.

Patricia having telephoned after they left the Metro Cinema to say that she would not be in till late, they did not hurry themselves and it was half-past two before they drove back through the now deserted streets to the Carlton.

The Long party were leaving Johannesburg next day, but the Bennetts had received a voluminous packet by air mail that morning and felt that they must take this last opportunity of dealing with the many details concerning their London business before setting off into the blue. Michael, therefore, had no idea when he would see Patricia again, for the Longs might well have left Zwart Modder by the time that his own party arrived. So although the hour was late he persuaded her to have a final drink with him in the palm court on the first floor before going to bed.

They walked slowly up the stairway and found the lounge practically empty. Only a few tables were occupied by couples who had strolled through from a private dance which was still in progress in rooms set apart for it down the corridor. To Patricia's annoyance, one table at the entrance to the restaurant was occupied by Wisdon and a couple of strange men, all still in their day clothes.

He caught sight of her and, leaving his two friends, strolled slowly over towards them. Then, ignoring Michael who stood up politely, and slightly rocking on wide-spread feet, he said with insolent familiarity:

'Hello, young Pat, I see you've found a boy friend. So that's why you turned me down this evening, is it?'

Patricia flushed and, ignoring his rudeness, waved her hand towards Michael. 'This is my cousin, Mr. Kane-Swift, of whom you have heard from father.'

The big man lurched a little as he clutched the back of a chair and, pulling it from the table, sank into it. 'So you're the young feller who's so anxious to risk your neck in the desert eh?' he said aggressively. 'But you won't find it like they say in the story books with palm trees and oases at the right moment and all that. It's just sand, my Buckoo, and rock and *toa* grass and not a ruddy thing to drink.'

Michael suppressed an angry retort with difficulty. Wisdon had appeared in none too good a light from Patricia's sketch of him, but this great drunken brute was infinitely more unpleasant than anything that he had pictured. He would have liked to counter the sneer with some curt, coldly insolent rejoinder, but felt that in the man's present state the least display of antagonism would precipitate an open and unseemly quarrel which he could not chance before the girl, so he replied quite casually: 'Oh, I don't know that we've many qualifications for this sort of job—before we finish up we may even be asking you to help us out.'

'There's no harm in *asking*.' Wisdon grinned unpleasantly, passing his tongue over his full protruding lips. 'But if you take my tip you'll cut it out. This is a man's job not the sort of thing for a kid like you.'

'Fortunately my half-brothers will be with me and both of them are considerably older than myself,' Michael replied mildly. He wished profoundly that this ordeal of having to keep his temper before Patricia would soon be over and the big brute leave them to themselves, but Wisdon proved garrulous and inquisitive. He tried, in a clumsy way, to pump Michael about the activities of his party since they had landed in South Africa, and made sly references, for which Michael wanted to hit him, as to the lateness of the hour and how unusual it was to see a couple of young cousins enjoying an evening together. After ten minutes, however, he declared that another drink was an immediate necessity and that since 'Little Galahad' had not offered him one, the best thing for him to do was to return to his own table.

Michael, or Little Galahad as Wisdon had dubbed him, crimsoned to the roots of his dark hair. Never before had he been accused of being shy in offering drinks, but little as he wished to drink at all with the flamboyant Mr. Wisdon, who had very obviously had more than his fair share of liquor already, he had been so occupied in keeping his temper, that the thought had not even occurred to him.

Wisdon heaved his big body out of the basket chair and, as he made a ponderous unsteady progress back to his two friends at the other end of the palm court, Patricia laid her hand gently on Michael's.

'Full marks, my dear,' she said softly. 'Full marks every time. How you stood for it I can't think, but it was marvellous of you.'

Her quick understanding brought an immediate ease to his ruffled feelings, but he could not suppress one outburst. 'Did you hear him? The bounder! He had the cheek to call me Little Galahad. I'd like to get my thumbs pressed well into the folds of his great fat neck.'

'I know you would, but Galahad's a name to conjure with. 'If I called you that you wouldn't mind, would you?'

He grinned a little sheepishly: 'I wouldn't mind anything that you cared to call me, but Galahad sounds a bit priggish, I always think, so I'd rather you stuck to Michael, but look here, I've simply got to talk to you.'

'Talk away,' she smiled. 'The air here is so different from foggy London that if I had only half the sleep I'm used to, I think I should be just as fit and fresh every morning. I don't feel in the least like bed, although I ought to have been there hours ago.'

'I can't say what I want to here.' Michael shrugged impatiently. 'The sight of that brute, slinging more whisky down his neck over there, gets me all wrought up. Come along to the writing-room.'

She raised her eyebrows and made a little comical grimace, but picked up her bag as he pushed back the table for her, and allowed him to lead her down the corridor on the right of the lift.

The writing-room was in darkness. Only a faint light penetrating through the windows from the street lamps, showed vaguely the double line of tables, the arm-chairs, and the illustrated weeklies scattered about in disorder. He did not bother to hunt for the switches but sank into a low chair and pulled her down on to his knees.

'You mustn't,' he said hoarsely. 'It's utterly impossible for you to set out into the wilds with a man like that.'

'Why?' she asked, accepting the situation quite naturally and putting her arm round his neck.

'The man's in love with you,' he declared angrily. 'I could see it in his eyes.'

'Don't worry, my dear.' As she lay close to him her fingers strayed for a moment in his dark wavy hair. She had been waiting to touch it ever since that afternoon when he had come down to see her at Surbiton. 'Father will be with me and I am quite capable of taking care of myself.'

'But if anything happened to your father?'

'Why should it?'

'I don't say anything will, but from all the accounts which we have heard of this place it sounds pretty grim. Honestly, Patricia, you ought to stay in Upington or Zwart Modder.'

'No, I'm going through with it, Michael. Father wants me to stay behind as well. He was saying so only this morning but I don't see why I should. Men have such extraordinary ideas about women. To be one of the few people who have ever reached this place will be a tremendous thrill, and since I'm in this thing why shouldn't I enjoy it just as much as any of you men.'

'Yes, that's fair enough I suppose,' he agreed reluctantly, 'and I wouldn't mind if it were not for the fact that this fellow's going with you. He's dangerous, I'm certain of it.'

'I don't think so, really. You're making rather a mountain out of a mole-hill just because you like me quite a lot.'

'*Like you!* Good God! I love you, Patricia. You must know that, and you love me too. Come on—kiss me . . . No not like that . . . properly! Just as you did an hour ago when we were at Aasvogelskop.'

'Michael . . . darling . . . we mustn't.' She struggled half-heartedly to resist his caress. 'Don't you see that nothing can ever possibly come of it. If you want to keep your home you've got to marry a rich girl, and besides we're cousins, so we just ought to hang on to ourselves terribly tight because we're falling desperately in love.'

'Oh, don't let's think of those things now. I want your kisses. Come on—kiss me again—that's better. Oh, Patricia. You're just as bad as I am—and you know it.'

As Patricia and Michael lay enlaced in a big arm-chair in the darkened writing-room, Wisdon was leaning over the table in the palm court towards his two companions. 'We've got to take them along in the party,' he insisted with a drunken leer, 'because that clever old devil made me hand over the necklace of monkey's skulls and the knobkerrie—and they're sticking to both like glue. But if the old boy doesn't come back who's ever to know about it? There's Bushmen, leopards, fever, thirst, a hundred reasons why he should peter out—as for the girl I'll tackle *her*.'

13

Armistice and Treachery

Five hours later Michael, his dark hair tumbled and his brown eyes still heavy with sleep, sat perched on the end of George's bed. 'Surely it is the sensible thing to do,' he pleaded.

'Well, if you're so set on it,' George replied a little reluctantly, 'but after the way the old hypocrite lied to us about not meaning to come at all I'm anything but keen to join up with him. He'll only try and play some dirty trick on us if we do.'

'But look at the advantages!' Michael stood up drawing his dressing-gown tighter round him. 'We've still got to find this witch doctor, and two clues will be more useful than one, besides the larger the party the less risk there will be when we have to cross that infernal desert.'

George sat up in bed brushing back imaginary hair from his almost bald scalp with one plump hand. 'Maybe you're right—anyhow let's hear what Ernie thinks about it,' he added, as his brother came out of the bathroom which the Bennetts shared.

Michael advanced his arguments again and Ernest, fingering his prominent Adam's apple, gave George a knowing wink.

'I'll lay there's quite a different reason, that he hasn't mentioned, in our Michael's head—Ask him what time he got to bed last night!'

'Oh, shut up!' Michael grinned a little sheepishly. 'Honestly, as the Longs have come out here after all we should be idiots not to join forces with them if Uncle Henry will consent.'

'Two heads are better than one I always do say,' Ernest agreed. 'Or eight than three for that matter, though I didn't much like the looks of those fellows that he's taken on to do the hunting.'

Michael shrugged. 'Yes, they're a tough looking couple and the fellow he brought out from England doesn't look much better, but you can hardly expect them to be anything else if they've been roughing it on the outskirts of civilisation most of their lives. All the same, if Uncle Henry trusts them, I don't see why we shouldn't, and if we do go with them we shall be saving ourselves all sorts of bother.'

'I'm not over keen but I'll admit its the common-sense

thing to do, so as far as I'm concerned you can have a shot at fixing it if George is willing.'

This grudging assent from the two brothers was quite sufficient for Michael so, having dressed, he went downstairs and was fortunate enough to find his uncle in the dining-room alone at breakfast.

He was a little frightened of Henry's steady unsmiling grey eyes and tight-lipped mouth but quite determined to press every argument which he could think of, to bring about an alliance between the two parties. The thought of Patricia a week's march from civilisation with only her elderly father between her and Wisdon made the skin under his curly hair prickle. By hook or by crook he had got to arrange a sinking of the differences between Henry Long and the Bennetts so that they might all travel together.

His uncle listened to all he had to say with a non-committal expression. Then, after twenty minutes, when Michael asked him frankly how he viewed the suggestion Henry replied:

'I refused to accompany your half-brothers in the first place for a number of reasons. To start with this is an illegal business and the fewer people that I am concerned with in such an affair the happier I shall be. Buite frankly, I hoped to get out here well ahead of you, and gather all the necessary information before you arrived. If I had reached the Valley before you it is most improbable that you would ever have known if I had succeeded or failed in actually securing and marketing any illicit diamonds.'

'I quite understand that,' Michael conceded, 'but it hasn't come off, so what is there against our joining forces now?'

'Only personal prejudice,' Henry said gravely. 'I have no objection to you, my boy, but your half-brothers are such a talkative couple that by some indiscretion I fear they may give the entire game away at any moment, and it would annoy me intensely to be arrested because the Bennetts do not know when to hold their tongues.'

'I think you're doing them rather an injustice,' Michael protested. 'They know the risk as well as any of us and I've found them close as oysters about the reason of our visit to South Africa whenever we've been talking to strangers. Besides, even if what you say is correct, the more of us there are in the party the more chance of our intervening if George or Ernest are tempted at any time to be a little indiscreet.'

Henry nodded: 'There may be something in what you say but, although I hardly like to mention it, there is a further reason why I have avoided being mixed up with them. This does not apply to Ernest and, if you were not pressing me so much I would not rake up old skeletons at all; but I happen to know that when George first started in business he was mixed up in one or two very shady transactions, and so you can understand that in a matter of this kind I would far rather not be associated with him.'

'Have you any proof of that?' asked Michael with a flash of spirit.

'None.' A dry smile lit Henry's face for a moment. 'You can believe it or not as you like, but I am quite satisfied in my own mind that what I have said is true.'

'I see.' Michael's eyes fell to his uncle's coffee-cup and for a moment he rubbed his short, almost snub, nose with a thoughtful forefinger. Then he lifted his head and looked Henry straight in the eyes. 'Still, I think you'll agree that quite a number of successful people have done some rather doubtful things at the beginning of their careers and then gone perfectly straight afterwards.'

'That is so and I confess that I have heard nothing against George for many years now.'

'Then why not forget it and come in with us?' Michael pushed this small concession home. 'We shall stand a far better chance of pulling this thing off if we all go together.'

'Yes, there is something in that,' Henry agreed slowly, 'but I must talk it over with Philip—Philip Wisdon, you know, whom I brought out from England to help me—before I give you any definite answer,'

'Splendid!' A broad smile spread over Michael's freckled face. 'Could we meet later on in the morning, then?'

'He has gone out already and I don't think he will be back

before lunch time but, if he agrees, we could all meet for a discussion this afternoon.'

'But I thought you were leaving Johannesburg to-day?'

'That was our arrangement, as I suppose Patricia told you, because naturally we do not wish to waste any time. If we did come to an understanding could your party be ready to leave with us?'

Michael shook his head. 'I'm afraid that wouldn't be possible. You see George and Ernest only got the draft balance-sheet of their Company by air mail yesterday, and it may be the last chance they will have to communicate with London for several weeks to come. They are devoting at least a couple of days to analysing the figures in it in order to draw up a report for their partners to present to the Shareholders at the Annual General Meeting.'

'Well, the main question of our joining up at all has yet to be settled and I will meet you in the lounge here at 2.30 if Wisdon agrees. If not, I will leave a note for you with the hall porter.' Henry pushed back his chair and stood up, thinking, as he did so, that he must consult Philbeach at once as to how they could best take advantage of this new situation. With this Michael had to be content and returned upstairs to report the result of his conversation to the Bennetts.

Afterwards, by the house telephone from his own room, he got through to Patricia and asked her if she could spend the morning with him but, to his disappointment, she told him that it was the only chance she had to get her hair done decently and even the fun of spending a couple of hours with him could not reconcile her to setting off into the wilds looking like a ghoul. In addition, she had both her father's and her own packing to see to.

He consoled himself with the thought that if his negotiations were successful he would soon be spending long days with her and urged her to do everything that she possibly could to get her father to agree to his proposals.

The Bennetts having settled themselves to their figures in the writing-room, he spent the morning walking round the principal streets of the city and afterwards took a taxi to the Zoo. Then, by a quarter past one, he was back at the Rand Club where he had been invited to lunch by his medical friend.

At any other time he would have been impressed by the enormous bar—said to be the largest in the world after the Long Bar in Shanghai—where at least a hundred big business and professional men were standing about drinking the famous Iceberg Cocktail of the Club; but his thoughts were focused upon the all-important meeting which he hoped would take place that afternoon.

By the fine double staircase he went up to the spacious panelled dining-room which, but for the blazing sunshine glimpsed between the shades over the tall windows, might well have been situated in Pall Mall. He did scant justice to an excellent lunch and, having been weighed in the famous chair and signed the book, he bolted his coffee and excused himself to his host, in order to get back to the Carlton by half-past two.

To his joy no note had been left with the hall porter for him so, collecting the Bennetts, he went at once to the palm court where he found his uncle, Patricia, Wisdon and the two strangers whom he had seen the night before, already assembled.

After a few preliminary remarks, principally between Henry and George, Philbeach's two companions were introduced.

'This is "Darkie" Rickhartz,' the big man announced, waving his plump hand towards a short, swarthy, bull-necked individual whose quick grin, as he nodded towards the newcomers without troubling to stand up, displayed a row of gold-filled teeth. 'And this is "Ginger" Plettenberg.'

Darkie might have been so named from his swarthy complexion and the short, close-cropped hair which grew square cut in a bristling fringe on his forehead, but he was obviously of pure European origin. Ginger Plettenberg, however, undoubtedly had negroid blood somewhere in his ancestry, despite his fair complexion and sandy curls. The grinning mouth, the long, loose-knit body and the shape of the skull all proclaimed it.

As they settled down, Philbeach announced cheerfully: 'Nothing like the cup of kindness to drown any little differences we may have had, eh boys?' Then he called loudly for a waiter, and when they had given their orders, he immediately launched into particulars of their plans.

His own party was leaving Johannesburg that afternoon for De Aar which they would reach the following evening and, changing trains at the junction, should be in Upington by the second night. Being all packed up and ready he was loath to put off their departure, and suggested that the Bennetts should abandon their business in order that they might all leave together.

George, however, would not hear of this and Ernest supported him. Both of them had spent too many years in the routine of business life to risk endangering their position in London for the sake of a couple of days' delay even if there was the possibility of a fortune round the corner.

For the moment it looked as if they had reached an impasse but Patricia saved the conference by reminding them that when they reached Zwart Modder they still had the problem before them of finding the witch doctor to whom the necklace of monkey skulls had belonged, and that even before that a certain time would have to be occupied in Upington, by the purchase of ox wagons and other necessities for their journey.

'Why,' she asked, 'should not the one party leave that afternoon as arranged and get on with the job while the other follow as soon as they are able?'

'That's true.' Philbeach flickered an eyelid at Darkie Rickhartz. The suggestion fitted in exactly with the plans that he had made with Henry that morning. 'We'll be lucky if we're ready to start out from Upington under a week.'

'Sure,' agreed Darkie with a flash of golden teeth.

With a swift smile Michael thanked Patricia for her suggestion and, on seeing the Bennetts nod, voiced his agreement on their behalf and his own.

Matters having been arranged thus, after a short discussion between George and Philbeach about the cost of oxen and necessities while the others exchanged notes of trains and timetables, the Bennetts left the group to return to their figures.

Michael remained and, when the time came to depart, accompanied the Long party to the station, where he procured flowers, books and chocolates for Patricia, but to his intense annoyance found that Philbeach had forestalled him in the purchase of all these things.

At length the train drew out of the station and, as he watched it go, Michael felt a shade of disappointment that he had not suggested accompanying them. Unlike the Bennetts he had no urgent business to detain him in Johannesburg but his medical friend had already introduced him to half a dozen people, all of whom offered, most hospitably, to entertain him in various ways during his short stay. In addition he felt that, having come out with the Bennetts it would hardly be fair to desert them at this juncture, particularly as he would be seeing Patricia again for certain now in four or five days' time; so he reconciled himself to her departure by the thought of the jolly parties and motor trips which he had already accepted to fill the following days.

From that Friday evening right over the week-end, up to Sunday night, while the Bennett brothers laboriously concocted their Company's annual report, Michael had little time to think of the problem which had brought him out to Africa. He was rushed from cocktail party to cocktail party where new friends, to whom he was continually introduced, pressed fresh invitations upon him. He danced at big private houses, bathed in the swimming pools of their lovely gardens, dined at one, supped at another, played golf and squash and watched the polo, and was taken to see a native war dance on Sunday morning; his five days in Johannesburg had fled all too soon.

The Bennetts, having completed their business, planned to leave Johannesburg on Monday for Upington via De Aar but, when Michael returned to his hotel from a party in the early hours of Monday morning, the night porter handed him a telegram which read:

> Have found guides for hunting expedition. Informed by them better to purchase wagons and start from Postmasburg Griqualand West proceed there and will join you West End Hotel. Love Patricia.

Michael thrilled at the last words in the telegram and then turned his attention to any alteration in their plans which might be necessitated by the wire.

The night porter produced a railway map and Michael saw that Postmasburg was a small town on the extreme southern edge of the Kalahari, at the termination of a branch line running from Kimberley. It appeared to be about a hundred miles east of Upington but no railway joined the two so evidently a stretch of desert lay between. However, the journey was considerably shorter than to Upington since they would not have to go all the way round by De Aar, and if Patricia had left Upington that day it looked as if she would be in Postmasburg on Tuesday night to meet them.

Immediately Michael woke in the morning he hastened in to the Bennetts' room to tell them of the wire, and when he informed them that the same express going south would suit their purpose as far as Kimberley they allowed their arrangements to stand—leaving Johannesburg by it shortly after breakfast.

All through the morning and the long, hot hours of the afternoon the train carried them southward once more across the barren, rocky waste of the Karroo where the sky-line was only broken by the appearance of an occasional kopje. In the evening they drew into Kimberley but they already knew that there was no prospect of being able to continue their journey that day, as no train left for Postmasburg until the following afternoon. They spent a comfortable night at the hotel and listened in the morning to the sad story of the manager who reported the ever increasing depression of the town owing to the fact that the Diamond Mines had been closed down for so many months. World recovery was not sufficiently advanced, he said, to absorb anything like the quantity of diamonds already lying in the companies' safes, without glutting the market, so there did not seem to be even a hope of reopening the mines for, perhaps, years to come.

Having ample time before their train was due to start, they walked out to see the giant crater of the principal mine which constitutes the deepest man-made hole in the world. Three thousand feet below them a line of abandoned trucks looked no larger than a string of peas, and all three felt a little excited at their first sight of the strange bluish soil from which the precious stones that held so deep an interest for them were secured. Even the two Bennetts, usually so talkative, maintained a thoughtful silence as they returned afterwards to the hotel.

Their journey in the afternoon was tedious in the extreme. For the most part the landscape was dull and naked while the same red dust which had plagued them so on the previous day, and on their way up from the Cape to Johannesburg, made them tired and irritable.

Arrived at Postmasburg they discovered the place to be a tiny dorp possessed of only one tin-roofed hotel, and, to Michael's disappointment, the Longs had not arrived nor was there any telegram to announce their coming.

On Wednesday Michael endeavoured to restrain his impatience. He had consulted the time-tables, and, if Patricia had left Upington shortly after she sent the telegram, she certainly should have arrived at Postmasburg on the previous day. The Bennetts, with their natural interest in commerce of any description, diverted themselves by long discussions with the landlord regarding the prospects of manganese which was the principal industry of the place.

On Thursday they, too, began to feel anxious about the non-appearance of the other party, and in the afternoon, George sent telegrams to the managers of the three hotels which Upington boasted. After dinner he received a reply from the *Gordonia* and with a scowl of disgust threw it across to Michael.

'There you are!' he cried angrily. '*Long party left here Monday for Zwart Modder*. From this hole we won't even be able to get to Upington before the week-end, and by letting them pull the wool over our eyes they've got ahead of us again by a clear six days.'

'But I don't understand!' Michael frowned at the paper.

'Don't you!' George stared at him contemptuously. 'Who was it that you gave away this place Zwart Modder to—and the names of the native guides—without getting a darn thing in return. Who suggested their going on ahead? Who sent the telegram which side-tracked us here? Why, that little chit with the goo-goo eyes—and she has fooled you properly!'

14

The Necklace of Kieviet the Witch Doctor

On the previous Saturday morning while Patricia was nearing De Aar, and Michael wandering from department to department in Anstey's big store in Johannesburg—hesitating between a dozen presents that he wanted to buy her, Sandy and the Van Niekerks were making final prepartions for their departure in Cornelius's plane from Pretoria Aerodrome.

All three had spent the last two days in making separate lists of such stores as they would require and procuring in the town such items of the final list as the Van Niekerks were unable to supply.

For food they must principally rely upon game which, by all accounts, was plentiful in the Kalahari; so they took a good supply of ammunition and armed themselves in case of emergency with modern automatics in addition to their rifles, as Cornelius's plane could well carry a good weight, in addition to the three of them and their black boy Willem,

Sarie bought a carefully selected assortment of tinned goods from her grocer, that she might be able to vary their meals as much as possible. Of fruit, rice, and fresh vegetables she intended to lay in a store on their arrival at Zwart Modder. Sandy was given the job of securing the most up-to-date maps of the southern Kalahari from the Government Department at the Union Buildings, and Cornelius spent the best part of Friday with a couple of first-class mechanics thoroughly overhauling his plane.

The journey from Pretoria to Zwart Modder, as the crow flies, was a little over four hundred and fifty miles, but there were certain portions of it where hills and air-pockets would make the going difficult if they took the direct route, so it was decided to make a slight detour and break their journey at the town of Rutland, just over the border of the Orange Free State.

They reached it well before luncheon and, having ample time on their hands, dawdled over the meal for a couple of hours, then they set out again and came to the neighbourhood of Upington early in the evening.

Below them were spread the fertile farm-lands bordering the tributaries of the Orange River but immediately Cornelius sighted the town he veered north-west and, after a further half-hour's cruising, there came into view a few rows of straggling houses which they knew must be Zwart Modder. He banked immediately, for the unusual sight of a private plane landing and being housed, perhaps for a number of days, on the outskirts of the place was certain to excite interest and gossip; so it had been planned that they should select a spot a couple of miles or more outside the dorp where they could form a camp.

A narrow stream of water in the broad bed of the Molopo River lay shimmering in the sunset as Cornelius found a suitable stretch of grassland near it where no house was visible. It was guarded from prying eyes by low ranges of hills, between which he brought the plane at a sweeping curve and, taxi-ing for some distance, came to a halt near a plantation of blue-gum trees.

Of the Longs' movements they knew nothing and there was no possibility of Michael's party arriving at Zwart Modder until the following night at the earliest so, with the material they had brought, they made their bivouac and Sarie, with old black Willem fetching and carrying for her, cooked a meal.

By the time they sat down to it night had fallen and they fed by the light of a fine camp fire which Sandy and Cornelius had made while the food was being prepared. Afterwards the myriad stars which nightly make the African veldt a paradise for those who, living in the cities, appreciate occasional solitude the more, came out above them. With the sentimentality that comes upon habitual town dwellers at such times, they sat cross-legged beside their fire singing those songs in chorus that have always been a subtle link between the old country and the new.

In the morning a fresh conference was held and it was decided that, in the afternoon while the two men remained at the camp, Sarie should go in to the dorp and put up at the inn. As the Bennetts and Michael had never seen her she could watch for their arrival without any fear of betraying the presence of the rival expedition. With luck she might be able to get in touch with them, learn what further plans they had made, and duly report their intentions. At four o'clock she set off, Sandy carrying her grip for her as far as the first houses of the village. As he handed it to her she said cheerily:

'Well, expect me when you see me. They may come in this evening but if they decide to buy their stores on their way through Upington they may not be here for a day or two yet.'

'That's no reason why you shouldn't come out to us again to-night,' he told her. 'Won't you do that anyhow?' His glance betrayed an open admiration as he stood looking at her—brown armed, brown legged—in her practical khaki shorts and open-necked blue shirt. A little of white skin showed above the sunburn at the roots of her hair as it was ruffled by the evening breeze.

'Not on your life,' she replied gaily. 'Do you think I'm

going to walk out to the camp again for the fun of seeing you when I can spend the night in a comfortable bed; besides, in any case, I've got to play my part, it's no good taking a room at the inn if I don't sleep in it.'

'I don't mind a walk,' he assured her quickly. 'What about meeting you here again, say at nine o'clock? Then we could have a stroll round the outskirts of this place together without any fear of the Bennetts or young Michael seeing us.'

She laughed then, tickled a little by his obvious eagerness, but quickly shook her head: 'If I'm strolling with anyone to-night it will be with your handsome cousin Michael that you've told me so much about, and not with you.'

'Oh, he's only a boy,' Sandy shrugged disdainfully. 'It's no good trying to make me jealous about him.'

'Thank you,' she gave a little mocking bow while her blue eyes danced with humour: 'It's interesting to know that you like me enough to be jealous of me, but if Michael is half as nice as you've made out I shall certainly take him on a little expedition to see our African moonlight, so you can think that over while you are singing songs with Cornelius at the camp.'

'Damn you!' said Sandy with a sudden grin.

'Damn me if you like,' she replied lightly. Then on a more serious note: 'But honestly it is my job to get in with these people and Michael is the obvious line of least resistance—don't you think?'

'Yes, the Bennetts are the most awful bores so if you're going to vamp anyone it had better be Michael. Poor boy! There won't be any resistance once *you* set to work.'

'He may think I'm perfectly hideous and not fall for me at all,' she said quite solemnly. Then as she turned to leave Sandy she swung round with a sudden laugh and called to him over her shoulder: 'Anyhow I promise you that I won't let him kiss me unless I think he's awfully nice myself!'

Sarie entered the inn and, since she had thought the whole situation out carefully beforehand, registered as *Miss* Aileen Orkney; then she made friends with the fat old wife of the Dutchman who owned it, explaining her presence by saying that she had come up from Johannesburg for a few days' rest cure and settled down to wait for the Bennetts.

Visitors were so few and far between at this tiny township on the fringe of the desert that, after the description Sandy had given her, it would be quite impossible to miss them, but the evening passed without their arriving and so she was compelled to kick her heels alone in the single reception-room and round the precincts of the small tin-roofed hostelry.

On the first night after Sarie left them Sandy had an opportunity of inquiring the reason for Cornelius's limp and learned that as a boy of sixteen the young Dutchman had volunteered for the special police during the miners' strike, which had developed into a red revolution, in Johannesburg in 1922.

A sniper, lurking in the church tower in Lilian Road, had shot him down just as the loyalists were making their attack on the last stronghold of the Reds in Fordsburg Square. The bullet had severed a sinew and left him permanently lame, but the disability did not interfere with his irrepressible gaiety, and Sandy found him a most delightful and amusing companion.

That night they had to be content with old black Willem's cooking. He scorned the camp fire and having discovered a large conical ant-heap nearby, set to work on the hard, cement-like structure with a chisel, hollowed out the top, dug a hole in the side and made a chimney connecting the two. By the time he had a fire going, which he fed through the hole, and his saucepan on top it made a first-class oven, but Willem was not the Van Niekerks' cook—only their garden boy—taken for his general usefulness and trustworthiness, so the stew that he produced was distinctly on the tough side.

In the days that followed, however, Sarie returned to the camp and, getting out her flat, round Dutch baking-pot fulfilled the boast that she had made in Pretoria by providing them with a dozen different succulent dishes.

She got out her ukulele too and while they lazed in the sunshine kept them merry with her singing, but for all their laughter, as Sandy listened to her clear contralto he knew that he was falling desperately in love with her.

Of all her songs he loved best the one after which she had been named 'Sarie Marais'. That lilting melody so dear to the hearts of all South Africans.

> 'O bring my trug na die ou Transvaal,
> Daar waar my Sarie woon.
> Daar onder in die mielies by die groen doringboom,
> Daar woon my Sarie Marais.'

Again and again he begged her to sing it for him and with smiling eyes she complied, but about the evenings she was adamant. Each night she returned to the inn to keep up her part of a girl who had come to Zwart Modder for a rest cure, and she flatly refused to allow him to accompany her.

Sunday had been the earliest conceivable day upon which the Bennetts might arrive, but it was not till Wednesday that Sarie's patience was rewarded. After dinner that night an ox-span drew up before the inn.

No one remotely resembling Michael or the Bennetts were among the new arrivals, but an elderly grey-haired man of middle height, in London clothes, stiffly descended from beside the driver and a pretty dark-haired girl dismounted from a roan horse, while of the three mounted men who accompanied the wagon the largest tallied exactly with Sandy's description of Roger Philbeach. Sarie decided at once that the old man and the girl must be the Longs.

After they had entered the inn, she moved to a better-lighted portion of the stoep, and when the newcomers had washed and fed she was not at all surprised at seeing the girl whom she assumed to be Patricia come out and, after a second's hesitation, pause before her chair with a low greeting.

'I do hope you'll forgive me, but are you Miss Orkney?'

Sarie smiled to herself; obviously one of the party had been examining the visitors' book. Then she said gravely: 'Yes, that is my name.'

Patricia sat down beside her and having introduced herself

went on at once: 'This is terribly interesting, I wonder if you are any relation to a *Mrs*. Aileen Orkney who used to live at the Cape and is now living in Johannesburg.'

'But, of course. I am her daughter,' declared Sarie, her blue eyes round with well-feigned astonishment.

After that Sarie's task was easy. Patricia introduced her father, Mr. Roger Philbeach, under the name of Philip Wisdon which was the only one she knew him by, and his two unprepossessing companions. All five gathered about Sarie and pressed her for any information which she could give regarding her mother's deceased friend, John Thomas Long.

On hearing the name she immediately exclaimed at Patricia's relative having left her mother £20,000, and then developed the part she had decided to play of a charming young girl, who was vague to the point of imbecility, doing a rest cure in this lonely spot after having danced herself almost into an asylum. But on going to bed she was able to congratulate herself on having established an acquaintance with the Longs which would enable her to watch their every movement.

In the morning she took Patricia for a walk up the only street of the dorp and along the few byways that led off it. Then Patricia took her round to the stable to feed her roan mare with carrots which gave Sarie a fine opportunity to develop her role by displaying a lively fear of the neat little animal's hoofs.

Meanwhile Philbeach, Darkie and Ginger busied themselves with inquiring at the native stores for the witch doctor Kieviet, and at lunch-time Darkie reported that he had traced the man. He was living in a small native settlement about a mile outside the town upon the river's bank.

Sarie, making her eyes larger and rounder than ever, played to perfection the part of the stupid innocent, so that when she asked to accompany them in the afternoon even Philbeach was convinced that she was only a girl greedy for sensations who wished to witness the mumbo-jumbo of a witch doctor, and, if possible, have her fortune told.

In consequence they allowed her to go with them when they

set off down the river bank at an easy pace made necessary by the semi-tropical weather. Their way lay principally through fields of lucerne which were broken, here and there, by large patches of wheat and occasionally the regularly planted trees of an orange grove. Bright butterflies of every size and hue fluttered in their path, and once a snake that Philbeach declared was a highly poisonous boomslang wriggled across the sandy track a few yards in front of them.

The heat of the early afternoon was such that although they took half an hour over their walk, they were all perspiring freely by the time they reached the circular palisade of rushes and wattle which surrounded the Hottentot village, except Sarie and, curiously enough, the bulky Philbeach.

'It's good to be in Africa again after all these years,' he declared loudly as they entered the enclosure. 'Can't think why I ever left it.'

No one replied to the observation but Ginger winked at Darkie behind the others' backs.

Both had known Philbeach, alias Wisdon, under yet another name when he had been compelled to fly the country eleven years before. They were well aware that only the long interval during which he had been cloaked in the respectable guise of a wine merchant's traveller, had enabled him to obtain a fresh passport and consider himself secure from recognition now he had returned to his old happy hunting ground.

One of the many children playing in the sand at the entrance was questioned by Philbeach but the little, yellow, pot-bellied caricature of humanity only grinned broadly, for he understood neither Basuto nor Afrikaans. A woman joined them, to whom at last they succeeded in making their meaning clear, and she led them into a circular, open space in the centre of the village. From one of the mud huts which gave upon it a wizened, mongolian-faced native, at whose belt a mixture of ostrich feathers, strings of beads, cowrie shells and leopards' teeth dangled, was produced. He had just been aroused from his midday sleep and was none too pleased to see them, but upon Philbeach producing the customary offering of whisky, which it is illegal for the natives to purchase in the ordinary way, he became almost embarrassingly anxious to serve them in any manner possible.

Sarie stood in the background, but she listened with strained ears while Philbeach questioned the man in a mixture of dialect and Afrikaans. He produced the necklace of monkeys' skulls, and told him that he was anxious to talk with one Kieviet, to whom he understood the thing belonged, and who was reported to be living there.

The Hottentot cast covetous eyes upon the strange ornament that Philbeach dangled before him and hesitantly touched the largest skull with his forefingers; then he gave a rueful sigh.

'It is the necklace of Kieviet the Witch doctor, but he talks no more with any man. Three moons ago we buried him by the river's bank.'

15

Sarie Plays a Part and Two Lovers Quarrel

It was a crestfallen party that sat down to dinner that night at the inn. They had been lucky in tracing two out of three of the owners of the strange clues that John Thomas Long had left behind him, but one of these had emphatically refused to set out into the Great Thirst again and the other was dead. They had no hope of getting the kaross which was the only other clue left.

Although Patricia had come so far her journeys by train and car had given her little appreciation of the size of Africa. She was all for setting off into the desert and trying to find the place on the slender information that N'hluzili had given them, but Philbeach roared with laughter at the very idea of starting upon such a hopeless quest.

'Might roam that wilderness like Moses for forty years and

then not find the place we're after if we hadn't got a guide,' he said, and Darkie tittered rudely.

'Guide or no guide, I guess the young lady don't know what she'll be letting herself in for, if we go up country on trek.'

'That's none of your business,' Philbeach took him up sharply; 'you're paid to make things easy for us, not to shoot off personal remarks.'

'No offence, no offence,' Darkie muttered, but he gave an il!-concealed wink towards Ginger.

'Obviously we must have a guide,' Henry declared firmly. It was a constant irritation to him that his daughter had insisted upon accompanying him on the trip, but since she was paying her own share of the expenses he could not very well object.

'That's so,' Philbeach agreed; 'but now that we've reached the jumping-off place there must be someone here who knows roughly where the Valley is supposed to lie and has talked with the old man's guide. If we could only find this "some-one" it might be worth our while making a trek into the interior on the off-chance that we'd strike lucky.'

'Yes, yes,' Ginger leaned forward across the table. 'We visit all the native kraals hereabout, eh?—we find someone who can help us for certain if we spend a little time like that.'

'A little time is right,' Philbeach nodded his large head; 'it'll mean two or three weeks' steady grinding work but I don't doubt we'll raise somebody who can tell us something before we've done.'

Sarie's air of innocent stupidity had taken the others in so completely that they were talking freely before her and now she listened to this conversation with dismay. The one thing which Sandy had dreaded seemed about to happen. Philbeach and his friends—this striking-looking girl, and her morose father, were on the point of exciting the entire countryside by a house-to-house inquiry about a legendary diamond mine. By the time they did set off up country, half the population of Koranna Land would be hastening in their tracks and the Union police taking a lively interest in the proceedings. It was up to her to stop that if she could.

Having rapidly evolved a plan, she went into the back-room after dinner and asked the telephone exchange to get her a Johannesburg number. Some twenty minutes later, her call came through. She had a meaningless chat with one of her best girl friends and, returning to the stoep, informed the Longs that she had just been talking to her mother.

Then she told them she had consulted her about their difficulties and that Mrs. Orkney had proved most helpful. She remembered that the bushman guide who had accompanied John Thomas Long came from King George's Falls, a hundred miles from Upington down the Orange River; and quite neat a white settlement called Kakamas.

Patricia was overjoyed and wanted to act on this information immediately. She pressed Sarie to join them on their expedition, but Sarie kept up her part of a girl whose one idea was to return to the gaiety of Johannesburg as soon as possible.

Philbeach called to their landlord, who came out and joined them on the stoep, and asked him in Afrikaans for particulars about the journey to King George's Falls.

The man was a little surprised that, having declared their intention of setting off to hunt in the interior, they should now have decided to turn south again to see the Falls. He told them, however, that they should certainly not miss it since it was the most wonderful sight for many hundred miles around, if not in all South Africa. The great flood of the Orange River poured over the cataract into a vast basin no less than four hundred and fifty feet below, which provided a spectacle only to be rivalled by the great falls at Lake Victoria, and Niagara in America. They should proceed back to Upington in their out-span, he suggested, and from there they could get the narrow-gauge railway down to Kakamas from which the great falls were only some ten miles' distant.

Asked what sort of accommodation they would be likely to get in Kakamas the landlord said that he did not know if there was an hotel, but the place was a notable colony for poor whites, founded by the Dutch Reformed Church on the fertile banks of the Orange; so there would be plenty of people only too willing to take them in for the sake of a small payment.

When Philbeach translated for the benefit of Patricia and her father, Henry said:

'Well, that sounds all right, so we'd better set out again first thing to-morrow, but what does he mean by *poor white*?'

'It's easy to see that you haven't been here long,' Philbeach laughed. 'Poor whites are one of the biggest problems of this country. You see, the old Boer farmers all lived like patriachs and when they died they had the habit of splitting up their property into equal parts for all their sons and, like the Bible folk, there was generally plenty of them to split up amongst. That was all right, of course, in the early days, when some old Dutch had a farm of fifty thousand acres with slave labour into the bargain, but if you get a system like that going on for three or four generations it ends up with the heirs getting a mealie patch apiece, and that's not enough for any man to live on. Most of them have no schooling so they sell their bit to a brother that's got more guts, and drift into the towns, hoping to get some sort of job. Unfortunately, the type of work the poor white is capable of can be done better and cheaper by niggers, so they form a class apart as unemployable and unemployed.'

'But what happens to these poor people?' Patricia asked.

'God knows,' the big man shrugged his shoulders. 'They drift about the country, a curse to everyone and a thorn in the side of the Government. Sometimes they do a hand's turn for a week or two with farmers who are getting in their crops, or a little casual labour in the mines. Other times they wash the up-country river beds for alluvial or do a bit of prospecting on their own, but there are said to be over a million of them and, since they're becoming a menace to the country, the powers that be are trying to get them settled back on the land like at this place Kakamas that we're going to.'

Sarie, delighted with the success of her stratagem, praised Patricia for her courage in persisting in roughing it with the men. Giving the first address that she could think of in Johannesburg, she pressed the whole party to come and visit her mother and herself when they returned there then, still chortling with inward mirth, went up to bed.

In the morning she came out to wave them farewell as the slow-moving oxen set off down the short village street. Then, since Michael and his party had still failed to put in an appearance, she decided to visit her brother and Sandy at their camp.

When she told them her news they roared with laughter at the thought of Roger Philbeach, alias Philip Wisdon, with his two friends and the Longs, trekking southward again to Upington on a complete fool's errand, but their amusement was considerably subdued when Cornelius pointed out that Kieviet had been duly run to earth, and found to be lying several feet under it. Their principal hope in that direction had been completely shattered. What were they to do now?

They also agreed that it would be madness to attempt to find the place of the Great Glitter unless they could trace one of the guides who had been on the expedition ten years before or could follow one of the other parties in their plane. However, when Michael and his party did arrive with their leopard skin they might be more fortunate than the Longs, so Sarie, Sandy and Cornelius decided to wait for a few days before attempting to search out a native guide on their own.

In the days that followed, the three continued to lead the simple life. A nearby pool of clear fresh water some fifty feet in circumference, from which a narrow outlet gave on to the Molopo River, provided excellent bathing. Afterwards, they sat or lay upon the hot rocks, sunning their bodies to a more golden brown while they smoked and laughed and chipped one another. The two men did a little mild shooting in order that they might not encroach unduly upon their tinned stores, and old Willem, under Sarie's supervision, produced some of her specialities for their evening meals.

On the second night after their departure for King George's

Falls, the Longs' out-span crawled back into Upington. Henry was already heartily sick of this primitive and wearisome mode of travel and Patricia was a little sore from the long hours in the saddle to which, much as she enjoyed riding, she was unaccustomed. Both were glad to see again the small town with its three comfortable hotels.

Patricia had an additional reason for her pleasure since she believed that her father had left a message for Michael in Upington, asking him to wait there until they sent back a runner from Zwart Modder with the result of their inquiries for Kieviet.

Her face, tanned now after these long days of exposure to the sun, had a happy glow as she handed over the little roan to one of the native boys and ran up the steps of the *Gordonia*. She was confident that even if he were out at the moment she would be seeing Michael's snub nose and freckled face again in an hour or so.

The pseudo Mr. Wisdon watched her enter the hotel. Dismounting from his horse, he winked at Henry. 'Trouble for you, my boy, if Pat discovers why her young man hasn't turned up!'

Henry shrugged as he brushed the dust from his neat dark coat. 'How can she? Michael's party could only have arrived at Postmasberg four nights ago and even if they are getting suspicious now it will take them a couple of days to come on here. If you remember, we counted on that telegram delaying them at least a week.'

'Still, say they've rumbled us and are here already—what do you mean to do?'

'You can leave me to deal with my own daughter,' Henry replied gruffly. 'She came here against my wish and she will have to do as she is told if she wants to go any farther. I only concealed the fact that you were Philbeach from her to spare her feelings. I told you long ago that is she found out about the knobkerrie I should give her the choice of going home or accepting the situation.'

The big man nodded and followed Henry into the hotel. He had been delighted with the result of his stratagem for sidetracking the Bennetts but he was now a little afraid that they might have come on to Upington sooner than he expected. If Patricia and Michael got together again he would have all the trouble of separating the parties once more, for he was quite determined that if Darkie, Ginger and himself did set off into the Kalahari only the Longs should go with them. He was convinced that old Henry had a pretty useful packet tucked away in England and if they failed to find the Valley there were ways in which he could be made to cough up a nice hunk of it. Keep him on a short ration of water out there in the desert until he signed half a dozen cheques, then Darkie and Ginger could do the necessary while he saw to clearing them and getting the cash out to the Union. If he could collect another £5,000 from Henry in addition to the £5,000 he had inherited from John, the total would provide a sufficient income for him to settle down quietly, and Philbeach realised that he was not getting any younger. Besides, there was the girl. Roger Philip Wisdon Philbeach had seen the traces of powder on Michael's lapels that night in the Carlton after she had been up to Aasvoglerkop. He wanted some of that powder himself. 'Her own cousin, too!' he found himself thinking, and curiously enough he was a little shocked.

To Patricia's intense disappointment Michael was not staying at the *Gordonia* nor could the people in the office tell her anything about him. Weary after her long day, she undressed and enjoyed the luxury of a warm bath, where she lay for some little time thinking the matter over. Philbeach and her father only shrugged their shoulders when she commented at dinner on how extraordinary it was that the others had not yet reached Upington, so afterwards she excused herself on the plea of tiredness, but instead of going straight up to bed, she slipped out of the side door, bent upon inquiring at the other two hotels in case Michael had gone to one of them through some misunderstanding.

She walked quickly down the street and turned into the entrance of the Imperial. The first thing that caught her eye was Michael seated on the veranda—a long cool drink in his hand—talking to his two half-brothers. Forgetful for the moment of everything except that she had guessed aright and found him, she ran up the steps and cried cheerfully:

'Michael! So you are here, after all !'

He rose a little stiffly. He had liked her—believed in her —yes, damn it, loved her, but she had tricked him. On every mile of the long journey from Postmasberg the Bennetts had pointed out the various ways she had fooled him. Firstly, she had weedled the name of Kieviet out of him. Secondly, he had told her old John's jumping-off place—Zwart Modder —and she had not told him a damn' thing in return. She had been the first to suggest that her own party should go on ahead, and finally it was she who had sent the telegram. He could hear Ernest's Cockney witticisms at his expense ringing in his ears still, and forty times in the last two days he could cheerfully have strangled the Bennett brothers. As she came up to the table they regarded her curiously but left it for him to speak.

'Yes, we're here,' he said, without the flicker of a smile. 'I suppose you imagined that we were still kicking our heels in Postmasberg?'

'Postmasberg! Why, where's that?' she exclaimed a little nervously. She was disconcerted and upset by the complete change in him.

'Oh, *you* ought to know. It's that rotten little dorp you sent us to.' He stared at her, a hurt look in his dark eyes.

'I don't understand,' she gasped.

'Do you mean that you didn't send us a telegram telling us to go to Postmasberg and wait for you there?' George asked, his voice full of sarcastic unbelief.

'No! How absurd! Why should I do that?' Patricia was almost on the point of tears. She was disappointed and entirely at a loss to account for this unsympathetic reception.

'It was signed in your name, anyhow,' Michael declared coldly, 'and the reason's pretty obvious. You meant to shanghai us there, so that you could get ahead of us again in spite of the arrangement that we fixed up.'

'No! No!' she assured him. It was gradually dawning on

her that Wisdon must have used her name to deceive the others. 'I didn't, honestly . . . I didn't even know that you'd had a telegram. . . . It . . . Why . . . It must have been that man that father took on before we left England. We went up to Zwart Modder four days ago. They told me a message had been left for you to wait here until we sent a runner to tell you what luck we'd had there with the necklace.'

Ernest's quick eyes were fixed steadily on Patricia's face and, feeling quite certain that she was not lying, he endeavoured to bridge the misunderstanding which obviously lay between them. 'Come on, now. Let's be reasonable,' he said, pulling his collar from under the big Adam's apple with a characteristic gesture. 'Young Pat's been led up the garden path, I reckon, and if that's so we've got no quarrel with her.'

'No, none whatever,' Michael agreed a trifle more amiably, relieved that there was a possibility they had misjudged her. 'But will you tell us what has been going on during these days that we have been delayed.'

'Of course, I will. I have no idea what game Wisdon is playing. I can only suppose that he didn't mean it when he agreed that we should join forces. We've been up to Zwart Modder and found Kieviet, or rather we've found out that he died three months ago, so that hope is gone.'

'Well, if you're being honest,' George cut in, 'it would be interesting if you'd tell us what new plans you've made now.'

'Of course I'm being honest,' Patricia protested. 'I can only tell you everything I know. When we arrived at Zwart Modder we had an awful stroke of luck. There was a Miss Aileen Orkney staying at the hotel and, seeing the resemblance of the name to the one in Uncle John's Will, I got hold of her at once. It turned out that she is the daughter of the original Aileen Orkney. She's a stupid, empty-headed sort of girl but she was most awfully sympathetic when she heard Kieviet was dead and that we had had all our trouble for nothing. She telephoned to her mother in Johannesburg and landed the information for us that the boy, who was the only other survivor of the party besides N'hluzili and Uncle John, lived at

King George's Falls. We are going down to see if we can find him to-morrow.' She paused suddenly—was it possible that they still didn't believe her? Surely Michael would know she was telling the truth—it was like a nightmare to see the disbelief in his eyes. She stammered out—'I've told you everything. I don't care what you do!'

As Michael listened his mouth drew down into an angry sullen curve. Here she was, with this glib explanation, trying to draw another red herring across the trail.

'Thank you for nothing!' he exclaimed rudely. He was bitter in his disappointment and only thinking of hurting her as much as she had hurt him. 'We're not quite fools enough to be taken in by you twice. You seem to forget that we met Mrs. Orkney in Johannesburg and happen to know that she never had a daughter!'

16

The Leopard Skin Kaross of Ombulike the Hottentot

Three days later the Bennett party arrived at Zwart Modder. In spite of the purchase of a nice little cob in Upington, Michael did not enjoy the journey. He was in the depths of despair about his break with Patricia, and the Bennetts had added to his distress by warning him not to let his affair with her become too serious because not only was she his first cousin but her parents had been first cousins too. He had not known that before but now, even if he could patch up their quarrel, which he was anxious to do, it put all prospect of marriage out of the question.

The Bennetts, too, were distinctly sobered by their first taste of journeying in a springless wagon which progressed in a series of jolts and was drawn by a long span of sixteen slow-moving oxen, but as neither of them could ride there was no alternative.

To supervise their out-span they had engaged a tall, loose-limbed Kaffir boy, who spoke a little English, and two Sesutos, one of whom could cook after a fashion. The other, the voor-trekker, walked in front of the oxen, cracking his whip.

Johnnie, the head boy, duly delivered his passengers, who kept him and his two underlings in a perpetual cackle of laughter, at the tin-roofed shanty which served for a hotel at Zwart Modder.

The place was two full days' journey from Upington and, having had to spend the day following their interview with Patricia in securing their equipment, it was not until five days after the Longs had left that they arrived at the tiny dorp on the banks of the Molopo.

The Van Niekerk party had now been at Zwart Modder for nine days and, Michael's party having failed to put in an appearance, they had decided, only that afternoon, that Sarie should leave the inn to join them in the camp and that they would now set about trying to find a guide on their own.

When Sarie went in to collect her things and settle her bill, Sandy persuaded her to let him go with her in order to carry back her bag. and they were just having a cocktail together before their departure when the Bennetts plodded wearily up the steps.

The first person they set eyes on was Sandy. He was just inside the front room, leaning against a small bar, his way-ward lock of dark hair tumbled forward across his forehead. Sarie, seated nearby on a stool, looked, in her khaki breeches, the image of a film star all ready to walk on the set in a jungle picture.

'Well, well!' George exclaimed. 'You're a sly one and no mistake, trying to kid us that night at Simpson's that you never meant to have a cut at *you-know-what*, and then turn-ing up here after all.'

Sandy realised that he was caught but put the best face on the matter that was possible. 'I'm not here for what you think,' he said amiably. 'It's a copper proposition which has brought me north, but I'm glad to see you all the same. May I introduce my wife?—Darling, these are my cousins, George and Ernest Bennett and Michael Kane-Swift.'

Sarie's blush would have done credit to a peony. There was nothing to be done but accept the situation; so in her new role as Mrs. McDiamid she greeted Sandy's row of cousins.

Sandy, chortling inwardly at the sight of Sarie's flushed face and the furious glance she shot at him, was in high good humour. 'What are you going to have?' he cried, with a sweep of his arm towards the modest array of bottles in the small bar.

'Double Scotch for me, thanks,' Ernest replied promptly. 'But I didn't know you had a better half. This *is* a surprise.'

'Didn't you?' Sandy grinned genially. 'Well, we saw so little of each other in London it's quite possible that I never mentioned it. But, as a matter of fact, we've been married some time—I've got three children as well as a wife, you know.'

George's semi-circular eyebrows went up towards his bald forehead as he looked at the sylph-like Sarie. 'My! you do look young to be the mother of three.'

'Oh, two of them are twins!' said Sandy airily. Upon which Sarie gave him a hefty kick on the shin under cover of the table. A sudden spasm crossed his tanned face but he suppressed a yowl of pain and went on quickly: 'Seen anything of the Longs? They were up here five days ago.'

'Yes,' Michael nodded. 'We met them in Upington. They pitched us some absurd story about having met Mrs. Orkney's daughter here and that they intended going down to King George's Falls, but, of course, that was only to put us off the track.'

'Why do you think that?' Sandy asked, pushing back the dark lock with a quick sweep of his hand.

'Because we know there is no such person. We met Mrs. Orkney in Johannesburg, and she has no daughter.'

'What do you intend to do now then?' Sandy inquired.

'Hunt every kraal for miles round until we can run a certain witch doctor to earth,' said Michael promptly.

Sarie's face broke into a smile. 'If it is Kieviet you are looking for,' she said, 'we can tell you where to find his family but the old man himself is dead.'

'May I ask how you know that, Mrs. McDiamid?' George asked quickly.

She flushed again at the manner of his address and, lowering her eyes, began to flick the dust off her field-boots with a riding switch: 'Because Sandy met the Longs when they were here and his cousin Patricia told him so. The landlord here will direct you to the kraal where old Kieviet used to live. It is only about two miles up the river.'

'Come on now! Drink up, all of you,' Ernest interjected. 'The next round's on me. Then, how about a bit of a wash and a spot of dinner?'

'Sorry,' Sandy shook his head. 'But my wife and I are staying with the man whom we've come up to see about this new copper mine. We can't dine, but I'd love another drink. If you like I'll take you along to Kieviet's kraal myself tomorrow morning.'

'That's decent of you. We'd be much obliged,' George agreed.

The words were hardly out of his mouth when Sarie, seeirg an excellent opportunity for a come-back, smiled sweetly up at Sandy:

'I know that you can't dine, darling, because you've got your business to attend to but I'm sick of hearing you talk copper so if I may I should love to accept your cousins' invitation.'

Sandy groaned inwardly. His jest had cost him the evening with Sarie. As an additional pin-prick she looked swiftly at her wrist-watch and exclaimed: 'You must run, my sweet, it is half-past eight already.'

With as good a grace as possible Sandy said good-bye, promising to call for them in the morning. Just as he was about to go, Sarie delivered a parting shot.

'Don't wait up for me, dearest, will you? I'm almost certain to be late, it's so seldom that I have anybody new and nice and interesting to talk to!'

He paused beside her, a little smile hovering over his full mouth, then he stooped and, catching her unawares, gave her a smacking kiss on the side of the mouth. With a cheerful flourish of his broad-brimmed hat as he strode out of the door he called over his shoulder: 'Be as late as you like, my dear. I'll tell the servants not to call us in the morning.'

Sarie was not late, despite her threat. The Bennetts were tired after their long day and went early to their room, while Michael, whom she did her best to intrigue purely for the fun of annoying Sandy, proved moody and unresponsive. Believing her to be Sandy's wife, it would never have occurred to him to flirt with her even if he had been in a mood for flirtation. Yet he liked her, and in some strange way she reminded him of Patricia. She was taller, of course, and fair with blue eyes, whereas Patricia was dark; Patricia's nose was distinctly Roman too, while Sarie's was straight, but there was something about the sweep of her eyebrows and the tilt of her chin that made Michael see the other girl in his mind more distinctly. In fact he felt that but for their colouring they might have been sisters.

He had revolved the problem of Patricia's treachery in his mind unceasingly. One side of him refused to believe that it was anything more than a misunderstanding—the other, prodded by the Bennetts, advanced arguments which seemed fatally convincing. He only realised how much he loved her when he found himself constantly inventing fresh excuses in palliation of her fault.

Sarie was determined to make her self-elected husband pay for his trick. If Michael had fallen in with her plan she could have hit back by making Sandy jealous. This gambit having failed, she pretended when she got back to camp that, far from thinking the matter funny, she was deeply offended. This was not easy, for Sandy had told her brother of the episode and Cornelius greeted her return with loud laughter and earnest inquiry as to the well-being of her twins; but with a little air of dignity which she could so well assume at times, she succeeded in sending Sandy to bed quite miserable in the belief that his jest had cost him her friendship.

In the morning she refused to accompany him into Zwart Modder, so he set off, more dejected than ever, to pick up the Bennetts and take them to the Hottentot kraal. They found no difficulty in seeing the medicine man whom Sarie and the Longs had spoken to a few days before. Michael unpacked his leopard skin kaross and placed it in front of the man while Sandy asked the bushman in Afrikaans if he knew to whom it had once belonged.

The yellow, wrinkled Hottentot shook his head but said that if they were prepared to wait for an hour or two he might be able to ascertain. Then, sitting in the space before his mud hut, they witnessed a curious ceremony.

The women in the crowd brought him certain dried herbs in a pot and a long pipe. The pipe was filled with the herbs and he began to smoke while a dozen younger men gathered round him and squatted down on their haunches in a circle. While the medicine-man smoked placidly in their midst, holding the leopard skin kaross between his hands, the others began a low chant in response to one who acted as their leader. Each time they droned out a few sentences of this weird litany, in reply to a queer staccato question which the leader flung at them, they swayed a little in a bowing motion which gradually increased in rapidity until their heads almost touched the ground. The witch doctor swayed in union with them until suddenly, with a little grunt, he pitched forward senseless upon his face and lay motionless on the ground. The others ceased their chanting, his pipe and his herbs were collected, and they left him there—sprawled in the dust before his hut. The four Englishmen sat silently at a little distance waiting to see the result of this strange performance.

After a time the sun became so hot that they were forced to move into the shadow of the reed and wattle palisade. Then when the man had lain motionless for nearly an hour his feet and neck began to jerk. A woman went up to him and, placing his head upon her knees, poured some liquid from a small kalabash into his mouth; he sat up and looked about him.

Sandy strolled over and asked him if he would now be able to help them further. He nodded slowly, handing back the kaross to Michael, who had joined them.

'This,' he said, 'belonged to a white man of great height and fine presence. . . . One who was as a lion for courage, but he is no more, and died in a country far from here beyond the great waters.'

'Before that?' Sandy prompted.

'Before . . . it belonged to one of my people. . . . One who is still in the prime of life. . . . He lives in the kraal beyond the hill-top and his name is Ombulike.'

When Sandy translated this to the others and told them that they must make the old man a handsome present for his trouble, George exclaimed: 'I bet he knew all the time that the thing belonged to one of his neighbours. He went through all that palaver just to get a bit more out of us.' But Ernest was obviously impressed by the Hottentot's powers of divination and answered in a hushed voice:

'Don't you believe it. How could he have known that part about Uncle John being dead and having died in a far country? I think it's a miracle, but there you are. I always do say truth is stranger than fiction.'

'Anyhow, he may have told us what we want to know,' said Michael, paying the witch doctor lavishly. 'Shall we walk across the hill to the other kraal now?'

Sandy agreed to accompany them and the distance was soon covered, but not before all four were streaming with sweat for the sun was well up in the heavens by this time. The second Hottentot kraal was very similar to the first. Primitive mud huts and a crowd of small, yellow, shrivelled, monkey-like people. Sandy once again acted as interpreter and they soon found the man whom they had come to see.

He was a sinewy little creature with high cheekbones and a triangular face of the pure Hottentot type, with no trace of negro about him. His small quick eyes held a humorous, friendly glint and he could speak both Afrikaans and a few words of English. He listened patiently to all that Sandy had to say and then replied, without hesitation, that he was willing to undertake the journey again if it was at the request of the brothers of his Great Master.

Asked how soon he would be prepared to start, he picked up the leopard skin kaross which they had shown him when they arrived and twisted it round his shoulders. Taking an assegai and a little skin pouch which held his knife, pipes, tobacco, charms and drugs, from just inside the doorway of his hut, he stood before them, announcing abruptly: 'One day is as another.'

The three half-brothers were overjoyed that the first half of their mission had now really been accomplished. They had actually succeeded in securing one of the men who had been with their uncle when he obtained his marvellous fortune. Now it was only a matter of reasonable luck, coupled with considerable endurance, before they felt that they too would be leaving South Africa as rich men. Sandy was equally delighted but hid his own satisfaction under congratulations to the others as they made their way back to the village, the Hottentot following.

At the inn a surprise was in store for them. The Longs' party had arrived in their absence. When Patricia had reported Michael's statement that there was no such person as Miss Aileen Orkney they were convinced that they had been tricked and sent upon a fool's errand. They had decided to follow the Bennetts back to Zwart Modder—keep an eye upon their doings in case they secured a trustworthy guide—and, in the meantime, scour the native kraals in the hope of obtaining one themselves.

As Michael caught sight of Patricia and her father seated on the stoep he stopped dead in his tracks and the Bennetts automatically stopped with him. Their faces went an angry red at the sight of their detested uncle. Sandy, who had not seen the Longs since he left London, was greatly amused at the encounter and, turning to Michael, remarked gaily:

'So your rivals have turned up again? But I don't see the chief crook. What can have happened to Philbeach?'

'Philbeach!' Michael echoed. 'What the devil are you talking about?' While Ernest put his hand to his Adam's apple and croaked an astonished 'Eh?'

'Didn't you realise?' Sandy said quickly. It was on the tip of his tongue to add: 'I haven't seen him, of course, and if I had I'd have knocked him down,' but it flashed into his mind that he could not give away the fact that he had guessed Wisdon to be Philbeach from Cornelius's description of him in Pretoria. The Bennetts were not supposed to know that he had ever been in communication with the Van Niekerks at all, much less that they were both in the immediate neighbourhood, so he went on casually: 'I know, because I saw the great brute when the Longs were here before. I understand that they have taken him on as their guide, philosopherr and friend.'

'By Jove!' Michael's hands clenched as he realised the position. 'Things are even worse than I thought. I met him in Johannesburg and he called himself Wisdon then. If it's the same fellow who knocked you out with the knobkerrie in London, I was right about his being a crook. The Longs can't possibly know that it's Philbeach whom they've taken on, and I'm going to warn them at once.'

At that moment Sarie came gaily round the corner and, ignoring Sandy entirely, intercepted Michael as he moved towards the stoep. 'Hello!' she cried, 'what sort of luck have you had?'

Michael was forced, in common politeness, to stop for a moment and tell her of their good fortune in having found Ombulike and in having persuaded him to go with them. Then, getting free of her as quickly as he could, he strode towards the stoep.

Patricia had noticed the four men almost as soon as they halted and began to talk together in the street. To see Michael and the Bennetts again was no surprise—but Sandy! So he too had arrived here on the edge of the Kalahari. Then the girl who called herself Aileen Orkney but who Michael said was a fake joined them—yet there he was talking and laughing with her as though they had been friends for years.

Oh! how Patricia suddenly envied her that divine supple slimness, the air with which she carried herself, the chic with which she wore her well-cut riding kit. Her heart began to pound in her chest and her breath came with difficulty as she saw this bronzed Athene openly flirting with Michael beyond the fence which railed off the dusty garden. Then, her eyes made doubly acute by jealousy, she suddenly noticed that Sarie was hatless even beneath that blazing sun. The girl must be a South African, not a doubt of it, and Patricia had seen her face somewhere before, but where? The fine straight features, the golden hair, the look of lazy, aristocratic self-assurance. . . . As Michael turned away it came in a flash, the bright cheerful room in Pretoria—Cornelius Van Niekerk —this was his sister—the resemblance was too striking for her to be anyone else.

Instantly a jumble of confused conclusions seethed in Patricia's mind. Sandy had the Van Niekerks in his pocket— they had refused information on receiving his cable and had gone into this thing with him the moment he arrived. Michael had got all that he knew from them—Sandy had shown a soft spot for him even in London—the two parties were acting in concert—Michael must have wired them from Johannesburg to put her own party off the scent—that was why the Van Niekerk girl had posed to them as Aileen Orkney—but why then had Michael gone to Postmasberg?

Patricia could not answer that—but there was no time to think. Michael was already at the garden gate. The thought of a scene in front of her father appalled her so she ran down the steps and along the path to meet him.

'Patricia,' Michael said urgently, as they came face to face, 'I've just heard something . . .'

'I don't know what you've heard and I don't care,' she cut him short in a low, angry voice. 'I don't want to have a row with you in front of Father—that's the only reason I came out here when I saw you meant to speak to me. Only to tell you that I never, never want to see you again.'

'But listen!' Michael protested. 'I've only just learned that the man whom you call Wisdon is actually Philbeach—you know, the crook who knocked Sandy McDiamid out in London.'

Her hazel eyes half-closed in a sneer of unbelief. 'You fool,' she said softly. 'Do you think that you can take me in with that sort of tale? I suppose you imagine that if we were idiots enough to believe you it would prevent our going on with our journey and leave you a free hand to start off on your own.'

'No, no.' He shook his head with a worried frown. 'If anybody's tried to do that sort of thing it was you, side-tracking us like that at Postmasburg, but I mean this honestly.'

She laughed then, but it was not her usual pleasant, friendly laugh, it was full of bitter anger and dillusion. 'It is likely that I should believe in your "*honesty*" after the way you managed to have us sent back to Upington? If we hadn't met you there we should be at King George's Falls in two days' time, and look, there's your little friend whom you put up to do the business talking to those precious Bennetts now.'

With a furious gesture in Sarie's direction Patricia swung on her heel and, leaving him, stamped back up the steps into the inn.

17

Kalahari Picnic

Henry Long could not hear what Patricia and Michael were saying but he could see from their flushed faces and low, angry voices that a first-class quarrel was in progress.

He watched it with considerable pleasure. Three nights before, his daughter had accused Philbeach and himself of sending the telegram which had side-tracked the others to Postmasburg. When he admitted it she had given vent to such an extraordinary outburst that it had even shocked him out of his cold impassivity for the moment. She had been brought up in the belief that God delegated a portion of His inscrutable wisdom to all parents. He had never even considered explaining any of his actions to her and was exceedingly annoyed that she should suddenly not only demand full details of his motives, but charge him with dishonesty into the bargain. He had refused to discuss the matter with her and told her that he was not prepared to explain his actions to his own daughter; moreover, that he had never wanted her to come on this expedition and it would obviously be better if she packed up and went home immediately. Patricia had grown sulky then and had continued so all through the trek back from Upington. He was quite indifferent to her moods but furious that after all these years she should suddenly question his integrity. Guessing that her interest in Michael had been the mainspring of her revolt, he was heartily glad to see them quarrelling now.

As Patricia ran up the steps, leaving his nephew open-mouthed at the bottom of the path, Henry followed her into the hotel. He had seen the Bennetts standing in the street and had no desire to face an open altercation.

Michael's anger at the way Patricia had just spoken to him swamped all his more tender feelings.

When he had discovered that Wisdon and Philbeach were the same man, his first thought had been to warn the girl he loved not to venture into the wastes of the Kalahari with such a character.

Even if she had tricked him over the telegram and some story of a girl called Orkney—he had not allowed his hurt feelings to interfere with his desire to protect her. Either one loved or one didn't, and nothing could prevent him doing his best to serve her whatever she did.

Patricia's own perverseness and her harsh words to him seemed to have finally ended their friendship.

With a rueful shrug he turned away, but as he approached the group in the street he suddenly began to wonder what Patricia could have meant by saying that it was Sandy's wife, under the name of Miss Aileen Orkney, who had sent them off to King George's Falls.

'Mrs. McDiamid,' he said hesitantly, as he joined the others, 'did you meet the Longs when they were here a few days ago?'

Sarie was quick to sense the danger. 'No,' she lied glibly. 'Did the girl you were talking to think she knew me? In the distance she probably mistook me for a girl called Aileen Orkney who was staying at the inn when they were here before. She had the same tow-coloured hair and dolly-blue eyes that Sandy says I've got when he's angry with me.'

'That's right, Orkney was her name,' Sandy declared. Then, quick to realise that he had got to get Sarie out of it before they asked her any more awkward questions, he drew her arm through his and added: 'Come on, darling, we mustn't stay here talking—it's time for you to bath the twins.'

Ernest grinned. 'Now that's what I like to see. A real family man, isn't he?'

George mopped his red face with a damp handkerchief and nodded, but his small quick eyes held a sudden look of distrust as he shot at Sandy: 'Queer hour to bath babies—isn't it? In the middle of the day.'

'Some people might think so,' Sandy agreed airily, 'but Sarie has a bee in her bonnet about baby culture. She's got a little book all about them by an old German called Pumpernickel which she follows religiously and, to make them good South Africans, we play them to sleep every night with records on the gramophone in Afrikaans.'

'Well, just think of that!' Ernest nodded understandingly. 'One half of the world doesn't know how the other half lives, and that's a fact.'

Sandy seized the opportunity to hurry Sarie away before they became further involved in explaining the matter of Miss Aileen Orkney.

When they had passed out of the village Sarie quickly withdrew her arm from his. With a frown creasing his forehead, he shot a covert glance at her.

'Sarie, why are you being so beastly to me?'

'Twins!' she exclaimed angrily. 'Do you ever expect me to forgive you that?'

'Oh, hang it! I was only joking.'

'Perhaps. But it's not the sort of humour that I appreciate.' She eyed him curiously, amused at the quick droop of his sensitive mouth and the wayward lock of hair which had again fallen forward over his eyebrow.

'I'm sorry,' he said. 'I didn't mean it. You know I didn't. And I'll apologise a hundred times about that kiss. I wouldn't have done it for worlds if I'd been serious.'

She halted suddenly in her tracks beneath a big blue-gum tree—swinging upon him with an angry light in her blue eyes.

'So you wouldn't have done it had you been serious, eh? That's a pretty compliment, I must say!'

Sandy halted too. Tall and lean, he looked down at her with a troubled expression in his brown eyes. 'What do you mean by that?' he asked miserably. 'And what the devil am I to say? You're sore because I took an unfair advantage to kiss you and now you say it would have been uncomplimentary if I hadn't.'

'All right,' she smiled to herself at his crestfallen air. 'Would you like to make it quits?'

'Yes, I would, though I don't know what you mean, but I'd do anything to have you smile at me again.'

'Would you?' she suddenly reached up and slipped her arms about his neck. 'Then I'll give it you back,' and with a sudden smile, she kissed him on the mouth.

'Sarie!' As she tried to slip away he was too quick for her and caught her to him. 'Sarie, you've asked for this and, by

141

God! you're going to get it.' With one strong arm he held her firmly against his chest and tilting her chin with his free hand he pressed his mouth on hers.

For a moment her eyes showed fright, then she let herself hang, limp and unresisting, until at last he let her go. She laughed again then—a little, uncertain, broken laugh.

'At midday!—really you should be ashamed of yourself!' But he only pulled her arm through his again as they set off down the track and for the two miles back to camp, though both their hearts were beating furiously, neither of them said another word.

Cornelius was waiting for them with a midday meal of eggs and fruit already prepared. Sandy told him of their doings in the morning and of Michael meeting Patricia Long at the gate of the inn on their return, in short jerky sentences, while Sarie maintained an unnatural silence and busied herself as much as possible with the service of the meal.

They decided that now Sarie was suspect it would be inadvisable for her to meet either the Longs or the Bennetts again and that as Sandy also might have to face some difficult questions it would be best if Cornelius kept the other parties under observation. They had no idea that Patricia already suspected Sarie of being a Van Niekerk, so thought it unlikely that any of the visitors at the Zwart Modder inn would recognise the booted, khaki-clad young Dutchman, with his broad-brimmed hat and air of having lived on the veldt all his life, for the smartly-dressed young man that they had met for a few moments in Pretoria, unless he met them face to face.

About three o'clock, Cornelius set off and Sandy watched him limp away in the direction of the dorp with a happy grin. It was not that he disliked the young Dutchman's company—far from it—but he wanted to be alone with Sarie.

'How about a stroll down to the river?' he asked immediately.

'No, I shall be too busy this afternoon,' she replied, without looking at him. 'I'm going to make some mebos.'

'What here!—nonsense! It will take days.'

'Of course not, silly—but at the house of a young farmer's wife whom I met at the inn before the place became crowded out by your hordes of relatives.'

'Oh, do it another day,' he pleaded.

'No.' Sarie shook her golden head. 'She started it three days ago and the apricots will be dried by now and ready to crystallise. I promised for this afternoon. Besides . . .' she added, looking at him over her shoulder as she moved away, '. . . I'm very fond of mebos.'

To Sandy's annoyance she did not return until the evening, by which time Cornelius was already back. He had found out that the Bennett party intended to set out the following morning for Noro Kei, a salt pan around which there were a few bushmen settlements. He had not found it necessary to risk recognition by speaking to any of them but had obtained his information from their head boy—Johnnie.

As they sat round the camp fire that night Sandy would have given his eye teeth for ten minutes alone with Sarie, but she curtly rejected his suggestion of a stroll and in her brother's presence he could say nothing to her. Cornelius, finding them both unresponsive to his talk, suggested making an early night of it as he would have to be up with the dawn to ascertain if the Bennett party actually stuck to their present intention; also, what the Longs would do in the circumstances.

Sandy left them for a few moments. He had a patch of wild flowers in his mind that grew only a little distance from the camp. With the aid of his torch he managed to find them and, picking a few hastily, ran back with them. When Sarie relaxed her limbs and slipped her short-sleeved shirt over her golden head in her bivouac ten minutes later, she suddenly noticed them arranged in a neat bunch upon her pillow.

Cornelius left the camp before the first rays of sunlight had come over the eastern hills of their sheltered valley, and returned before Sarie had finished preparing their breakfast.

The Bennetts were off, he reported, laughing a little at the discomfort they would experience on the hard seat of their wagon. Michael accompanied them astride a nice little cob, and the Hottentot—Ombulike—together with three nigs—made up their party.

Half the population of the village had been present to watch their departure on the little-used track towards Noro Kei, but the Longs had not put in an appearance until half an hour after they had gone. Then they, too, had assembled their out-span; Patricia, Wisdon, and his two friends, mounted on horses, the old man perched uncomfortably beside a native driver, and two other natives with them. By that time another quarter of the population of Zwart Modder had turned out, including the rural policeman, to watch them with a vague, silent interest as their wagon took the tracks of the one which had preceded them. Evidently the Longs meant to follow the trail which was to be blazed by the Bennetts.

'What's the drill now?' Sandy inquired.

'Sleep,' declared Cornelius positively: 'no need for us to start until well into the afternoon. We know the direction they have taken and it will be as easy as winking for us to pick them up from the plane after they have experienced a really jolly day, such as our ancestors had when they decided to do a bit of voor-trekking.' He swallowed his breakfast and then disappeared into his bivouac.

Sarie avoided Sandy carefully and a few minutes later she was also lying upon her camp bed, not to sleep, but to think a little about the events of the previous day. She had liked Sandy the very moment that she had set eyes on him. She adored the tall, cavalier swing of his walk and the brown, humorous eyes in his tanned face. She liked his casualness and the gay, devil-may-care manner in which he had rushed her into that absurd situation two nights ago, and his stupid verbiage about her imaginary twins. But did she like him enough? That was the question. Sarie held some wilted, scentless flowers to her freckled nose.

Sandy meanwhile busied himself with the preparations for their departure. They had come well supplied with water-containers purchased in Pretoria, and he was careful to see that every one of these was filled to capacity from the rocky pool of fresh clear water on the banks of the Molopo. After he had re-packed them carefully in the body of the plane beside Sarie's stock of rice, mealies and tinned goods, he made a journey to the village and procured as much fruit in the way of oranges, grapes, avocados and bananas as he could carry, by which time old Willem announced the midday meal and the other two were roused from their slumbers, real or pretended.

They waited until an hour before sunset, knowing that they could catch up the ox-spans of the others after a few miles' flight. Then Cornelius set the plane in motion and they rose gently over the low hills which had been such a convenient shelter to them.

He climbed up to three thousand feet, not wishing the other parties to be aware of their presence if it could be avoided and, half an hour later, picked them up. The first party was already out-spanned and the other trekking towards it laboriously along the sandy track. They hovered in the heavens far above until a solitary horseman rode forward from the second party to a low bluff and evidently spotted the Bennetts' camp, for, turning, he galloped back to the Longs, who then out-spanned about a mile in the rear.

Cornelius brought his plane to rest in a sheltered dip some miles from both camps and an hour later they began their evening meal. Sarie gave them Sasaties which she had prepared the previous day and Sandy exclaimed:

'By Jove, these are good. How in the world do you manage to get such flavour into mutton?'

'It's the last you'll get for some time,' she smiled, 'but you shall have the recipe if you like it.' Then, immediately they had finished, to Sandy's chagrin, she disappeared into her bivie.

When he crawled into his own a little later he found a sheet of paper pinned to his pillow and written on it in a flowing scrawl:

145

SASATIES

Ingredients

1 Fat Leg of Mutton.

2 oz. of good curry powder.

½ cup of vinegar, or the juice of 3 lemons (if not to be had, an oz. of tamarind drawn on a cup of water gives a very pleasant acid).

A teaspoonful of sugar.

A cup of milk.

½ dozen lemon or orange leaves.

2 oz. of butter.

1 medium sized onion.

3 dozen skewers, cut out of a bamboo, or iron skewers.

Salt to be added when skewered.

Cut up the leg of mutton in little pieces an inch square, brown the onion, cut in thin slices and fry in a pan in fat or butter. Mix all the ingredients well with the cut-up meat in a deep pan or basin; leave it for a night or longer, and when wanted, place the meat interspersed here and there with fat on the skewers. Place the gridiron on wood coals to get very hot, then grill the sasaties a nice brown. Serve *hot* with rice. The gravy to be well heated in a saucepan and served with the sasaties. *A very favourite picnic dish at the Cape.*

This may interest your wife *if* you are ever lucky enough to get one who can cook.

S. v N.

With a low laugh Sandy thrust the paper inside his shirt and lay down to doze off happily into a sound sleep.

Early in the morning they were in the air again watching the departure of the two contingents. Then they descended and slept, chatted, or played the radio during the long hot hours of the day, leaving the others to their weary toil. They picked them up again in the evening on the fringe of the wide marshes that spread for many miles about the native settlements at Noro Kei.

Sandy had little chance, in such surroundings, to be alone with Sarie, but that second night he caught her for a moment beyond the glow of their camp fire, and sized both her hands in his. With no word said, he drew her to him and kissed her feverishly, but she broke away, giving him a violent shove, and the next second was seated beside her brother, laughing and talking just as though nothing had happened.

After they left Noro Kei they settled into a steady unvarying routine. Each morning, from a high altitude, they watched the two outspans as they crawled laboriously one after the other through the grassy waste to the north-eastward. Then, descending, they whiled away most of the day in their camp, reading, telling stories, and listening to Sarie's songs or the dance music that was relayed from Johannesburg and Cape Town through their portable wireless. The two men did some mild shooting—enough to keep Sarie supplied with provender for her pot—without unduly wasting ammunition, and she was able to give them a fine variety of good dishes. For their meat course, Tassel, Piggie haspot, stuffed baby marrows or stewed Duiker, and for a sweet—Wentel Jeeftjes, Tameltijes with Naartje peel. Pumpkin Poffertjes, Angels' Food or Rys Kluitjes with preserve.

In the evening they would break camp, take the air again to see how far the others had succeeded in hauling their cumbersome wagons during the day, and then descend a few miles farther into that trackless waste to choose a new sleeping place.

The scene changed little. To the east and more central portion of the desert stretched vast tracts of impassable bush, but the area through which they were journeying consisted of undulating country covered with coarse *bushman* grass. Occasionally, from the air, they saw large limestone depressions which Cornelius said were believed to have been hollowed out by the action of myriads of elephants indulging in mud baths during past ages. The only vegetation other than the grass consisted of small patches of Tasma, a species of wild melon which grew more infrequent as they advanced. Sometimes during the midday heat other scenery would

appear on the horizon but they knew it to be nothing but a mirage.

Day after day Sandy sought for some opportunity to get Sarie to himself, even for a few moments, but after that one episode at Noro Kei some devil seemed to have entered into her. If Cornelius was not with her, old black Willem who did the chores of the party was. With a fertility of imagination which amazed him utterly she never failed to find some urgent matter which needed her immediate attention whenever he endeavoured to lure her from the camp during the day-time. At night she seemed to take an open delight in covertly mocking him, secure in the knowledge that they dared not move beyond the circle of camp fires for fear of the wild beasts, whose coughing roar, as they padded softly up and down only a few hundred yards away, provided nightly a grim serenade before they slept.

On the fourth day out from Noro Kei, they raised a long jagged line of mountains, hazy and blue on the northern horizon. In the three following days the wagons crept steadily towards them. On the seventh day, and the ninth from Zwart Modder, they saw from their vantage point in the air, during their early morning flight, the Bennetts' outspan disappear into a narrow defile. Its sides rose sharply to rocky *krantzes* standing out clear and sharp in the sunshine against the higher levels which swiftly mounted to the main range. An hour later the Longs' wagon had also entered the valley and Cornelius was just about to search out a suitable spot in which to land for the day, when, with a loud series of bangs from the carburetter, his engine petered out.

Sarie's cheeks drained of their colour as she gripped Sandy's hand, the whites of Willem's eyes showed round with fright in his shiny black face.

Cornelius peered anxiously downward and in frantic haste began to search the ground below them for a decent landing place. He knew that the light patches meant loose sand into which the plane would pitch, bury her nose, and perhaps burst into flames. The dark ones indicated more solid ground. Seeing a likely spot at the entrance of the valley in which the wagons had disappeared, he steered for it as the machine, losing speed, began to plane swiftly down.

They bumped, lifted and bumped again, then taxied some two hundred yards, but he managed to pull up just in time to avoid a stretch of nasty rocky ground that lay ahead.

'What's happened?' cried Sandy, scrambling out.

Cornelius sat back in the pilot's seat for a moment, mopping his perspiring face. 'God knows!' he muttered, then he began to examine his engine.

For half an hour the others stood round him, holding nuts and spanners while he laboured in the sweltering sun. At last he gave a despondent shrug. 'The inlet valve spring is broken and I'm afraid it's impossible to mend it.'

'But surely you've got a spare?' Sandy's voice was a husky whisper.

'No.' Cornelius shook his head. 'One can't carry spares of everything—and it's no good my trying to kid you; we're absolutely stuck.'

'Oh, hell!' groaned Sarie. 'We're nine days out from Zwart Modder—we'll never make it—yet we'll die if we stay here.'

18

Kalahari Hell

Up to the time of leaving Zwart Modder all the English heirs of the late John Thomas Long, had, in their various ways, enjoyed their visit to South Africa. Henry's appreciation of colour, which had made him a life-long collector of pictures, found a quite satisfaction in the wonderful variety of scenery and the magnificent sunsets. The Bennetts' commercial sense had been aroused to keen interest by the great modern buildings and teeming industry of Johannesburg. Michael had had an opportunity of tasting South African hospitality and, like Patricia, had been constantly enthralled by the changing scenes in the cities and townships which they visited. For them, too, there had been the discovery of each other, so that up to the last few days they had been living on top of the world.

But soon after they had left the last outpost of civilisation they began to see something of a very different Africa. The sun streamed down and the earth lay dry and quivering beneath it. The gentle oxen plodded on with maddening slowness while flies, coming from no one knew where, swarmed and buzzed about their eyelids. The so-called track to Noro Kei seemed at times to disappear entirely, but the natives were always able to re-discover it by methods of their own.

The country through which they were passing was an endless succession of low valleys. For hours on end they crawled towards the crest of a brown ridge, sharp cut against the fierce hard blue of a cloudless sky, only to find when they had reached it that another exactly similiar lay before them. As a choice of evils they could sit sweltering in their shirtsleeves beneath the wide hoods of the wagons or trudge beside them and bear the penalty of a fiery burn on every exposed portion of their bodies. In the hours that followed it was just as though their limbs were being grilled before a slow fire.

Each day the same routine was followed by both parties. They were up by sunrise and on the move soon after, making the most of the cool hours of the early morning. By eleven o'clock—already weary—their eyes smarting from the ceaseless glare of earth and sky despite dark glasses, they halted and out-spanned, nibbled a little fruit and crouched in the narrow patch of shade underneath the wagon. It was too hot to sleep, their throats were too dry to talk, and their minds dulled by physical discomfort to a pitch where even reading was impossible. At four o'clock they would limber up and set off again, trekking on over the rough parched grass which seemed to survive miraculously despite the utter absence of any water in that desolate land. An hour after sundown they would once more out-span and form their camp for the night.

Michael and his head boy, Johnnie, shot game—principally

consisting of small buck—for one party, and Philbeach, Darkie and Ginger for the other. But the native cooks seemed to know only one method of preparing it and after a few days they all became heartily sick of the half-raw, fresh-killed meat which was put before them each evening. They talked for a little in the circle formed by the camp fires, which the natives lit all round them to scare away the wild things of the desert. Then, as the African night closed down they crawled into their bivouacs to face new tortures.

Their arms, hands. and faces, swollen and slightly puffy, seemed to glow with a devouring inward fire from the sunburn which had caught them in the daytime. Although after a first experience they took every precaution, it seemed impossible for them to avoid exposing themselves to those white-hot, blistering rays, however careful they were. Then, in the darkness, while they endeavoured to snatch a little uneasy sleep there came the warning ping that nightly signalled the onslaught of myriads of mosquitoes. Oil of citronella, anti-insect lotions and all the things which they had provided seemed no protection against these ferocious enemies. In vain they tossed and turned, burying their heads until they stifled beneath their coverings and then with hasty, bitter violence sat up to slap their hands, necks and faces, in the hope of driving off the pests. The low infuriating hum continued each night above their prostrate bodies, until, exhausted from lack of sleep, they rose again to face another gruelling day. In addition they felt depressed and heavy from the quinine they were forced to take as a precaution against fever.

In the Bennett party it was George who took the discomfort most to heart. All his jovial cordiality seemed to drop away under the rigours to which he found himself subjected. The first day out he and his brother had been badly sunburnt, and while Ernest joked philosophically about his reddened neck and forearms, George proceeded to take it out of Michael who, as the only sensible member of the party, had had the forethought to exercise reasonable precautions.

As time wore on George began to persuade himself that he had never meant to come at all but that Ernest and Michael had cajoled him into joining them, and he annoyed the others by a greedy disregard for their wish to economise the supply of water. At all hours of the day and night he poured copious draughts of lime juice and water down his throat and, despite Michael's warning that it was unwise to touch alcohol before sundown, he laid his hands on their gin so heavily that after five days the half-dozen bottles which they had brought were finished.

To add to their troubles their native guide, Ombulike, lost his way on the sixth day. They had found him untiring at first. He tramped doggedly on ahead of the wagons, his naked feet appearing callous of the burning earth. Then, after four days, he started a bout of dagga smoking which made him stupid, lazy and quarrelsome. Michael, who was watching the sun, became convinced that they were going the wrong way. After a heated argument with the little yellow Hottentot he succeeded in turning the convoy in the direction in which he imagined their goal to lie.

On the seventh day they passed out of the monotonous rolling grassy plains and entered hilly country. They wound through great mountainous, treeless gorges where at times rocky *krantzes* overhung their heads, and seemed to be entering one of the circles of Dante's Inferno. Although in the grassy waterless wilderness they had seen no trace of man, it at least gave the impression that they might come upon great herds of cattle with attendant ranchers or some isolated farmstead; but here there was the utter eerie loneliness of stark Nature in her most unfriendly role. It was a world unrealised by modern man—primeval, terrible, and with something ghostly about it even under the blazing noonday sun. The rocky cañons shimmered under the relentless glare, not even a lizard was to be seen sunning itself upon those dry stones, bleached by an eternity of blinding light. The place seemed haunted by some evil, menacing power as though all the bad souls that ever lived and died were congregated there, resentful of this intrusion upon their privacy; watching with silent malevolence for an opportunity to crush these humans who had ventured into their domain.

There were times when Michael felt an overwhelming desire to scream rather than suffer that .dread, appalling silence any longer. Once, he loosed off his gun simply in order to shatter the eerie stillness. The report echoed back again and again from the stark rocky walls that hemmed them in and George, half-delirious from alcohol, and fever engendered by mosquito bites, came bounding out from the back of the wagon where he had been lying in a semi-stupor.

The least movement in that grilling heat caused them to sweat profusely and now his sudden activity made a hot dew break out all over his body. It streamed from his bald forehead and drenched his scanty clothing. In a fit of ungovernable anger he wrenched the long whip from the native driver's hand and lashed out at Michael. With an angry laugh the boy cantered out of range of the long throng, but the episode made him even more thoughtful than before about George's condition.

Gently nurtured as he had been, and the idol of his mother, these nightmare days were one long agony to him, but with a determination which must have been inherited from the uncle who had undergone this same physical distress ten years before, he set his teeth and resolved to keep a sense of proportion. He and the Bennetts hated each other now as men are apt to do who are cooped up together for a considerable period under extremely trying conditions, but he knew instinctively that their best chance of succeeding lay in talking as little as possible, sinking their own individualities, and concentrating all their energies in plodding like automatons towards their goal.

In those long nights when his limbs smarted from the blistering sun and the mosquitoes buzzed overhead, he thought much of Patricia. His anger against her had evaporated again and he could only feel now a little sad that anyone so lovely and apparently so frank could lend herself to such despicable treachery. He visualised again that night when he had held her in his arms at Johannesburg and, like a nightmare vision, the red coarse face of the man he now knew to be Roger Philbeach loomed up, leering at him in the close, hot darkness.

He knew from the horsemen who occasionally appeared against the skyline in their rear that the other party had followed them into this great barren area of the Kalahari. As he dozed after desperate attempts to drive off the insects, he saw her in his imagination, somewhere out there upon the trackless veldt, plagued as he was himself by heat, thirst, mosquitoes—and worse—unprotected, but for her father, from those small, dark, lecherous eyes of Philbeach's which had swept over her so revoltingly that night in the palm court of the Carlton.

In the second party Patricia, despite an abundant supply of face lotions and ointments, was suffering equally. If she neglected to grease her face, neck and arms at night she found that she paid for it by a skin as dry as sandpaper in the morning. If, on the other hand, she used the creams which she had brought, they seemed to clog the pores of her skin so that at times she felt she would suffocate with the stifling heat which came more from inside herself than from the baking ground or fiery sky. The perfumes of these preparations were designed to give added attraction to beauty in the social round of a normal world. Here they aroused the lively interest of every insect, all of whom inflicted on her their particular variety of irritation, bite or sting. Worst of all, perhaps, the use of water was restricted entirely to drinking and, although she tried washing with sand, she found it a hopelessly inadequate substitute. As the days wore on she began to loathe her body. She became sick and disgusted with the ever-increasing filth and stickiness which she had no means of removing from it.

In addition to her physical discomfort, she was suffering considerable mental distress, for the situation between her father and herself was distinctly strained. When she had cooled down after her last angry scene with Michael she had asked Henry if Wisdon was actually Philbeach. He admitted that fact but refused any explanation and Philbeach seemed to exercise such a strong fascination over him that he would not listen to Patricia's plea that they should secure some other white man to accompany them on the expedition. He told his daughter once more that she could stay behind if she liked and since this was no business for a woman he would be heartily glad if she did.

Even if she had thought of drawing back that would have settled it, for Patricia was just as pigheaded as it was possible for any young woman to be. With her small Roman nose cocked in the air she had marched out of the room, slamming the door in her father's face. At this exhibition, so alien to the manner of the meek and obedient daughter he had known in England, Henry had been livid with righteous anger and the two had hardly spoken to each other since.

Within a few hours of their leaving Zwart Modder, Patricia realised that she had been unjust to Michael in accusing him of deliberately setting the Van Niekerk girl to mislead them. Every now and again Darkie or Ginger rode on ahead to observe the doings of the forward party—and neither Sandy nor the Van Niekerks were with them.

She began to worry then about Michael and, knowing how unused he was to roughing it, her heart ached at the thought of what he must be going through during these days and nights of unaccustomed strain and fatigue.

Unwelcome as Philbeach's presence might be in her own party, at least he was competent in ordering their arrangements and with occasional assistance from Ginger seemed to find no difficulty in providing adequate supplies of game for their consumption. But how, she wondered, were the others faring? Neither of the Bennetts could handle a gun, she knew, and none of the three had any experience of the ways in which the most acute hardships of this ghastly pilgrimage could be lessened, or at least made bearable.

In her imagination she saw Michael toiling on daily under this sweltering sun, the sole provider for his party's pot, and when night came on the only one among them with any knowledge of horses or cattle. He would also be called upon to nurse the useless town-bred Bennetts through the hundred petty worrying problems of their journey.

Philbeach continued to press his disagreeable attentions on her, and the open stare of admiration with which he now regarded her as she moved about their temporary camping places was horribly embarrassing. He seemed to have no conception of how to set about making love to her in a normal fashion, although that would have been bad enough, but just stared at her out of his little eyes embedded in fat or endeavoured to joke with her in a rough sort of humour. Once when he caught her alone behind the wagon he tried in a clumsy fashion to kiss her. After that she took extra care never to be far from her moody, silent, father who, curiously enough, seemed to support the rigours of the journey better than any of them.

The insects apparently took no interest in his dry, parched skin. He did not drink as the other men did each night to dull the aching of their sun-scorched bodies. He economised his energies by the simple process of lying absolutely still upon a pile of matting in the bottom of the wagon, protected by the hood from the blazing sunshine, as it rumbled on hour after hour. Silent and uncomplaining, he suffered the other hardships with a grim determination to reach that valley where his brother had gathered a fortune from the ground.

On the seventh evening out from Noro Kei they reached the foothills of the great mountain range which Michael's party had entered in the afternoon and halted a little after sundown in the entrance of a desolate valley.

The usual wearisome routine of which they were all so heartily sick was gone through and then they settled down for the night. After an hour or so Patricia fell into an uneasy sleep, tossing and turning on her palliasse in the narrow bivie. She awoke with a start to find a burly figure bending over her outlined by the faint light of breaking dawn which filtered in under the canvas flap.

'Quiet—don't make a noise now.' Philbeach thrust a hand over her mouth and wriggled down beside her 'You're going to be nice to me—see! 'cause I can't damn well stand this any longer.'

With a violent jerk she wrenched her head away and let out

a yell of repulsion and loathing as he threw himself upon her; his week's growth of stubbly beard rasping her chin.

Next moment Henry thrust his head and shoulders through the narrow opening of the low bivouac. In his right hand he clutched his ancient service revolver.

'What's all this?' he demanded harshly.

Philbeach released the struggling girl with an angry grunt and swung round on his knees. 'Put that damn' thing away, you old fool—it might go off.'

'It might,' Henry agreed dryly. 'You had better come out of that.'

'All right—give me some room then,' Philbeach snarled, from where he was crouching beside Patricia. The low, pointed roof of the little tent made it impossible for him to stand upright and as Henry moved aside he crawled out into the open.

'Now!' Henry shot at him in a fierce undertone. 'There's to be no more of this sort of thing—understand!'

'Oh, cut it out,' the big man shrugged, endeavouring to pass the matter off with a sudden guffaw of laughter. He had no wish to quarrel with Henry at the moment. 'I was taking a walk round and mistook the girl's bivie for my own—that's all. There's nothing to make all this song and dance about.'

Henry thought it policy to accept the explanation but jerked his head towards the rising sun. 'I should have thought there was plenty of light to see by—anyhow, why aren't the others about yet? It's time we were moving.'

'We're not moving,' Philbeach announced abruptly. 'I talked it over with Darkie and Ginger last night and we don't mean to go any farther.'

'Why?' Henry suddenly thrust out his jaw in a stony curve. 'Another two days now and we should be there.'

Philbeach waved a lumpish, grimy hand towards the towering mountain range, broken here and there by gaps and gorges. 'That's why!' he said with a sudden grin. 'The heat's bad enough here on the plain but it will be fifty times worse once we enter those damnable valleys.'

'I've come for those diamonds and I mean to get them,' Henry muttered thickly.

'All right—but the other lot's ahead of us—isn't it?' The grin broadened on Philbeach's heavy face. 'I mean to let them do the dirty work. If the stuff is there they'll find it and be back here inside five days. All we've got to do is to sit pretty here and take it off them when they turn up again. Then you'll have a chance to loose off that pop-gun to some purpose, or you can watch me and the boys if you prefer to see some really pretty shooting.'

19

The Underground River

Michael meanwhile was plodding on. The going now was more difficult than ever and he was compelled to lead his horse. The wagon creaked and groaned as, with a lop-sided motion, it lurched along, first one wheel and then another mounting the small boulders which were so numerous that it was impossible to circumvent them all. Every ten or fifteen minutes it got stuck completely and the whole party had to turn to with long poles which they thrust under the axles. Then, levering with all their might, while the sweat streamed down their bitten and swollen faces, they heaved it bodily over the obstruction and proceeded once more.

George was at the whisky now and drinking to such an extent that he was of little use although he caused endless bother to the others by his continual whining complaints. Even Ernest, who was devoted to his brother, rounded on him savagely on the second night after they had entered the mountainous region, and with blazing eyes wrenched a bottle out of his hands. The quarrel developed until both were snarling at each other in furious animosity and Michael, sitting nearby, a silent spectator of the scene learned, from the mud which they slung at each other, enough of their past transactions to realise that at least there was some foundation for what his uncle had told him in Johannesburg of George's dubious commercial beginnings. That night, when both the brothers were tossing in a fitful sleep, he climbed into the wagon and, securing the remaining five bottles of whisky, deliberately smashed them against a rock.

The following morning, when George discovered what he had done, there was another angry scene and the elder Bennett began to revile their mother for having deserted Ernest and himself to run away with Michael's father. Michael, now livid with rage at these insults to a mother whom he adored, snatched up his riding whip and would have used it relentlessly upon the podgy, swollen body of his tormentor had not Ernest intervened, first physically, and then with a recurrence of his quick Cockney humour which neither of them had heard for days.

This outburst seemed to ease the feelings of them all, and during that morning George was certainly better for having been deprived of the chance to drug himself with alcohol.

They halted at midday half-way along one of those endless rocky valleys and Ombulike came up to Michael who, despite his youth, all the natives had come to regard naturally as the leader of the party. He pointed with his stick to the end of the depression. In the blue, dancing heat it seemed to merge into the further mountains. He said one word: 'Water!'

The thought of water—not the meagre ration of lukewarm, unsatisfying liquid with which they had to content themselves four times a day, but cold, fresh, spring-water to drink without stint and perhaps even enough in which to bathe their sore parched bodies, filled them with such excitement that they determined to curtail the noonday halt. At two o'clock they set off again along the great boulder-strewn valley, where every stone reflected the torrid heat of that vast naked sun, and by a little after four they rounded a great mass of rock to find a swift, broad channel of water rushing in swirling eddies below them.

With frantic haste they scrambled down to a ricky ledge and, flinging themselves upon it, plunged their faces into the cool refreshing stream, gulping up great mouthfuls of that heaven-sent draught. Then, throwing off their clothes, they slipped from the ledge and, with infinite contentment, felt it gurgle over their red, dust encrusted bodies.

When they had dressed again an utterly new spirit seemed to have descended upon the party. Their quarrel of the morning was forgotten and they found themselves laughing together just as they had in that other, brighter world before they had ever started out into the desert. All three agreed to press on, keeping as close to the river bank as they were able and, after an hour of following its course through a stony defile, they came to a place where it ended suddenly. A vast wall of rock, several hundred feet in height, towered above their heads. It shut out the sun, and at its base the rushing waters poured into a great dark cleft where they disappeared from view.

Ombulike came forward and pointed with his stick to the entrance of that gloomy cavern into which the tossing waters surged. 'That way,' he said, 'is the way great master went— I wait for him here.'

Michael nodded, looking towards the Bennetts. 'He's right,' he agreed slowly. 'This is the place, I've not a doubt. Look! It is exactly as it is described in Hedley Chilver's book, "The Seven Lost Trails of Africa".'

'Well, I don't like it,' said Ernest frankly.

'Nor do I.' All the renewed cheerfulness which had brightened George's fat face for the last hour had drained from it as he went on: 'Surely there must be some other way except by risking our necks going into that beastly hole.'

'There is.' Michael lifted his face to the beetling crags which cut sharply into the blue sky above their heads. 'Once they have reached the valley people have managed to climb out somehow. They couldn't swim or steer a raft against this current, anyhow, but we might wander for months among all these desolate cañons before we could ever find a way into the one beyond.'

All three stood for a few moments watching the roaring current as it frothed and eddied against the rocks before disappearing into the great hole. The time had come when they must risk their lives unless they meant to turn back empty-handed, and it was Ernest who first gave them a lead. 'Well, chaps,' he jerked out, fingering that prominent Adam's apple, 'nothing venture, nothing have—so I suppose we've got to risk it.'

'All right—I'm game,' Michael agreed, although he paled a little under his brick-red tan at the thought of venturing into those dark, fearsome waters. 'I should think the best thing we can do is construct a raft from all the gear that we have got in the wagon. The current will carry us along but we can check the speed and fend ourselves off from the rocks and corners if we take long sweeps. It may not be so bad in there if we're able to light our way with the torches. Come on, let's get busy.'

They still had several hours' daylight before them, so it was decided to make the attempt that afternoon rather than wait until the following morning. They set to work at once to make as solid a raft as they could of packing-cases, tent poles and all the odds and ends of timber which they had with them.

When it was completed George looked at those evil, rushing waters and then at the others. 'Is it necessary that we all should go?' he muttered a little thickly. 'Someone ought to stay here to keep an eye on the niggers and the wagon. At least, I think so.'

Michael nodded. 'Yes, that's sound enough. Two of us should be able to gather enough stones for the three of us to live in comfort for the rest of our lives, so there's no need for us all to risk our lives. The third can stay here and if the others aren't back in forty-eight hours he can make up his own mind whether to take a chance and come after them or beat it back to civilisation.'

Ernest strolled over to the wagon and, taking a Lett's Diary from the pocket of his coat, tore a leaf from it at random. Then he divided it into three, and twisting the slips of paper, threw them in a hat. 'There's three dates there,' he announced, 'so let's make it odd man out. There'll be two evens and an odd or vice-versa. I don't know which, myself, but Michael is the youngest so he can have first pick.'

Michael drew a paper and, unfolding it, saw that he had drawn the eighth of August. Ernest took another and drew the seventh.

Both of them watched George covertly but with burning interest. If he drew the sixth, Ernie would have a prolonged chance of life but, if he drew the ninth, it was Michael who would remain behind. George unfolded the paper and handed it over with a little grunt. Printed upon it in clear blue lettering was August sixth. So Michael was destined to take his life in his hands with George for a companion while Ernest stayed behind and waited the result of their desperate undertaking.

Filled with the urge to get this wretched business over rather than sleep upon it, Michael led the way down to the raft which was already floating in a little bay sheltered from the rushing current, with Ombulike keeping a watchful eye upon it.

While Michael and George gingerly balanced themselves upon the raft, Ernest carried down sufficient stores to last them for two days on the far side of the mountain—Michael's gun, with a supply of ammunition wrapped in a waterproof sheet, and their electric torches. They would have to go without bedding since the structure was barely buoyant enough to carry their own weight and that of their supplies. In the evening light the Kaffirs stood round, grinning a little to each other at the complete madness of men who would venture into such a place. Ernest, with unusual soberness, bade them good-bye and good luck—then they pushed off.

The instant they left the shelter of the little backwater the flood caught them, and, whirling them about, carried them rapidly along the fast-flowing stream. In a moment Ernest's figure was hidden by a jutting rock at one side of the opening, and the next the evening light, bright upon the red verdureless boulders, had been cut out and only a semi-circular glimpse of the landscape remained as the rushing torrent bore the frail raft into the darkness.

With astonishing speed the opening appeared to decrease in size, then, as they passed a bend in the tunnel, it was completely blotted out and they were left racing along on the bosom of the underground river in Stygian blackness.

When they started they had been carried away so swiftly that neither had thought to use their torches, but now, as he crouched beside George on the raft, Michael produced his and shone the beam before them.

At its opening the arch of the cave had been at least twenty feet above the water's edge but now he saw with sudden anxiety that it was no more than a few feet above their heads and every moment, as the raft rushed on, it seemed to become lower. With an awful misgiving the thought flashed into his mind that they had no knowledge of the time of year at which old John had preceded them into this fearsome place. Perhaps at that season the river had been lower, and now, if it was in spate, there might come a point in the tunnel where the waters actually met the roof, in which case their fate was sealed. It was impossible to turn back, for the sides of the cave were sheer and glassy. No projecting crag offered the least hand-hold at which they might catch to stop the wild progress of their rickety float. With a sudden cry George lurched against Michael, who sprawled forward, dropping his torch with a splash into the hissing water, but George still held his. In its beam Michael guessed, with a horrible feeling of repulsion, the thing which had caused his half-brother to cry out. It must have been another of those huge blind vampire bats which, with spread wings, was fluttering towards them. As George ducked to dodge the brute the beam of his torch jerked upwards to the low roof above them and to his horror Michael saw that there were scores and scores of the loathsome creatures hanging head downward from it within a few inches of his hair. The roof was lower now and it would have been impossible for them to stand upright since it was no more than four feet above the seething water. Both had slipped down to their full length on the raft and, while George gripped the remaining torch with both his hands, Michael staved their frail craft off from the solid walls of rock as they were raced round corner after corner. In the bright shaft of light to the front of them a flat head with gaping jaws suddenly appeared. The raft caught it as it swept past and the water-serpent disappeared from view.

A hanging bat struck Michael's head, another fluttered between them, and a third brushed George's shoulder. The roof was shelving still more steeply towards the stream and although they were lying flat upon their stomachs they were knocking the loathsome creatures from their resting places as they shot past. The air was fetid with the smell of them. In the few moments that followed both went nearly mad as they fought off a whole flight of those monstrous blind inhabitants of the subterranean cave which squeaked and fluttered as they dashed into their faces.

The end came suddenly. Only a few seconds after they had passed out of the bat-infested area the roof took so sharp a dip that there was no longer hanging space enough for them between the stone and the rushing waters. With bulging, terror-stricken eyes George peered ahead of him to where, in the clear-cut arc of the torchlight, the rock and river seemed to meet. Michael buried his head in his arms with the awful feeling that, whatever he did, there was no hope of his seeing daylight any more.

Next second his elbow was caught on a projecting snag of the slimy ceiling. The raft was going at such a pace that he was torn bodily from it. The icy waters of the subterranean river closed over his head and when he came up gasping from the freezing shock of his immersion, George—the raft—and the light, had disappeared. All about him hung a stifling black-velvet blackness. He struck out wildly, grabbing frantically at the rocky side of the cavern in search of a hand-hold. It was damp and slippery and the current was sweeping him along at such a pace that even when he managed to clutch at a protrusion in the surface he was torn from it and hurried once more along the nightmare waterway.

For hours, it seemed, he fought and struggled without success. Then, when his strength was ebbing from him, he glimpsed a lightening of the pervading murk. Where before it had been solid black it now seemed to have taken on a faint tinge of greyness. No sooner had he realised that than he was swept round a corner and saw full daylight entering from an opening at the far end of the tunnel. With incredible rapidity he was carried towards it until the scene framed in the arch of light stood out clearly, revealing the tops of a blue range of mountains in the far distance. A thunderous roar filled his ears and that sound warned him of a new peril. The underground river did not flow on into the valley beyond but descended from the mountainside in a great cataract. Next moment he might be hurtled hundreds of feet down some uncharted waterfall into the depths below.

The roar increased to a deafening thunder as he battled to reach the side of the cave. Where the wall split into fragments at the entrance his desperate fingers fastened upon a jagged rock. At his side the torrent curved and fell in a foaming cascade to pitch and break into flying spray and seething whirlpools a hundred feet below. For a second his life hung in the balance, then he got a foothold and with a final effort dragged himself free of the clutching waters to throw himself exhausted upon a ledge of rock.

How long he lay there he did not know, but when he recovered sufficiently to scramble farther from the danger, the sun was setting. By its fading light he managed to pick his way from ledge to ledge down into the valley, to the side of the great pool into which the spate of that terrifying river crashed and roared unceasingly. In the still waters beyond the raging whirlpool and white hissing foam a portion of the raft lay becalmed, resting upon a slight projection in the river's bank. There was no sign of George and as Michael looked around him in the evening light he knew that he would never see that confident, self-assertive smile again.

He searched the shelving shore of the small inland lake into which the waters tumbled but could see no trace of that fat, cheerful half-brother who during these last days had shown another side to his nature and been such a curse to their party. Then he rescued the remaining timbers of the raft and to his surprise found that the store of provisions which they had tied upon it in their waterproof ground-sheets were damp but safe. Carrying them ashore, he sat down beside the lake to make a solitary and miserable meal.

While he ate he glanced about him. This must surely be the place he had come so far to find. It was like a giant oval pit some two miles long and half a mile wide hollowed out of the solid mountain. At the end he had entered, the lake filled its bottom, then, gradually narrowing into a foaming spate, rushed headlong down a short slope to disappear underground once more in the base of the cliff face. The sides of the great crater were sheer and precipitious, so that while he felt that he would at least be safe from wild beasts there, he doubted his ability to scale those towering walls of rock which hemmed him in.

That this was the place for which they had been seeking he had no shadow of doubt, but where were the diamonds? To all appearances it differed in no way from those barren valleys through which they had made their way on previous days. Munching a bunch of grapes he strolled about disconsolately, kicking up the pebbles on the foreshore of the lake.

With a sudden surge of fury it came to him that old John must have obtained his fine fortune somewhere else and left the letter only with the idea of intriguing his avaricious brother Henry. He recalled the taunting challenge in the last paragraph. Yes, that was it. John's impish humour had turned to malice at the last and he had tried to tempt Henry into spending some of that fortune which he had hoarded penny by penny, knowing full well the bitter days of scorching heat and nights of suffering he would go through, yet find nothing for all his pains in the end.

Even the afterglow of the sun had vanished now, and in this desolate valley there were no grasses or scrub, which he could gather to make himself a couch. He hollowed out a place in the sand in which to sleep but, weary as he was, slumber refused to come to him.

George's terrible fate weighed upon his mind and the utter hopelessness of his own situation. He was separated from Ernest and the outspan by that great treeless mountain and ringed in by a dozen others, all of which looked impossible to climb. Even if he could break out to the southward at the far end of the valley there were miles of mountains before he could reach the plain, and he would still be many days' march from the fringe of civilisation. His stores were no more than could support him for three or four days at the utmost even if he cut himself down to the barest ration which would maintain his strength. Once he left this flowing river how long would the contents of the water bottle, which was still strapped upon his hip, last out? His rifle and ammunition lay somewhere at the bottom of the pool beneath the thundering torrent. Only his pistol remained with which to face the wild beasts who ranged the summits and valleys beyond this gargantuan pit, should he ever succeed in climbing out.

He sat crouched in the hollow that he had made for himself, his head in his hands, his elbows on his knees, desperate and desolate. He longed to live, yet doubted his capacity to crawl like a fly up those frowning cliffs. He cursed himself for a fool ever to have believed the fantastic story that this hidden valley contained the fabulous wealth which they had dreamed of for so long.

A couple of hours dragged by while he wrestled with his bitter thoughts in the darkness. Then the moon rose above the crest of the mountains, drenching the valley with a strange, unearthly light. It shone as only an African moon can, with the clarity of pale, whitish sunlight, round Michael's despondent figure.

With haggard eyes he looked about him, almost driven insane by the injustice of this dead uncle who had sent him, out of sheer malice against his family, into this desert hell.

Frantically he sought a way, a break in the surfaces, a cleft, a funnel by which he might attempt to scale those seemingly impassable barriers which held him imprisoned.

Then, suddenly, his eyes became fixed upon a gleaming light no more than a yard beyond his feet. As he looked there were other—dozens—hundreds scattered along the foreshore of the lake—round, oblong, irregularly-shaped stones, catching and reflecting the gentle glow of the moonlight.

With a sudden staggering heartbeat he realised the truth. His uncle had not lied. He was sitting there utterly alone—surrounded by enough diamonds to ransom a dozen kings. He had found it. He was there—in the valley of fabulous wealth —the 'Place of the Great Glitter'.

20

The Valley of the Leopards

Sandy and the two Van Niekerks stood beside the useless aeroplane, their faces tense with anxiety. None of them dared to put into words the frightening thoughts that were coursing through their minds. They were seven days' march from the nearest native settlement at Noro Kei but unlike the other parties they had no wagon, no oxen, no horses. How could they possibly carry a sufficient supply of water, let alone food, upon their backs for such a journey? To add to the appalling difficulty of their situation, Cornelius's limp would not allow him to cover half the ground in a long day's tramping that any physically perfect man could accomplish.

'Only one thing for it,' Sandy tried to make his voice sound as cheerful as possible. 'We'll have to sit here until one of the other parties returns and get them to give us a lift back in their outspan.'

'Hell!' exclaimed Sarie, cutting at her riding boot viciously with her crop. 'To think of this happening after we've been kidding ourselves for days that we had the laugh of the others. How I shall hate having to put my pride in my pocket and cadge a lift off the Roman-nosed girl, or that awful George Bennett.'

'Pride—nothing!' her brother said philosophically. 'Sandy's right and it's the only thing to do. If I thought there was a sporting chance of you reaching the Noro Kei pan I'd tell the two of you to clear out right away and leave me to take the chance of picking up one of the wagons, but I'm dead certain you couldn't make it, so heroics on my part are quite uncalled for.'

In a forlorn hope that they might yet be able to substitute some other spring for the broken one they spent the morning taking down various parts of the plane and experimenting with such spares as Cornelius had with him. By the time old Willem announced the midday meal they had to abandon the attempt as completely hopeless.

After they had fed they set about preparing a camp. As they might have to occupy it for a number of days they exercised more care in the selection of its site than they had for their previous temporary halting places.

The mountain range into which they had seen the leading outspan disappear early in the morning was only a few miles' distant and the place where Cornelius had been forced to land was a sandy patch surrounded by the broken ground of the rising foothills leading up towards the peaks.

After a thorough reconnaissance, Sandy discovered, some half mile distant from the plane, a place where two great chunks of rock formed a clean natural hollow facing towards the south, so that even at midday they gave a good patch of shade several square yards in extent. The position had the additional advantage that they would be protected at night upon two sides from prowling wild beasts. Fires would only be necessary across the entrance.

Cornelius having approved it, they set to work to carry all their stores, arms and ammunition from the plane to their new camping ground, while Sarie occupied herself in searching every crevice in the rocks for small snakes, scorpions, and other dangerous reptiles, whose home they were invading.

By nightfall their arrangements were complete and, with the fires burning brightly beyond the half-circle formed by the two great rocks, they sat down to a haunch of springbuck which Sandy had shot early that morning.

Once more as he looked at Sarie's face, gentle and shadowed in the flickering light of the fires, Sandy was seized with an appalling longing to have her in his arms again. But it was impossible for him to tell her what was in his heart in her brother's presence and he knew that it would be madness to suggest her going for a stroll with him beyond the glowing circle of light cast by the fires. Already the nightly serenade had commenced out there in the darkness. The woof, woof, woofing roar of a lion came from the nearby valley and the hideous laughing bark of a hyena, slinking after the offal that the lion would leave, rent the stillness in the intervals. As Sandy stared out into the darkness between the fires he thought, every now and again, that he caught a glimpse of two round yellow watchful eyes reflected in the blackness by the glow of the flames. A leopard perhaps, or a cheetah, lurking out there ready to spring should one of these two-legged creatures that had invaded its solitude venture beyond the protective circle of light. He could only hope that some chance might come for him to get Sarie on his own during the daytime.

Next day it came. As he was crawling from rock to rock, his rifle held carefully in front of him, on the look-out for a gemsbok or dik-dik for their pot, he came upon a wagon abandoned there in the desert.

The woodwork had been bleached white by the relentless

rays of many thousand days' exposure to the sun. The canvas of the hood had rotted but the hoop-shaped uprights which had supported the material showed stark against the sky-line with a few tatters of the decomposing stuff hanging from them.

As he walked over to it he saw nearby, half buried in the sand, a few enormous bones, obviously the oxen that had been attacked and devoured by leopards. When he examined the wagon he found that several packing-cases still remained where they had been left upon its floorboards and, without waiting to investigate further, he returned at once to the camp. He was convinced that he had found the relics of his uncle's last venture. A grim memento of his unknown relative.

Cornelius was also out after game in a different direction so Sarie was there alone except for old Willem. Immediately Sandy told her of his discovery she was all agog to walk the mile or so over the crest to see this relic of a past adventure with him.

Both remained silent as they trudged along. Sandy was biding his time and Sarie knew it, but in any case it was too hot to make any unnecessary effort at conversation.

When they reached the wagon Sandy sprang up into it and, holding out his hand, pulled her after him. Then, still maintaining that silence which now had something electric and unnatural about it, they began to break open the half-dozen cases. The letters J.T.L. were branded on the sides, so there seemed no doubt that Sandy was right in his supposition. They had little hope of finding anything which might be of any use to them after all these years but they emptied them one after the other out of curiosity.

One contained nothing but a large ham bone picked clean by ants. Others held rows of water bottles, the contents of which had long since evaporated, but towards the front of the wagon they came upon a small iron box which, after some difficulty, Sandy managed to prise open with his knife. At first they thought it might contain money but evidently their predecessor had taken that with him. A single copper coin showed that the little box had once been used as a safe deposit. Now it contained nothing but old papers, some faded bills and a few bundles of letters.

Sarie took one packet and Sandy another, then they settled themselves underneath the vehicle in the small patch of shade provided by it and began to read the dead man's correspondence.

'These are love letters!' said Sarie after a moment. At the word Sandy dropped his packet, pulling her quickly towards him.

'Love letters!' he ejaculated. 'It's about love that I've been trying to talk to you for days. You've been a perfect little beast to me, Sarie, but I believe you do love me, don't you?'

'Of course I do, stupid. Haven't you seen that from the beginning?' She suddenly dropped her eyes and hid her golden head upon his shoulder.

'You darling!' Sandy tilted her chin and kissed her violently. 'I knew it, I knew it,' he cried exultantly, 'but why have you been so devilish cruel to me all this time since we left Zwart Modder?'

'I haven't,' she protested, a provocative twinkle in her eye. 'It's just that you never seemed to want to speak to me!'

'You little liar,' he caught her to him again and pressed his bronzed cheek against her own. 'You've been deliberately avoiding me.'

'Have I?' she laughed suddenly. 'Well, perhaps I have. It's been fun to tease you when we sit round the camp-fire in the evening, but I'm not avoiding you now, am I? And I like to listen to your voice when you're excited, so tell me some more.'

At sunset Cornelius became anxious about them both for he had returned to their rocky home over an hour before, but it was not until the gorge was full of gathering shadows that Sandy and Sarie put in an appearance.

On the following days they seemed to have developed a most extraordinary interest in the derelict wagon. Soon after breakfast each morning they set off to it and, except for a brief spell at lunch-time, did not return to camp until falling dusk made the surrounding veldt a dangerous place to linger in.

Cornelius understood perfectly what was going on. He liked Sandy and, although they said nothing to him of their feelings for each other, he was unselfishly glad to see that a strange delirious happiness appeared to protect the two from the crushing anxiety which was weighing upon himself.

Their food supply caused him no concern. Sarie had brought iron-rations for a month and with the game they shot these could be eked out to double that time if necessary. For water, too, they had no immediate need to worry. Used with strict economy they had sufficient to last for several weeks, but the gathering of enough fuel to maintain their nightly bonfires was proving a real difficulty.

In this treeless hollow on the edge of the great blue mountain range there was no verdure of any kind except an occasional cactus and a few small withered shrubs which grew in the depths of the rocky clefts. The great areas of *toa* grass over which they had passed were a full day's march behind them. They were marooned in that great sandy waste, of which the Zulu Induna had told Philbeach when he spoke of the leopards devouring old John's cattle because they were unable to keep up sufficient fires to protect them.

After three days they had searched every cranny for a couple of miles around and burnt the last twig which they had uprooted. On the fourth night a good half of old John's wagon, flaring like a tinder, was consumed with terrifying rapidity, while the beasts howled dismally beyond the glare.

Sandy and Sarie were compelled to seek out another nook for those long and intimate conversations which they held each day. They seemed oblivious of the terrible danger which was creeping upon them but Cornelius, seated upon a stony crag from which he could overlook most of the country towards the mountains, searched the shimmering, heat-soaked distances with desperately anxious eyes. If the Longs or the Bennetts failed to appear in a few hours now he knew the next morning they would be forced to attempt to cross the many miles which separated them from Noro Kei on foot, carrying what little water they could on their backs.

Early that afternoon his heart suddenly missed a beat for a little cloud of dust at the entrance of the defile announced the coming of one of the wagons. Slipping from his knobbly perch, he hobbled with a limping run the mile that separated him from the others and arrived, steaming with sweat, to tell them his good news.

Sandy and Sarie were lying closely embraced, apparently asleep. They started up immediately he appeared, both flushing crimson, and hastened back with him to a depression between two hillocks through which it seemed certain that the approaching convoy would emerge.

As they watched it advance towards them they saw that it consisted of an outspan and three horsemen. Obviously then it must be Philbeach and the Longs. In another few moments they were able to distinguish the riders and recognised them as Philbeach, Darkie Rickhartz and Ginger Plattenburg. A frown of annoyance creased Sandy's brow as he realised that he would have to beg a lift from the treacherous devil who had cracked him over the head in London.

On seeing them standing there, Philbeach galloped forward and reined in his horse some ten yards away. His grimy, mosquito-bitten face broke into a grin as he recognised the despondent party.

'Well,' he said brightly, 'out after diamonds after all, it seems! I had an idea you meant to try your hand.'

'We've tried and failed,' Sandy said evenly. 'Our plane broke down. Have you succeeded?'

'Do you think I'd tell you if I had, with the police waiting for the lot of us after the way we all stuck around asking for trouble in Zwart Modder?'

'You have, then?' Cornelius cut in dryly.

'That's nothing to do with you, young Dutchie,' the big man laughed unpleasantly.

'Where are the Longs?' Sarie asked suddenly.

'They met with a bit of an accident,' Philbeach informed her, still grinning. 'Old Henry and the girl would go strolling round at nights outside the camp-fires, though I warned them not to, and one night a leopard got them. The old man was a deader even before he had a chance to shout. Like a fool, instead if running for it, young Pat tried to pull him away from under the brute, so it turned on her and savaged her too. We did what we could for her but she lost a lot of blood. She petered out before the morning.'

'I see,' said Sandy slowly. 'Have you seen any sign of the other party?'

Philbeach nodded and stuck out his unshaven chin from which ten days' growth of beard sprouted. 'Yes, and they're sunk too. I reckon another leopard must have come on them sudden and scared the oxen. Anyway, two days' march back in those God-forgotten mountains we came on their wagon tracks which seemed to have skidded on the narrow ledge. When we looked over, there was the whole caboodle, wagon, oxen, horses and men tangled up in no end of a mess a hundred feet below us in the gorge.'

Darkie and Ginger rode up beside him as he finished describing the tragedy which had overtaken Michael and the Bennetts, and the plodding oxen in his outspan came to a halt a little distance in their rear. Darkie sat grinning in his saddle at the unfortunates and Ginger stared at them with his round black eyes that looked so strange in his fair, hairless, almost leprously white face.

Seeing nothing else for it, but filled with the bitterness of defeat, Sandy said slowly: 'Well, I owe you one for what happened in London and had we met anywhere else you would have got it all right, but we're on our uppers at the moment, so I'm prepared to forget the past. You've won—whether you ever secured the diamonds or not, so I give you best. We'll keep still tongues in our heads and give you a free field to get the stuff out of the Union if you've got it. Now you can have the satisfaction of giving your defeated rivals a lift back to the nearest place where we can have a civilised drink.'

'Thanks,' Philbeach leered at him with undisguised amusement. 'I don't need any promises about still tongues. Yours will be still enough anyway this time next week or there-abouts.'

'What!' exclaimed Sandy. 'You don't mean that you're going to leave us here to die?'

'Why not?' The big man had seen Cornelius's hand slip to his hip where he carried his pistol and next second he had drawn his own, covering the three.

'No nonsense now,' he barked, 'or you'll be dead even before your water gives out.' Then he turned towards his companions. 'If there's a little shooting to be done, I reckon we can show them something, don't you, boys?'

Ginger laughed as he, too, lovingly fingered his automatic. 'I'll say so, Chief, but we wouldn't mind giving little blondy a ride back if she's prepared to pay her passage, would we?'

'Go to hell, you swine!' Sarie shot at them from between white lips.

'If there's any hell in this world or the next we're leaving you to enjoy it,' Philbeach countered. Then, with a jerk of his pistol, he motioned the outspan to proceed.

Ten minutes later it had disappeared over the crest, leaving the Van Niekerks and Sandy to face their last night behind the protective barrier of fire from the remaining timbers of old John's wagon. Then . . . eighty miles of desert or . . . the leopards!

21

Death in the Sunshine

Henry Long raised no protest at Philbeach's proposal to hold up his nephews when they returned out of the Valley. Ordinarily he would have cavilled at open robbery, but despite his care of himself his resistance had been lowered by sleeplessness and a mild attack of fever. As he faced the big, beefy giant outside Patricia's bivouac he realised for the first time how foolish he had been to ignore her warning and place his trust in such an unscrupulous partner. But the natural cunning which he hid under half-lowered eyelids still remained to him. Come what might he was determined to secure his share of this amazing wealth which had enabled his brother to spend the last years of his life in reckless luxury. If Philbeach would not risk penetrating farther into the grip of this terrible country, the others would be certain to return with a fat consignment of uncut diamonds if they ever found the Valley. Let Philbeach and his friends hold Michael and the Bennetts up then if they chose, for his nephews had never meant a thing to him. He would keep out of it and felt confident that he could protect himself and Patricia with his own revolver. Getting the diamonds was by no means an end of the business, for when they got back to Zwart Modder the stones would have to be smuggled out of the country. If Philbeach refused to split with him he could always threaten to hand him over to the police.

After they had breakfasted, however, Henry was under the unpleasant necessity of having to tell his daughter about this change in their plans. She was horrified to hear of his decision and implored him either to turn back or order the convoy to proceed at once.

Philbeach strolled up in time to catch the last words of her desperate appeal to Henry and laughed openly at her anxious, harassed expression. Frenzied with fear now both for herself and Michael, she stood up and lashed him with her tongue, telling him, in a spate of angry words, how she loathed, hated and despised him.

Her outburst did little good, for Henry shrugged non-committally. His mind was made up and he was determined to conserve his energy rather than dissipate it by a useless wrangle in the rapidly increasing heat. The other only grinned and turned away to join this henchmen who were seated beneath the shadow of some out-crop at a little distance from the wagon.

Now that they were no longer faced with those gruelling journeys day by day, when horizon seemed to melt into horizon as they trudged on beside the wagon, life became a trifle easier. Patricia reaped one benefit at least from the new situation. Philbeach's open declaration that he would not scruple to hold up the other party and, if necessary, actually fire upon them, had at last awakened Henry to the danger of their own position, and to the fact that the time might even come when he would have to protect himself from this man in whom he had previously trusted. The result was a bridging of the estrangement which had recently existed between father and daughter.

During the days that they spent in the narrow entrance of the valley which led to the beetling crags, beyond which the others were sweltering on their way towards the hidden fortune, Henry behaved with a kindness and consideration to Patricia which she had never known in him before. Once again she came to believe that in some strange way she was herself to blame and had quite misjudged his motives.

After Philbeach's attempt upon her on the first morning of their halt Henry saw to it that he had no other opportunity to molest her. He even exerted himself to go for short walks with her across the rough, broken ground in the early morning or the comparative cool of the evening, and arranged that she should share his bivouac for the future.

Darkie, Ginger and Philbeach took turns each day, posted on horseback at the bend of the valley from which they could see a mile or more along it, in order to watch for the convoy. On the sixth afternoon Ginger came galloping back to report that a little column of dust which could only indicate one thing was visible in the distance.

Philbeach had long since made his dispositions. Darkie and Ginger were to conceal themselves one on each side of a narrow gully through which the wagon would have to pass. He would halt the convoy himself and demand that any stones which they had secured should be handed over. At the least sign of any resistance the other two were to blaze away with their rifles from the rocks above without further warning.

Patricia, before whom they had openly discussed their intentions, had no difficulty in guessing what the outcome of the business would be. Philbeach did not mean the others ever to get back to Zwart Modder. By riding out alone he intended to provoke his victims to a fight in order to afford a reasonable excuse for the others to shoot them down. Michael, she felt convinced, would be certain to put up a fight for the wealth which he had secured after these terrible hardships. He was even more certain to do so if he thought that he only had one antagonist to tackle. Night after night she woke shuddering, her hair damp with perspiration, from an awful vision, partly dream and partly conjured up by her half-waking imagination. She saw herself standing behind a rock in the valley mouth . . . she heard the crack of rifles and saw Michael pitch from his saddle as the bullets thudded into his chest . . . then she saw herself rushing towards him as he lay on the ground with blood streaming from him.

Somehow she had got to stop this terrible nightmare becoming a reality. So she also made her plans, ready for the terrible moment when the wagon should at last advance out of that deathly valley.

Immediately Philbeach had posted his men and started to walk towards the gully, leading his horse by its bridle, she ran towards her own little roan and climbed quickly into the saddle.

Next second she was off, galloping madly down the stretch to the corner beyond which the wagon should emerge at any moment.

As Philbeach caught the sound of her horse's hoofs he swung on his heel and yelled at her to halt. She took no notice and, lowering her head, raced past him just as he raised his rifle and bellowed:

'Stop!—damn you!—or I'll shoot.'

Henry, who was standing twenty yards behind him, rushed forward to knock up the rifle, but he was too late. A crack like a whip echoed again and again through the rocky pass and Patricia felt the roan lurch beneath her. She grabbed at its mane and then another shot rang out, this time from Ginger. With a heart-rending neigh the little beast collapsed beneath her, shot both in the near hind quarter and through the head.

She pitched from her saddle a dozen yards away and, sprawling along the ground, tore her hands and gashed her knee upon some outcrop. She staggered to her feet and, her shoulders hunched, her eyes starting from her sockets, her hair streaming behind her, began to run; petrified with fear that any second she would receive a bullet in the back, yet still determined to reach the corner and warn the oncoming party.

'Stop, d'you hear? If you don't, I'll shoot you,' yelled Philbeach. He gave Henry a savage push which threw him to the ground and then sank on to one knee to take better aim with his rifle.

Henry sprang up again and thrust his revolver into his red, brutal face. 'I'll kill you,' he cried desperately, 'unless you put that rifle down.'

Philbeach shrugged and lowered his weapon. 'All right—you'll kill me, eh?' he sneered. Then, with a simulated lurch, he fell against Henry and wrenched the revolver from his shaking hand. 'Now get after her and bring her back,' he thundered. 'If you don't I'll out the two of you.'

Henry's lined face went grey as he realised that he was now defenceless and that this great hot sweaty man with the hard small eyes meant every word he said. He turned, as Philbeach raised the rifle again, and began to run after Patricia.

Panting with her exertions she raced on, half-blinded by the perspiration which streamed into her eyes; then she caught her toe upon a snag of stone and pitched forward to her full length on the ground. For a moment she lay there half-stunned and gasping, but struggled to her feet again. The corner was now only fifty yards away but her fall had given Henry a chance to decrease the distance between them and he was hard behind her, shouting as his breath came in quick, painful gasps:

'Stop! Patricia. Stop, or he'll fire again.'

With her heart pounding in her breast, limping a little from the pain in her bleeding knee, she dashed round the bend only to discover that there was no wagon to be seen. Another bend about half a mile distant shut off a large portion of the Valley from view, and it was in the open space beyond this that Ginger must have sighted the convoy.

As she stopped, leaning for support against a rock, a solitary figure on foot came round it. For an instant she thought it was Michael, then that it must be the Hottentot whom they had secured to guide their party. Half-blinded by dust and sweat, she could hardly make out the figure at all for a moment. As she was still straining to clear her eyes that she might see more plainly, Henry came up beside her and, seizing her by the arm, almost swung her off her feet.

It was only then that she caught sight of the great, tawny, sinuous leopard that stood within a few feet of her, just by the rock where she had halted. It was staring at her with evil menace in its great yellow eyes.

As the brute sprang she screamed and fell sideways. There was a snarling roar, a horrible choking gurgle and, as she tried to fling herself farther back upon the ground, she saw that the great cat was whirling round and round with her father underneath it. The fore-claws were buried in his shoulders and the hind ones tearing at his body.

She screamed again, half-mad with terror. The leopard suddenly stopped gyrating, then, seizing Henry's neck in its great teeth, it shook him like a rat. A rifle cracked, the leopard leaped sideways across her father's body and then Patricia fainted.

22

The Land of the Great Thirst

After Michael had made his amazing discovery he began to pick up some of those strange stones which lay all about him glowing dully in the moonlight; soon he put the few that he had gathered down, for an utter weariness descended on him again and this time he fell into a sound healthy slumber.

When he awoke the sun had already topped the mountains. Having bathed in the river, he set about making preparations for his attempt to rejoin Ernest. He now found that only the half-light of the evening, when he had arrived in the Valley, had prevented him from realising at once that it was indeed the place which he had undergone so much hardship to discover.

On the sandy shores of the lake into which the great waterfall thundered there seemed to be a curious opalescent sheen. It had all the colours of the rainbow, and little points of light struck his eyes from all directions. As he stood there, the solitary inhabitant of that strange hidden cañon empty of man and beast alike, he realised why it had been christened the 'Place of the Great Glitter' by those native discovers who had penetrated to it in past times and preserved the legend in their tribes for posterity.

He spent the whole of the early morning hours in gathering the precious stones; contemptuously disregarding the smaller stuff and those with a reddish hue which he knew to be garnets until he had picked up as many really fine specimens as he thought he would be able to carry. He then scrutinised each one of the glassy pebbles through a magnifying glass, which he had brought for the purpose, in order to assure himself that every one *was* a diamond. He had taken the trouble to study the specimens in the British Museum with the greatest care on the morning before he left London, and, as far as he could ascertain, none of his final selection contained a serious flaw.

Then, instead of trying to sleep through the midday heat, as had been his custom during their days of journeying, he stripped off his clothes and lay down in the shallow waters at the river's edge, with his head sheltered from the sun by a slab of projecting rock. He had already made up his mind by which funnel he would attempt to scale the rocky walls which hemmed him in, but it might be hours or even days before he could reach the outspan. In the latter case his greater danger, apart from wild animals, lay in the limited quantity of water which he would be able to carry; but his education, if not profound, was at least enough for him to know that the mouth is not the only way by which the body can obtain the liquid which it requires.

Until the previous afternoon he had been unable to wash even his face, let alone his limbs, for days past, so that the skin of his whole body had become dry and parched. Now, by allowing it to soak for several hours, he hoped to adjust the deficit and by these means economise to the lowest point the ration which it would be necessary for him to drink once he set off on his journey.

He made a hearty lunch, even cramming himself to satiety after his appetite had vanished, knowing that he would not be able to carry all the supplies which he had rescued from the piece of raft. Then, making a careful selection from the rest, he made up a packet and tied it to his belt. The diamonds he distributed as evenly as possible about his person and, having filled his water bottle to the brim, he knelt down and drank from the river until he could drink no more. After that he took George's ground sheet and his own and, forming them as well as he could into bunchy sacks, filled both with water, tying their outer edges together firmly with a piece of string. He strung the two bags upon his back in the manner of a rucksack and then, feeling far more like sleep after his heavy meal than scaling mountains, he began the ascent of the funnel.

His progress was easy to begin with but as the rough walls

grew steeper his difficulties increased, added to which he began to suffer acute pains in his stomach from the excessive amount of water that he had drunk.

The heat was intense and at one time he almost gave up the ascent. However, he laboured on with grim determination and, his fingers bleeding, hauled himself on to the top of the precipice where he lay panting and exhausted. When he recovered a little he glanced at his watch and found that his climb had taken something over two hours and that the time was now ten past five.

He pulled himself together again as soon as he was able and began to make his way round the top of the steep cliff that edged the valley in the direction of Ernest's wagon. At one point he found himself faced with a yawning chasm, so was forced to make a detour of some three miles before he could circumvent the gulf, but just as the sun was setting he arrived on the top of the enormous rock face of the mountain through which the underground river ran. There below him, like toy animals, he could see the grazing oxen, but the wagon was hidden from him by a projecting ridge. Even if Ernest or the natives were on the look-out for him they would not be able to see his signals from where he stood. He realised that it would be necessary for him to make a detour of many miles in order to reach Ernest, as the mountain on which he was standing was sheer cliff down to the opening of the underground river.

For half an hour he shouted, yodelled and hallooed, while from time to time he threw chunks of rock down into the gorge in the hope of attracting their attention, but all his efforts proved unsuccessful. At that distance it was obviously impossible for them to hear his voice and the stones that he hurled fell, as far as he could judge, a good three hundred yards short of the nearest oxen.

As the afterglow faded he became anxious for his safety. Here, on the high levels, which communicated on either side with steep but easily-negotiable slopes, he would be exposed to the attack of any wild thing that prowled the hilltops in the night. His only hope of safety lay in finding a cave in which he could shelter during the dark hours. He abandoned his attempt to attract the attention of the party lying hundreds of feet below him, and began to search in frantic haste for a suitable shelter in which to spend the night.

His water bags flapping behind him, he ran along the uneven ground of the flat-topped mountain. No break in the bare inhospitable tableland seemed to offer a likely shelter, so he covered the best part of a mile in fifteen minutes towards where the mountain broke into clefts and gullies. Yet even here he could find no place which was altogether suitable. For days, it seemed, he had passed caves by the hundred in the stony hill-sides, yet when his need was so urgent he could not find one that would answer his purpose.

He stumbled and slipped from slope to slope, the loose shale sliding from beneath his feet and tinkling down the mountain side, while darkness closed in around him. At last he reached a depression between two summits and, peering anxiously among the boulders that strewed its bottom, made his way as quickly as he could along it. The bed of the hollow opened into a junction where several others led off from it and here at last he found an opening in the rocks where, with reasonable luck, he might pass the night in safety after he had barricaded the entrance.

He started to shift the nearest large stones that he could carry and after an hour he had erected a five-foot barrier. Then, wriggling through the small hole he had left into the pitchy darkness of the shallow cave, he closed that too and then sank to the floor utterly worn out. He had no torch or matches, so had to take his chance of the cave being free of small reptiles, but he was so weary that he hardly thought of it. His head pillowed on his arm, he dropped off to sleep.

In the early morning he awoke with a feeling of weight across his thighs and, lifting his head, was terrified to see in the faint light that filtered between the stones of his barricade a large yellow snake, sleeping comfortably upon his body. The brute was about three feet long and had the flattened hooded neck of a cobra.

He gazed at it in fascinated horror, straining to keep his

body perfectly still for fear that the snake should wake. He racked his brain for a way of dealing with it, but it seemed that his mind had gone completely blank except for a mental picture of the reptile raising its head at any moment to strike.

The pistol which he had carried through the journey was still strapped to his hip and he could reach it, he thought, without disturbing that yellow length of coiled evil, but it would be impossible to shoot at it without wounding himself in the leg. If he suddenly threw himself from under it he felt that the chances were all against his being able to draw a bead upon its narrow head before it had bitten him.

The awful tension was broken a moment later by the snake waking despite his care. It raised its head and began to uncoil itself lazily with a queer gliding motion. Tense with horror, he waited, expecting it to strike, but it slid gently off his legs and with a swift wriggle disappeared into an opening formed by two stones a few feet farther along the cave. It was apparently content at having enjoyed the hospitable warmth of his body during its night's slumber.

In frantic haste Michael knocked the top stones of the barrier out, and, clearing the rest, raced twenty yards down the slope. When he pulled up, shaking slightly from his horrible experience, he realised that he had left his water bags behind him. With cautious steps he approached the cave again and, peeping over the wall of rocks, saw that the snake had come out of his hole at the sound of his flying footsteps. It was a yellow Kalahari cobra, one of the few varieties of the species found outside India. Coiled on its tail, it sat there watching him with its beady black eyes. Its head, raised a foot above the ground and arching back, swayed slightly from side to side and its long forked tongue flickered in and out with incredible swiftness. But he was in a far stronger position now as the barrier gave him chest-high protection and, seizing a big flat stone, he flung it as the snake reared up, crushing its head between his missile and the side of the cave.

Having secured his water bottles and the belt with his small store of provisions, he sat down to a modest breakfast and then set out on a fresh attempt to rejoin Ernest and the outspan. On seeking for the entrance to the depression down which he had come the night before he was faced with a new difficulty. In the semi-darkness he had been unable to mark any distinguishing landmark, and all five of the hollows which formed a junction at that spot looked so similar that he did not know which to take. With an awful feeling of despondency he realised that he was completely lost in the heart of the great uninhabited mountain range.

After some deliberation he decided that his best hope lay in taking the sun for a guide and trying to break out of the mountainous area back towards the plain. If he failed to find the outspan in the next twenty-four hours Ernest would have left the river and his last hope would be gone. By striking to the southward and sticking to the high ground as far as possible he would at least stand some chance of picking the convoy up on its return during the few days that his water would last.

That morning he trudged along a sandy hillside, then climbed a rocky barrier where he lunched and rested for a few hours in the shadow of a crag. In the afternoon he pushed doggedly on from valley to valley, often having to make wide detours, but gradually nearing the open ground of the southern Kalahari.

That night he selected his resting place while he still had ample daylight and, having made certain that it contained no noisome occupants, he made another barrier in front of the entrance. As night drew on, the long-drawn howls of the prowling beasts echoed eerily through the stillness and once he heard the soft patter of padded feet and then long snuffling breaths as some large beast sniffed his scent only a few feet away on the far side of the heap of boulders which shut him in. He was so weary from his long day's tramping that even while he strained his ears to listen for the noise again he fell asleep.

In the two days that followed the conviction grew upon him that he would never look upon a human face again. His boots were cut to ribbons on the jagged rocks, so he bound pieces of the blanket round them to protect his bruised and bleeding feet a little. He stumbled wearily on from one ravine to another and examined horizon after horizon in a vain search for Ernest's outspan. There were no streams or tracks, no wooded heights to vary the monotony of that hellish country, only endless vistas of scorching rock, boulders and pebbles beneath a sky of white-hot brass. The water bags which he had made out of the ground sheets proved a terrible disappointment. Their contents evaporated rapidly as the sun beat down upon his back, and more of their contents was lost in this manner than the amount he drank. By the third evening, only his water-bottle remained to him.

At times, as he pushed one foot doggedly in front of another, he was even tempted to throw away the diamonds which weighed so heavily in his pockets but if he did so and relieved himself of their few pounds' weight, it would not materially better the prospect of him being able to find his way out of this awful solitude. He felt that if he were doomed to die in that infernal region he might just as well carry them until the end.

The heat was so overwhelming that for periods he became semi-delirious; singing to himself snatches of long-forgotten songs as he plodded on, his head reeling and his body one great ache from blisters, burns and bruises.

It was in this state—his head hanging low upon his chest —his feet dragging mechanically, that he heard two rifle shots ring out. At first his mind was too far out of control to realise the fresh hope of succour that they brought him. He only stared about him vaguely. Nothing stirred within his area of vision but, recovering a little as the sound of the shots echoed and re-echoed along the gully, he suddenly grasped the fact that human beings must be near and, moreover, in the direction in which he was going.

With stumbling steps he began to run, terrified now that they might move off in another direction before he could reach them. As he rounded a corner he saw a little group of figures half a mile away. He had lost his dark glasses in the underground river and his eyes were so strained and bloodshot from the long days in the frightful glare that he could not make out the figures clearly but he ran on towards them, shouting and waving wildly to attract their attention. Before he had covered a quarter of the distance his bandaged foot slipped upon a small boulder and, crashing forward, he struck his head against another, knocking himself senseless.

When he came round he thought at first that he must have dreamed the whole episode, for the valley was once again empty as before, but the pain in his head soon assured him that he had actually fallen. Immediately he struggled to his knees he realised that the diamonds had gone from his pockets.

The sun was considerably lower in the heavens, so he knew that he had been unconscious for some time; even so, the people who had robbed him and left him there to die could not have yet got any great distance. A mad, wild rage, which made his heart catch in his throat at the thought of the way in which he had been treated, filled him with a sudden renewal of energy and, completely forgetful that in his present state he could not have stood up to a well-grown girl, he set off at a brisk pace to pursue and attack his despoilers.

At the bend where he had seen the figures he pulled up short as he nearly stumbled upon the bodies of Henry and the leopard. Both were dead, his uncle being terribly mutilated. He paused for a moment, quite bewildered by this fresh shock; then, seeing his uncle's water-bottle, which was half-full of lime juice and water, he took a long pull at that glorious nectar and stumbled on.

By five o'clock he found, with sudden overwhelming relief, that he had at last passed out of the clutches of those grim mountains and before him, gently sloping, lay the foothills with patches of sandy plain in the distance. His mind was so confused by his sufferings that the hopelessness of attempting the seven days' march back to Noro Kei without transport, food or water never occurred to him, nor was he capable of seriously considering who the people were who had robbed him of the diamonds and left his uncle unburied. The figures of Philbeach, Sandy, Patricia, George, Darkie and all the others who had played any part in this desperate adventure danced a fantastic can-can in his head. The one thought that hammered in his mind was that he must catch up somehow in order to get back those diamonds which he had purchased at such a price in blood and toil.

Wild-eyed and haggard, he was still striding gamely forward when a voice hailed him from a nearby slope.

'Hello you there! Come here a moment.'

He swerved to the right and whipped out the gun which they had not troubled to remove from his hip then, blinking his eyes, stared at the man who was advancing towards him.

'Hi! Steady on with that thing,' called the man—then, with a sudden shout: 'By Jove, it's Michael!'

Michael lurched forward a step, still pointing with the gun. 'You've got my stones, you blackguard,' he croaked. 'Give them back to me or I'll shoot you.'

'You're dippy,' said another voice quite close behind him, 'and if you don't drop that gun I'll plug you where you stand.'

Swinging round, Michael saw that another khaki-clad figure held him covered with a rifle.

The first man walked straight up to him and took him gently by the arm, as he said kindly: 'You poor old boy, you look about all in—surely you know me?—I'm Sandy.'

Michael passed a weary hand over his dust-encrusted face and then shook his head from side to side. 'Of course I know you,' he muttered huskily, 'but I've been through the hell of a time. Everything in my head seems to be muddled up. Weren't you with the crowd who pinched my haul of diamonds and left old Henry's body to rot in the sun?'

'Of course not,' Sandy assured him. 'But I can guess who did. Come on, Cornelius, let's get back to camp.'

The two of them practically carried Michael back to the niche between the two big rocks, where Sarie was just beginning to prepare the evening meal. Immediately she saw him she left it with an exclamation of pity at his terrible state.

She forbade him to talk any more for the moment but

used some of their precious water to bathe his face and the best part of a bottle of witch hazel on bandages to wrap round his blistered arms, then insisted that he must rest at least until dinner was ready.

The cooling bandages, the brandy and water which they made him sip, and more than anything the incredible relief of finding himself once more among friendly humans, aided his recovery. After he had rested for the best part of an hour, Sarie came over to ask him if he felt up to joining them at dinner and by that time his mind had cleared to a reasonably normal state.

Over the meal he told his story from the time when they had left Zwart Modder up to an hour before when Sandy had spotted him staggering along through the desert. Then Sarie gave him an account of all that had happened to her party.

Michael's brain had only just begun to function properly again and, immediately Sarie spoke of Philbeach and the lies he had told, his thoughts flew to Patricia.

Actually, although he had no means of knowing it, she had fainted almost at the same moment as himself.

When she came to she was lying on her back in the wagon upon the heap of matting that Henry had occupied for so many sweltering days. The wagon was jolting gently onwards and through the back of it Patricia could see sufficient of the landscape to know that they had turned southwards once more.

At the sudden memory of her father's terrible fate she raised herself with a loud cry. Philbeach rode up and, dismounting from his horse, hitched it to the back of the wagon, then climbed in beside her.

'Don't try to talk now,' he told her with rough kindness, 'you'll feel better by and by.' Then he gave her drink of water and, producing a little bottle with some tabloids from his pocket, made her take four of them.

The drug was potent, for she had hardly begun to wonder if they had held up Michael after all, or if the shooting had been sufficient to warn him of his danger, when she dropped into a heavy sleep.

When she awoke it was night. The camp fires were gleaming and she could hear Darkie and Ginger laughing together. Still half-dazed from the effect of the drug, though not sufficiently to prevent her remembering the shattering events of the afternoon, she sat up and climbed out of the wagon.

Philbeach saw her at once and, as he strolled over, she suddenly realised with an awful quickening of her heart the full horror of her position.

He came quiet close to her but did not touch her, and said amiably: 'Feeling better now? I wouldn't fret yourself about the old man too much. All of us have got to die some way and I reckon he had had his innings.'

She nodded silently, and then he added quietly: 'You and me's going to be good friends from now on, aren't we?'

'I hope so,' she replied almost in a whisper.

'I hope so too. For your sake as well as mine,' he went on firmly, 'because it lies with you. Either you treat me decent from to-night on, and I'll look after you, or else you'll get what's coming to you all the same, and when I've done with you I'll hand you over for Darkie and Ginger to have a cut at. Now get back in the wagon and think it over.'

23

Blood *is* Thicker than Water

As Sarie finished her story, Michael, filled with an awful apprehension for Patricia now, exclaimed:

'There was only the old man there in the valley and the dead leopard,' he exclaimed.

'Well, Patricia wasn't with the Philbeach party when they passed here three hours back,' Sandy assured him.

'But the girl can't have disappeared altogether,' insisted Sarie. 'Philbeach said that the same leopard attacked them both and if they didn't trouble to bury the old man they wouldn't bother about burying her either. When they passed us she must have been in the wagon.'

'Good God!' cried Michael, springing to his feet, 'then she's alone now in the hands of that devil.'

Sarie looked across at Michael sharply. His face showed all the agony of mind which he was feeling and her thoughts flew to the other girl in quick comprehension of what she was likely to suffer at the hands of a man like Philbeach.

'Poor kid,' exclaimed Cornelius. 'I wish to goodness we could do something about it but without horses we're pinned down in this hell ourselves.'

'We've got to do something about it,' Michael cried, his eyes gleaming. 'We've got to. They're only three hours ahead, you say, so I'm going on.'

Sandy caught his arm as he was about to start out there and then. 'Steady on!' he said quietly. 'You haven't got a hope in hell even if you were strong enough to walk it, which you aren't. It'll be dark in less than an hour and the leopards would get you for a certainty.'

'I don't care,' Michael protested passionately. 'I've been too near death to worry about it any more. I'm going to take my chance on reaching her.'

'We are all pretty near death anyhow,' Cornelius remarked grimly. 'The rest of the old wagon and the packing-cases will just about keep the fires going to-night. We shall be up against it in real earnest about a couple of dozen miles south of here in a few days' time.'

'Then let's start now,' Michael urged.

'I'm sorry,' Sandy shot a covert glance at Sarie, 'I'd like to, Michael, but our chances are pretty slender as it is and I'm not taking one single risk I haven't got to at the moment.'

Sarie caught his glance and knew that it was her he was thinking of so she said slowly: 'I'm willing. If we do get out of this alive I shall never be able to get that poor girl out of my mind unless we make some attempt to reach her.'

An argument developed in which Cornelius, also thinking of his sister, backed Sandy up although he was secretly willing to have gone himself if they considered that his lameness would not be too great a drag upon the pace of the party. It was then that Michael suddenly thought of the aeroplane.

'Tell me more about your crash,' he said to Cornelius quickly. 'What actually did happen?'

The young Dutchman told him and added, with a shake of his head: 'There's no hope there, I'm afraid, unless you can find me a new inlet valve spring growing in this filthy desert.'

'It does sound pretty hopeless,' Michael agreed, 'but I'd like to have a look at it all the same because as it happens I qualified as an engineer, so it's just possible that I might be able to think of something.'

Darkness had almost fallen so they took some lengths of wood to act as torches in case they had to linger there for any length of time, and then walked the half-mile to the stranded plane.

With quick, efficient fingers Michael set to work on the engine. When he reached the broken spring he examined it carefully.

'I think I can do it,' he muttered with sudden excitement.

'*Ach,* how?' Cornelius inquired, a trifle sceptically.

'Look!' Michael held up the two halves of the spiral. 'When the broken ends come together they dovetail and screw into each other if pressure is put upon them, so the spring goes down to half its usual size without taking up any resistance; but by placing the rings at the top and bottom together in the middle, they cannot pass each other and the spring remains its normal length whatever pressure you put upon it.'

'By Jove, you're right!' exclaimed Sandy.

For an hour and a half they laboured in the darkening shadows, and for the latter part by torchlight. Then, at last, when they tested the engine it sprang into life with an even roar which thrilled every one of them and heralded new hope.

As Michael cut it off a voice suddenly addressed them out of the gloom.

'Well, the world is a small place, I always do say. Fancy finding friends in a place like this.'

'By all that's marvellous!' Michael exclaimed. 'It's Ernest. Good Lord! I am glad to see you. Where's that wagon of ours?'

'Cripes!' ejaculated Ernest. 'So you're here too!—I'd almost given you up for a gone-er.' Then he jerked his thumb over his shoulder. 'The wagon's back there, about a hundred yards away. I should have camped for the night half an hour ago only that I happened to see your torches. But where's brother George?'

There was a sudden awful silence, which was broken at last by Michael, who muttered: 'I'm afraid poor George . . .'

Ernest's distress was quite pitiful. For days he had given them both up as lost in that terrible underground cavern, yet he had delayed his departure from its entrance twenty-four hours longer than had been arranged in the hope of their return. He had never really admitted to himself that they must be dead. Now, from Michael's murmured words, the conviction went home that he would never see George again. It had been upon his brains that their prosperous little business was founded but Ernest looked up to him for many other reasons besides that and the two brothers had been inseparable friends all their lives.

They led him back to the camp and, while Sarie and Michael tried to comfort him as best they could, Sandy and Cornelius saw to the out-spanning of his oxen within the semicircle of their own camp fires. Then they went into conference regarding their next move. Ernest seemed to be too broken up at the loss of his brother to be of much use for anything and each second Michael was manifesting more impatience to be off in search of Patricia now that the plane had been repaired. In addition, neither Sandy nor Cornelius were prepared to leave Sarie behind alone with the native servants.

In consequence it was decided that while Sandy, Cornelius,

Michael and Sarie should start at once by plane, Ernest should be left at the camp to load such stores as they still had on to his wagon and, if they failed to return, proceed in the ordinary way next morning with old Willem as an addition to his party.

By the light of their flares the others set off again to the plane which, when they had started it up, purred so evenly that they could hardly think anything had ever been wrong with it. They climbed to a height of a thousand feet and almost immediately picked up the camp fires of Philbeach's party. The journey that had taken three hours for his slow-moving oxen was covered by the aeroplane in as many minutes.

Cornelius's anxiety now was to land the plane safely, since in the darkness they might easily have a nasty spill if they came down on broken ground. In any case, they could not hope to conceal their presence, for the roar of the engine would give warning of their approach, so he thought the best thing to do was to land as near the lighted patch as possible and taxi right up to it. As the plane bumped and bounded Michael and Sandy leaned from it with rifles at the ready and, as it ran lightly past the camp, they saw the others spring up from their fire in sudden alarm.

Philbeach and his friends had caught the sound of the plane a moment earlier but had never anticipated that it would come down practically upon them. Much less that their first warning of attack would be a rifle bullet whizzing over their heads as the plane came to rest twenty yards from the wagon.

The hands of all three instinctively moved to their belts, but before they could draw their guns the engine of the plane was shut off and Michael shouted:

'We've got the lot of you covered and we'll shoot if you move a hand.'

After that the whole thing was easy. Philbeach, Darkie and Ginger, realising that they were properly caught, were far too wise to risk a gun fight. The invading party climbed out of the plane and, while Sandy and Sarie kept them covered, Cornelius relieved them of their weapons.

Michael, heedless of the others, dashed straight to the wagon and a moment later he was fiercely pressing his blistered lips upon Patricia's.

By the time the two of them joined their friends, Cornelius had searched the robbers and recovered Michael's store of diamonds. As he ran his hands over Darkie again to make certain that he was concealing nothing else, Cornelius peered into his face and said slowly:

'I've seen you somewhere before? Yes, I remember, it was when my father, Judge Van Niekerk, sent you up for five years for a little job of arson—wasn't it?'

Darkie grinned, his gold teeth flashing in the firelight.

'That's right, Mister, but anyhow, the old Judge has gone on a longer stretch than that now, ain't he?'

'Perhaps,' Cornelius replied evenly, 'but there's just one difference. Wherever he is nobody can send him there again, whereas if you give me the least chance I'll see to it that you have another opportunity of sampling the air on the Break-water.'

When they had dealt with Philbeach and his friends and Michael had counted over the uncut diamonds to assure himself that they had secured the whole of his hoard, they held a short consultation beside the aeroplane.

'What's the next move?' Sarie asked.

'We have the choice of three,' Cornelius said quietly. 'We can rejoin Ernest Bennett, which doesn't seem very sensible since we'll only have to leave him again to-morrow morning now the plane's all right. We can push on to Zwart Modder, which must be about seventy miles to the south, but after all the excitement of these two expeditions leaving there we've got to remember that the police are on the look-out for our return and they'll ask all sorts of unpleasant questions, or we can fly south-west to Postmasburg, where nobody is expecting us. It can't be more than a hundred and fifty miles and in my opinion that's the thing to do.'

They had set off in such a hurry that no definite plans about what they were to do if they were successful had been arranged. Sarie thought that they should rejoin Ernest, otherwise he would have half a dozen anxious days wondering what had become of them. She also pointed out that if he overtook Philbeach's party they might hold him up.

'What with?' protested Sandy. 'We've drawn their fangs already and he is armed so they wouldn't risk interfering with him. Besides, he's got a first-class guide in Ombulike, three other native servants and our supplies as well as his own; he's on an easy wicket. Cornelius is right, but the question is, will the plane carry five?'

'As far as weight is concerned, it's easy,' Cornelius replied, 'because we've unloaded all our stores, but it means someone taking a hard seat and crouching in the back.'

Patricia gave a strained, uncertain laugh. 'I'll crouch anywhere, in an aeroplane or on an ass's back—to get out of this.'

'I still think we ought to return to Ernest Bennett, at least for the night,' Sarie maintained, but the question was decided against her because at that moment Michael, who had been leaning silently against the side of the plane, suddenly collapsed.

Only the imperative urgency of reaching Patricia had kept him going so long, and now the strain that he had undergone in the last days had proved too much for him.

'Got to get him to a doctor quick,' said Sandy as Patricia, with a low cry, knelt and lifted his head on to her knees.

'Postmasburg then,' Sarie agreed at once. 'It's much bigger than Zwart Modder and worth the extra half hour or so in the plane.'

'All right—but we'd best land somewhere outside it,' said Cornelius, as he hoisted himself into his machine. 'We've got to be devilish careful now we're running illicit diamonds, but if he is really bad when we get there we'll carry him up to the hotel somehow or to the doctor's place.'

The others lifted Michael up and then climbed into the plane, while Philbeach, Darkie and Ginger watched their departure with sullen interest.

The going was easy in the clear, starlit African night as they passed over those desolate miles of plain and bush. After an hour and a half's flying, Cornelius began to climb in order to pick up Postmasburg—another twenty minutes and they saw the lights of the little dorp gleaming to the left below them. The moon had risen now and enabled him to make a landing without mishap on a level stretch of ground some two miles south of the village.

Michael had slept during their flight but now he roused and declared that apart from over-tiredness he felt all right, so they decided to camp outside the dorp for the night and, after half an hour, during which the rest of the party collected dead branches to make protective fires, they settled down beneath the sheltering wings of the plane.

Michael was no longer sleepy now, and it seemed that new life had been given to him by their successful rescue of Patricia. His eyes were bright and feverish but he flatly rejected their suggestion of taking him into the town and insisted that he would be quite all right in the morning. Then he begged Patricia so urgently to leave the others and talk with him that she could not find it in her heart to refuse.

For an hour or more they sat together in the moonlight exchanging their stories, while every few moments he would interrupt their conversation to grab her hands with a new expression of his love. His fingers were hot with fever but his brain was lucid and a great contentment filled their hearts, but for one thing of which they were both thinking.

'Are you religious?' he asked suddenly.

'Not particularly. Why?' she questioned.

'You're not a Roman Catholic or anything of that sort, are you?' he went on.

'No, just an ordinary Christian, but why do you ask?'

'I only wondered,' he said slowly. 'I was thinking of all that business in the Prayer Book.'

A shadow clouded Patricia's face. 'I think I can guess the bit that you are thinking of.'

'Can you? I wonder.'

'Has it got anything to do with relationship?'

'Yes—blast it. You've hit on just what I mean.'

'The old religious prohibition doesn't trouble me much,'

she murmured, as she leaned her head against his shoulder; 'but if we married we ought not to have any children, and you've *got* to have a son, Michael dear.'

He nodded. 'Yes, it would be ghastly if we produced an idiot child, wouldn't it?'

A short silence fell, then Michael suddenly burst out: 'Oh, isn't it hellish that, now we've got the diamonds, there is still this ghastly barrier between us!'

24

Robbery under Arms

It was only with the greatest difficulty that Patricia managed at last to induce Michael to try and get some sleep. She was almost in a state of collapse herself by the time they settled down beside the others under the outspread wings of the plane, for it was eighteen hours since she had woken the previous morning on the fringe of the great mountain range. So much had taken place—the ambush, her wild attempt to warn the oncoming party, her father's death, the terrible hours which she had spent in the wagon after her talk with Philbeach, her rescue and the harrowing discussion with Michael, when she had been faced afresh with the fact that their double first cousinship made it impossible to marry—it seemed as though she had been living with her emotions strained to breaking point for weeks. The second her head touched the aeroplane cushion that had been put no the ground for her, she fell into the dreamless sleep of utter exhaustion.

Michael, however, could not sleep. His head was throbbing, a shooting pain kept stabbing him behind the eyes and his body was burning with fever. The strain through which he had passed had been too much for him and his temporary recovery after the short sleep in the plane proved only a prelude to complete delirium. Four hours later Cornelius, rousing as the sun came over the hills, discovered him wild-eyed and dishevelled, muttering incoherent nonsense to himself.

With as little delay as possible they got him to the small inn at Postmasburg, where he and the Bennetts had been marooned a fortnight earlier. Sandy and Cornelius put him to bed while Mr. Versfeld, the landlord, ran round to get the local doctor.

The latter, when he arrived, proved to be a tall, good-looking young Dutchman who had just completed his studies after passing through Cape University. He was of the new school, competent and practical, who believed in telling his patient's friends the truth in simple language, instead of hiding his views under a cloak of professional mystery. Moreover, when he learned that Sandy was a graduate of his own University he devoted himself to the case with particular enthusiasm.

The two girls took it in turns to nurse Michael and after Patricia had settled down in his room to take the first spell and the doctor had left, the other three, with welcome cooling drinks before them, held a conference on the deserted stoep of the small hotel.

Sandy had removed the diamonds from Michael's clothes, but none of the three felt they would be justified in taking any steps to get them out of the country before he was in a fit state to be consulted as to their disposal.

In his open-handed, generous way he had made a vague statement the previous night that they must all split up the proceeds once they could get them marketed; but Cornelius said that he hardly thought that this was enough for them to act on, and in any case Michael's share should be at least half the plunder since it was he who had actually secured them, while they had done nothing but assist him in retrieving them from Philbeach.

Sandy was now anxious and worried about the police. The goings and comings of the two ox-spans between Upington and Zwart Modder had, he felt sure, aroused all the curiosity which they dreaded and he considered it highly probable that, when the two wagons returned, the Union police would be on the spot to make inquiries about their doings.

Philbeach and Co. could probably be counted on to say as little as possible, but Ernest, on the other hand, might say too much. Immediately he got into Zwart Modder and found that they had not arrived he would assume that their plane had broken down again and start organising a search party to go out and hunt for them. In order to do that it was most likely that he would go at once to the local authorities and, with the thought of their safety overwhelming all other considerations, give a frank and complete history of the three expeditions.

If he did so, the fact of Michael having secured the diamonds would come out; Philbeach and Co. would be searched and the police, failing to find the stones, would immediately start casting their net all round the borders of the Kalahari to pick up the other party. Once that happened, their hope of evading the authorities for any length of time would be extremely slender and their chances of getting the diamonds out of the Union practically nil. In consequence, it was decided that Sandy should return to Zwart Modder in time to be on the spot when Ernest arrived, and prevent him mentioning the diamonds to the police.

If Michael was well enough the best hope for the others lay in disappearing completely from Postmasburg, leaving no trace behind them, before Ernest or Philbeach could come in from the desert.

They thought of taking him back to the Van Niekerks' house in Pretoria, but Sarie pointed out that if anything did go wrong at Zwart Modder that was the first place at which the police would inquire for them. Any hotel, big or small, would be equally dangerous since the police would circularise their descriptions.

All sorts of suggestions as to a possible hiding-place were made but turned down as unsatisfactory for one reason or another, until Cornelius suddenly thought of a property which he possessed at Orchards on the outskirts of Johannesburg.

It was a furnished house which had been left to his father by an aunt who had died some four years earlier; instead of disposing of the property they had let it at a good rental to the representative of one of the big British Insurance companies in Johannesburg. Quite recently their tenant had been transferred to Shanghai, so the place was now furnished but empty, and there was nothing to prevent them from breaking in and lying low there for a week or two until Michael was quite recovered and any interest aroused by the returning ox-spans had died down.

At first the young doctor feared that Michael was in for brain fever, but his effective treatment and the careful nursing of the two girls saved the invalid from that danger; and, although he was still weak the doctor declared on the sixth day that he was fit to be moved. Having taken tickets for Pretoria and publicly announced their intention of proceeding there, Patricia, Sarie, Cornelius and Michael left Postmasburg, while Sandy took a train a few hours later in the opposite direction back to Upington.

There he hired a horse and rode up to Zwart Modder once more, securing a room at the inn where Sarie and the others had stayed.

He soon found that his fears regarding the police were only too well founded, for he had not been there half an hour before Captain Moorries called to see him. The Inspector of Police was a tall, broad-shouldered man with a long, thin nose, crisp hair and a frank, disarming manner.

He asked Sandy to have a drink with him at once and apologised for bothering him but no sooner had the drinks been served than he began a long series of shrewd questions.

Sandy had been in Zwart Modder for some days, three weeks before. He had been seen in conversation with various other rather unusual visitors to such an out-of-the-way spot. A tall, fair girl, for instance, who had been staying at the inn under the name of Aileen Orkney and who, if the landlord was right, Sandy had introduced to some other people one night in the bar as his wife. The other people, again according to the landlord who had been serving the drinks, were Sandy's cousins. Two middle-aged fellows and a youngster. All three had set off the following day in an out-span for Noro Kei and had not been heard of since. Then there had been another party who had made two visits to the place; an old man, a girl, a big, bluff fellow and two tough-looking characters. The lady reported as Sandy's wife, or Miss Orkney if he preferred, had been seen in conversation several times with this other lot until they too had set off into the blue. There was nothing illegal, of course, in all this, but Captain Moorries felt that the whole business was a little queer and he would be very much obliged if Sandy could let him know—just as man to man—what all the excitement was about.

Sandy endeavoured to satisfy the inquisitive officer while actually saying as little as possible, knowing that any lies he told might be held against him later. He said that, in the first place Miss Orkney was not his wife, that had been only a jest on his part; the three men to whom he introduced her were certainly his cousins but he had been most surprised to meet them in Zwart Modder. He had only seen them for a little while and had gathered that they were about to set off up-country on a hunting trip. He added that he knew nothing of the other party.

'Quite sure it was only hunting?' The Captain's close-set blue eyes smiled into Sandy's over the rim of his glass.

'What else could it have been?' Sandy inquired, with assumed innocence.

'It wouldn't be a little illegal prospecting by any chance, eh?' The other's smile broadened.

'I shouldn't think so for a moment,' declared Sandy emphatically.

'You wouldn't, eh? Yet one of those cousins of yours made

204

a very queer remark about it being a surprise to see you here after you had said in London that you didn't intend to have a cut at the "*you-know-what*".'

Sandy's smile never flickered, but inwardly he was squirming as he cursed his stupid indiscretion in having talked to the Bennetts at all in front of the landlord of the inn who obviously understood English perfectly well although he never spoke anything but Afrikaans. 'I was only referring to a copper proposition that I thought of going into with my cousins when I was in London,' he lied glibly. 'When they ran across me here they assumed that I'd decided to go into it on my own.'

Captain Moorries nodded. '*Ach*, yes, what was the name of the copper man that you were supposed to be staying with when you were here before?'

'I wasn't—I've already told you that I was only playing a joke on my cousins.'

'Where *were* you staying then?'

'I wasn't staying with anybody. I was camping out—just on a little holiday—that's all.'

'Queer place to take a holiday, isn't it?'

Sandy shrugged. 'Some people might prefer Muizenberg or Durban or Mossel Bay, but I happen to have rather a liking for solitude—that's all.'

'Ever heard of a witch doctor called Kieviet?' the Captain asked suddenly.

'Yes,' Sandy admitted after only a fraction of a second's hesitation. 'I'm rather interested in the indigenous races of South Africa, so while I was up here I visited one or two of the native kraals.'

'Know a little Hottentot called Ombulike?'

'Yes,' Sandy admitted again.

'It seems that all these other people are interested in the indigenous races of South Africa too.'

'Maybe. Have another drink?' Sandy set down his empty glass. 'There's nothing unusual in that. Most English visitors to the Union like to see something of the nigs in their native setting, don't they?'

'That's so. . . . Thanks, I'll have the same again—and, as you say, tourists in the Union may like to see the nigs, but they don't usually come out here with the names of a couple and go to a lot of trouble to hunt them up.'

'Well, I'm sorry, but I'm afraid that I can't enlighten you any further,' Sandy said evenly. Upon which the police officer swallowed his second drink and stood up.

'Staying here long?' he inquired just as he was about to depart.

'I don't know,' Sandy hedged. 'Just for a few days, I think.'

'Right-ho!' the other nodded. 'Perhaps I'll be seeing something of you a little later on.'

When Sandy went to bed that night he was extremely thoughtful. His encounter with Captain Moorries had shaken him quite a bit. The old man did not seem to know anything about their aeroplane, although one could never tell just what information the police did or did not possess. For a momemt apparently the Van Nierkerks were not under suspicion, but all the others very definitely were, and he foresaw a whole packet of trouble when Ernest and the Philbeach party arrived back.

It occurred to him then that the inquisitive Captain was probably having the track to Noro Kei watched, hoping to secure the suspects outside the dorp on their arrival before they had a chance to get in touch with anybody else and plant any stuff they might have. It was nine days now since he had last seen Ernest, so if all was well the chances were that he would be arriving on the following day. In consequence Sandy determined to be up by dawn and ride out towards Noro Kei in the hope of meeting him before he could be got hold of by the police.

Next morning he put his plan into execution and while it was still dark saddled his horse and rode out north-eastward into the Kalahari once more. Not having to moderate his pace to the slow, laboured progress of an ox-wagon, he made good going and descried, at half-past nine, an out-span approaching on the far horizon.

The probability was, of course, that Philbeach had kept his lead of Ernest and that this was his convoy, but that did not disturb Sandy in the least. Philbeach and Co. had been deprived of all their weapons, whereas he had his automatic on his hip and, knowing that he might meet them, had taken the extra precaution of slinging his rifle over his shoulder before he started out. As he neared the approaching company he noted that there were no horsemen with it. A native trudged some fifty yards in front, and then another—the voor-trekker—waving his long whip. Unless some accident had overtaken the mounts of Philbeach and his friends this must be Ernest's party after all, and so it proved to be.

Ernest was overjoyed to see him, for he had quite made up his mind that Sandy and the rest must have crashed somewhere behind him in those limitless miles of sand and prairie. Despite acute discomfort and a bout of fever from which he was suffering, he had pushed on in the hope of being able to organise a rescue party in Zwart Modder before the others died of thirst.

They out-spanned at once for the midday rest, during which Sandy told Ernest all that had happened and, between them, they concocted a story for Captain Moorries. If the police searched the whole outspan they would find no diamonds, so both felt reasonably certain that, after being questioned, they would be allowed to go. Then, having disposed of the ox-wagon and paid off the natives, they could proceed at once to the house outside Johannesburg where their friends were lying concealed.

At half-past three they in-spanned and moved on their way again, arriving at Zwart Modder by seven o'clock. Ernest had not seen Philbeach during his entire journey and so the two could only assume that he had struck off in another direction after reaching Noro Kei; but the big, red-faced adventurer had made the last stage of the trek in the early dawn and arrived at Zwart Modder shortly after Sandy had left it, passing him on a different track through the outskirts of the dorp.

As Sandy and Ernest entered the inn, Philbeach, with Darkie beside him, was leaning on the bar.

'Here they are!' he exclaimed to a third man, who was half-hidden behind the open door, a sudden smile of triumph lighting his coarse face.

The other was not Ginger, as Sandy had assumed in the twilight, but Captain Moorries. He stepped out into the open.

'So there you are, Mr. McDiamid. I've been hearing all about you and your friends this morning. It seems that, not content with illicit prospecting, you've been going in for robbery under arms. I've a warrant here for your arrest.'

25

Gandhi's House

Sandy had expected trouble; but to be arrested like this on a charge of highway robbery left him speechless and aghast. That Philbeach should have the audacity to lay any information after his own performance almost passed belief, but the tall Captain Moorries obviously meant exactly what he said and stood there, his hand resting upon the butt of his pistol, his tight mouth grimly shut, ready to act instantly should Sandy show the lest sign of attempting to resist arrest.

'Good God!' Sandy exclaimed, with an attempt at a laugh that broke off short in his throat. 'You can't be serious; you've no idea, Captain, who these toughs are.'

The police officer shrugged. 'They are perfectly legitimate prospectors and they've sworn an affidavit that, after their discovery of a new diamond field up in the Kalahari, you and some other persons held them up and robbed them of their samples.'

'What nonsense! They are no more prospectors than I am. Where's their licence?' Sandy mopped his brow.

'That is all in order,' declared the Captain, jerking his head in Darkie's direction. 'Mr. Rickhartz here has had a prospector's licence for some years, but I think you'd be well advised to keep anything that you have to say until you can say it to the magistrate in Upington.'

'Well, here's a go!' Ernest jerked up his chin and the Adam's apple wobbled in his excitement as he looked at the officer. 'Do I spend the night in Vine Street, too, or is it only my cousin that you're taking up before the beak?'

'Do you wish to charge this man as well?' the Captain asked, turning to Philbeach.

The big man shook his head. 'No, we've got nothing against Mr. Bennett—haven't set eyes on him since we left here best part of three weeks ago.'

'Very well.' Moorries relieved Sandy of his gun and touched him on the arm. 'You'll come along with me now and we'll put you inside the local lock-up for the night. You two,' he turned on Darkie and Philbeach, 'will be wanted day after to-morrow in Upington to give your evidence. So we'd best start all together round about seven to-morrow morning when I take McDiamid in.'

As Sandy was marched away Ernest caught his eye and, putting his fingers to his nose, made a rude gesture at the Captain's broad back.

Having watched their departure with a troubled look in his small, quick eyes, he demanded a drink of the landlord and, ignoring Darkie and Philbeach, carried it out on to the stoep, wondering what line of action he could adopt which would best help Sandy.

Following his cousin's lead, he had refrained from blurting out the truth, realising from all Sandy had told him since they had met that morning that any mention of the fact that they had secured diamonds must be rigorously kept from the police. Obviously, too, Sandy's intention was to take the brunt of the whole business upon his shoulders and, if possible, keep Michael and the Van Niekerks out of it.

Philbeach and Darkie would probably suborn their three native boys into supporting their evidence and, unless Sandy was prepared to involve his friends by calling them as witnesses on his behalf, it looked as though he was in an exceedingly tight corner.

At first he felt the only thing for him to do was go into Upington with the others and stand by in court, in case he was able to render any assistance. He did not know how the South African authorities would view such a charge and if they would allow bail or not. If so, he could offer to go surety for his cousin on a banker's reference. But would they accept him?

On second thoughts, however, it occurred to him that he could probably serve Sandy best by abandoning him for the moment and going as quickly as he could to the others at the address which, very fortunately, Sandy had given him in Johannesburg. Cornelius was a Dutchman and, into the bargain, the son of a judge, so he would be acquainted with the Law and far better able to decide what steps they should take.

Accordingly he got hold of the landlord's daughter, who did all the talking in English which was necessary in the little hostelry, and arranged through her the hire of a Cape cart and driver to take him into Upington the following morning. The matter was too urgent for him to waste a couple of days crawling back there in his out-span, and having seen the head boy Johnnie, he arranged to leave it parked in Zwart Modder for the moment.

Sandy spent a most miserable night of indecision and anxiety in the local gaol and early next morning was led out to mount his horse, which was attached to Captain Moorries' by a leading rein. With another officer, Philbeach and Darkie, the cavalcade started for Upington. Ernest took the same road an hour later in his hired trap.

It was a long day for both parties. Philbeach and Darkie

laughed and joked with the two policemen but as Sandy rode on hour after hour he became more and more despondent. Without telling the whole story and giving away the fact that Michael had actually secured a fine haul of diamonds—which would be immediately confiscated—he could see no way out of his wretched plight.

The Captain was a pleasant, kindly fellow, who provided him with drinks when they halted from time to time at the widely separated native stores, but could not resist the temptation to try and pump him. Having heard Philbeach's account of the plane and the party which it carried he was extremely anxious to get his hands on Sandy's confederates, and he felt quite convinced that if he could sift this matter to the bottom he would have a fine case of illicit prospecting and attempted diamond smuggling to his credit.

Sandy accepted the drinks and endeavoured to show his appreciation of the other's decency, but he kept a guard upon his tongue, fearing to be trapped into some statement which might involve the others; moreover, he was too mad against Philbeach to do more than pretend to any cheerfulness in his presence. Ernest, hot, dusty, anxious, and unable to exchange a word with his driver who talked nothing but Afrikaans, jogged on a few miles behind them.

At length as evening was closing in over the veldt with a magnificent sunset, they sighted the outlying farms of Upington. Sandy was taken to the police station. Philbeach and Darkie—warned to attend the court on the following day—took rooms at the *Gordonia,* while Ernest drove straight to the railway station.

Luck favoured him, for he found a train was leaving for De Aar under the hour and, having made a scratch meal at the station buffet, he boarded it with a feeling of immense relief that he was able to proceed on his way to consult the others so quickly.

Yet, although ten days had elapsed since his learning of it, the death of his brother struck him with renewed force now that he was safely back in civilised surroundings, and thoughts of his loss made him miserable throughout his lonely journey.

Arriving the following night in Johannesburg, he took a taxi straight out to the little house at Orchards and marched up the garden path to the highly-polished slab of stone before the front door, or rather the wire gauze construction which served for one, through which he could see a wide porch in which arm-chairs, a settee, and a gramophone were the principal furniture. Although he rang several times, there was no answer or sound of approaching footsteps so he stepped back a few paces and looked quickly about him.

The house was a one-storied building consisting of four rondavels—round white stucco replicas of the native hut—joined together by a large, square, central room. The whole was heavily thatched, so that its roof had the appearance in the distance of four conical hay-stacks set at the corners of one large square one. For a moment he was afraid that his friends must have left the place for some reason, but when he remembered that since they were living there in hiding they would naturally refrain from answering the front door, so he walked quickly round the side of the house, through a small orchard of orange, lemon, peach and nectarine trees, until he came on to a wide lawn, overlooking which he saw the back stoep, once more protected by wire gauze.

Here again no sign of occupation met his eye, but he had made quite certain from the taxi driver that this was the house he wanted so, feeling that if the others had gone they would be certain to have left some message there for Sandy, he put his shoulder against the wire door and heaved sharply until the flimsy lock suddenly snapped.

Inside he found a dining-room, upon the table of which four places were already laid for dinner. It was a lofty room, and in the semi-darkness he failed to notice that a partition which closed off the further half did not rise right up to the sloping ceiling. Picking up a silver candelabra he was just about to light it when he almost choked with fright. A voice had suddenly addressed him from out of the darkness six feet above his head.

'By Jove, it's Ernest.'

''Struth!' He looked up quickly. 'Is that you, Michael?

What the hell are you doing on the ceiling? You brought me heart right into me mouth.'

'We're in hiding and we wanted to make certain who you were,' Michael laughed. 'Switch on the light, old chap, you'll find them over there by the door.'

Considerably relieved, Ernest switched them on, and then he saw that beyond the partition a triangular loft occupied the portion of the roof which lay over the kitchen. The others were now scrambling down from it by means of an old iron folding ladder.

'Well, this is a rum place and no mistake,' he said after the greetings were over. 'Fancy having a loft leading on to the dining-room! Dirty, I call it!'

'This place is historic,' Sarie explained. 'Gandhi lived here once and he used to sleep up there with his goat.'

'Tell that to the marines!' Ernest winked a knowing eye.

'It's true,' Cornelius assured him. 'Gandhi used to sleep there, as Sarie says. He used to climb up that iron ladder to bed every night.'

'Go on!' Ernest protested. 'Gandhi's an Indian and not a South African nigger.'

'Perhaps. But he started all his stupid nonsense in this country, practised as a barrister her and this is the house he lived in . . . But where is Sandy?'

'Ah, now you've said a mouthful.' Ernest sank wearily into a chair and broke the news to them of Sandy's plight.

'The audacity of the brute,' exclaimed Michael when Ernest had done. 'After having robbed me himself! But we'll hoist him with his own petard now he has called in the law.'

'It's going to cost you your diamonds if you do,' Ernest remarked, 'and maybe they'll put us all in quod for illicit prospecting into the bargain.'

Cornelius shook his head. 'I don't think we need get wind up about that at the moment.'

'But we can't let Sandy be put in prison on a charge of robbery,' Sarie exclaimed. 'We's simply got to tell the truth and face the music.'

'Easy on, my dear,' her brother strove to pacify her excitement. 'Nobody is suggesting leaving Sandy in the lurch, but I don't think Philbeach and Co. will ever be able to sustain their charges. If you remember, I recognised Darkie as an ex-crook who had been sentenced by father and, when I go down to Upington and tell the authorities that, it is going to put quite a different complexion on the matter.'

'You'll have to explain what you were doing with your plane down there,' Patricia put in, 'and that doesn't seem to me as though it's going to be an easy job of work.'

Cornelius shrugged. 'I realise that, of course, but we must think out a really good story. After all, nobody apart from Philbeach's crowd have any proof that Michael actually succeeded in getting any diamonds. With luck, we may be able to persuade the police that we were only on an extended picnic to see something of the Kalahari, and that Philbeach has trumped up this charge through some old grudge against Sandy. The whole thing to me seems to hinge on our being able to wreck Philbeach's credit with the magistrate, and he's much more likely to believe me, as the son of Judge Van Niekerk, particularly as up to date I have had a perfectly clear record. All of you had better stay here and I will go down to Upington to-morrow.'

At this, the others exclaimed that they certainly ought to go too, in order to add their testimony to his, should it be necessary. But Cornelius was dead against that.

He maintained that it was all-important to keep the girls out of trouble if it were humanly possible, now that the law had taken a hand; that Ernest had a clean bill up to the moment, so it would be madness for him to get himself involved unless it was vitally necessary, and that Michael, having only just recovered from a very nasty illness, would be foolish at the present stage of events to face the tiring journey so soon after his recovery. He promised, however, that if the presence of any of them was urgently needed, he would wire from Upington.

After Cornelius had left them next morning, Ernest settled into the quiet routine of the little household. The place had several acres of garden and meadows attached to it; the whole property being fringed by a belt of pine trees planted originally as pit props for the mines. They were not overlooked by any of their neighbours and, apart from accident, might remain there for a considerable time without anyone guessing that the place was again being lived in.

Till now, in order to obtain stores without arousing suspicion in their own district, Sarie and Cornelius had walked to a different suburb each evening. In the daytime the two girls did most of the cooking and the chores while the men lazed in the garden, since it would have been highly indiscreet to risk hiring any native servants. Nevertheless, they had ample time to enjoy themselves, and their bruises, burns and sores acquired in the Kalahari were gradually healing. Day after day they sunbathed in the garden, protected from prying eyes by the long, pleached alley of vines on one side, and on the other by high banks of lemon verbena, salvias, gladiolas and dahlias which had been left by the late tenant. For hours they sat laughing, talking, sleeping and telling stories in the sunshine, while the gaily-coloured butterflies fluttered round them, their only anxiety the thought of what might be happening to Sandy and Cornelius.

More than a fortnight had elapsed since Patricia had lost her father and she was now recovered somewhat from the shock, while Ernest was gradually reconciling himself to the thought that he must order his future life without the help of that elder brother for whom he had had such a deep affection.

Sarie alone was restless and miserable. She was beginning to realise how much Sandy meant to her, and it gave her a new pang every time she saw Patricia and Michael stroll off together round the garden.

Now that he had succeeded in his quest Michael was bubbling over with plans for the re-establishment of Harcourt Priory on the grand scale and, for the time being while they waited news of Sandy, the cousins seemed to have tacitly barred any further reference to the close relationship which stood between them and happy marriage. Day after day they lingered, until the shadows fell, in a secluded corner beneath a lemon tree, oblivious of the call to dinner, laughing, talking, clasping hands and kissing between long intervals of blissful silence.

Meanwhile Cornelius had arrived in Upington, and to his satisfaction was allowed a short interview with the prisoner, at which he learned that Sandy had been brought up before the magistrate on the day that Ernest arrived in Johannesburg. He had been duly charged by Philbeach and Darkie but had applied for a postponement until his own solicitor could arrive from Cape Town to defend him. The request had been granted and the case adjourned for three days. He had wired to his lawyer who, arriving at De Aar Junction from the opposite direction within an hour of Cornelius, had come on to Uppington in the same train.

Cornelius then held a long interview with the solicitor at his hotel, in which they prepared an alternative defence for Sandy. A plea of 'not guilty' in the first instance and, if that failed, a decision to plead justification on the count of robbery should Sandy be sent up for trial, but when they came into court the following morning they found that their long deliberations had been quite unnecessary. Darkie and Philbeach were not present when the case was called and, since they failed to put in an appearance by three o'clock, to which time the magistrate had again adjourned it, the case was dismissed; Sandy's lawyer having given evidence as to his client's respectability, and an undertaking that he would appear again if called upon.

With a heartfelt sigh of relief Sandy left the court accompanied by his lawyer and Cornelius. Immediately they had had tea all three took the night-train back to De Aar, at which the lawyer left them to return south to Cape Town, while the two friends boarded the Johnnnesburg express.

They arrived at Orchards just before nightfall. Ernest and Michael gave them a rousing welcome and all four felt that the worst of their adventure was over. Michael had reached the 'Place of the Great Glitter', the others had helped him to get away with his precious haul, and Sandy had apparently managed to satisfy those dangerous police inquiries. It now only remained for them to lie low for a little bit, split up the diamonds, and each leave South Africa by a different route. They would meet again in London, on a date to be arranged, then Ernest's friend in Hatton Garden should be duly approached with a view to having the stones secretly cut in Amsterdam and placed on the market.

No sooner were the congratulations over than Sandy inquired for Sarie, and Michael told him that she had gone out with Patricia to secure their daily supply of necessities over in Rosebank before the shops shut for the night.

'You shouldn't have let them go alone,' said Cornelius sharply. 'I always went with Sarie when I was here.'

Ernest shrugged. 'Oh, they like being together without us men. Michael wanted to go but Patricia wouldn't let him, and I'm being a lily of the field these days—I work not, neither do I sin!' He laughed delightedly at his own jest.

'Sarie should have more sense,' said Cornelius abruptly. 'It will take them the best part of an hour to walk back here from Rosebank, and it will be dark before they turn up.'

'Well, what about it?' Ernest wanted to know. 'They're not kids to be frightened of the dark!'

'You don't understand,' cut in Sandy promptly. 'This is South Africa—not England—and white women should never be out after dark without their menfolk, because of the niggers.'

Michael looked quickly across at Cornelius. 'I thought you told me last week that you have a sort of curfew for natives and that they either have to be back by nightfall in their own settlement outside the town, or else in the houses if they're servants, unless they have a special permit signed by their master, who is responsible for their good conduct.'

'That's true,' Cornelius agreed. 'But there are always a certain number of bad blacks who evade the law and prowl round at night time, particularly out in these suburbs here. You must remember that we are the best part of five miles from the centre of the town.'

'Good God!' exclaimed Michael. 'You don't think there's a chance of any brutes like that attacking Patricia and Sarie, do you?'

'I don't think so,' Cornelius answered a little uncertainly. 'A white woman might leave her house after dark every night for a week and nothing would happen to her, because even out here, as you've probably noticed, every street is brilliantly lighted for that very reason, but on the other hand you never know, and I wouldn't even allow Sarie to walk up the street to post a letter after dusk.'

An uncertain, fretful silence descended on the party while they mixed drinks and waited, hoping every moment that they would hear the footsteps of the girls coming up the tessellated pavement of the garden path; but dinner time came and went, and they still had not put in an appearance.

By nine o'clock the men were seriously worried, and Cornelius muttered something about the Amalaitas.

'What's that?' Michael inquired.

'It is a Bantu word for a sort of secret society,' Cornelius replied, 'mostly composed of youths from the criminal section. It hasn't got any particular leader and is a nebulous sort of thing upon which nobody can put their finger. They roam about the streets at night with bicycle chains attached to the end of a long stick, which forms a most ghastly weapon. With one stroke of it they can practically sever your head from your body. Generally, they go for the black house-servants in the hope of robbing them of their wages, but every now and again you hear of them attacking whites.

'Stop!' cried Sandy, putting his hands over his ears. 'For God's sake, stop!'

By ten o'clock they had decided that although they were in hiding they must get into communication with the police. The telephone was cut off, the house being nominally unoccupied, but Cornelius got on to headquartes at a local telephone box and, ten minutes later, they were picked up by a police car, which took them all in to Johannesburg, where they made their despositions and gave full descriptions of the girls.

During the hours that followed, frantic with anxiety, they

were rushed by the police officers from place to place where dubious characters among the negro population were questioned, but all their efforts were unavailing. By morning, haggard and in the last stage of misery and apprehension, they were back at the house still without any news of Sarie and Patricia.

In a terrible despondency, they cooked a few eggs and knocked up a scratch breakfast, then, just as they were sitting down to it, the front door bell rang. All four left the table and ran to open it, thinking that it might be a policeman with some tidings, but it was only the postman who had dropped a single letter into the box and hurried away.

It was addressed to Michael. With trembling fingers he tore it open while the others crowded round him to read the few typed lines.

> 'By the time you get this both the ladies will have had an interesting night, but they seem to prefer your company to mine. If the feeling is mutual you will be at the White River Hotel, North Eastern Transvaal, at six o'clock to-morrow evening—bringing the stuff with you. If there is any funny business, or you fail to turn up, the little darlings won't be nearly so pretty when you do see them again.
>
> R.P.'

26

Illicit Diamonds

'Good God!' exclaimed Sandy. 'The swine!'

'Anyhow, they're safe,' Cornelius muttered. 'I've been picturing them with their throat cut after the Amalaitas had dealt with them.'

Michael put down the letter; his face had gone deadly white. 'But—what does Philbeach mean by both the ladies "had an interesting night"?'

'Don't worry,' Sandy comforted him. 'No harm can have come to them yet—there hasn't been time.'

'I should have thought there had been plenty,' Ernest said gruffly.

Cornelius picked up the envelope in which the note had been delivered. 'No,' he said, 'Sandy's right. This was posted last night in Johannesburg, immediately after Philbeach succeeded in netting the girls. He wouldn't risk staying in the town and since he's given us White River as a meeting place it's a thousand to one that they were on the road all night. It's every bit of two hundred and fifty miles to White River so they probably only got there early this morning.'

'Well, what are we going to do about it?' asked Ernest.

'Get a car and go up there right away,' Sandy replied promptly.

'Oh, hell!' Cornelius brought his fist down with a crash on the top of the gramophone that stood in the porch. 'To think that we've got to hand over the diamonds after all.'

'It's the only thing to do,' Sandy shrugged despondently.

'Oh, damn the diamonds,' exclaimed Michael. 'It's the girls I'm thinking of.'

Sandy gave a bitter little laugh. 'You're not the only one —so are we all. But I wonder how that devil Philbeach managed to run us to earth here?'

'Perhaps he shadowed you back from Upington,' Ernest suggested.

'No, he must have known before that,' Sandy said with conviction. 'The girls were already late when Cornelius and I turned up last night, so he must have sprung his trap for them just about the time we were coming out here in a taxi. He wouldn't have had the opportunity to prepare it if he had come in on the same train with us. It's much more likely that he shadowed you when you came up here five days ago.'

'How could he?' Ernest protested. 'He was spinning his yarn about you to the beak in Upington the morning after after I left.'

'I've got it—or at least, I think so.' Cornelius turned suddenly to Sandy. 'When you and Ernest met Philbeach at Zwart Modder Ginger wasn't with him, and I believe he had the whole thing figured out then. He planned to get you arrested and put you out of the way if he could, but he purposely refrained from charging Ernest—guessing that he would come straight to where ever we were hiding in order to let us know what had happened. While Philbeach was telling his story to the police at Zwart Modder, and you had gone out to meet Ernest on the last stage of his trek, Ginger was already on his way to Upington. Then he lay in wait there until Ernest arrived, and followed him up here on the same train. Directly he had traced Ernest to our hiding-place he must have wired Philbeach to join him in Johannesburg, and that is the reason why Philbeach failed to turn up to prosecute when you were brought into court the second time. If I'm right he would have had two clear days here in which to arrange the kidnapping of the girls.'

''Struth!' Ernest clapped him on the back. 'You *are* right, I'm certain of it. When I changed trains at De Aar I caught sight of a fellow in the distance who looked just like Ginger, but of course it never occurred to me that it could be him at the time. Then, when I drove out here from the station where was a yellow cab following behind which pulled up on the corner of this road about a hundred yards away just as I was paying off my driver. I'll bet a packet that was Mr. Ginger, too.'

'That's about it,' Sandy nodded, 'but we mustn't stand here talking. We've got to cover two hundred and fifty miles before six o'clock. I had better go along to the call box and phone up a garage for the best car we can get to be brought out here at once.' Without waiting for the others' assent, he pushed open the wire-covered door and strode off down the garden path.

'How about the police?' said Michael as Sandy's tall figure disappeared from view. 'Oughtn't we to let them know what's happened? They were awfully decent to us all last night.'

'Good God, no!' Cornelius made a shocked grimace. 'If you do that you'll have to give it away that we'ver got the diamonds, then we'll all be had on the illicit prospecting charge after all, and they'd confiscate the goods in the bargain.'

'What the hell does that matter, since we've got to give them up, anyway?'

'*Ach*, man! don't be an idiot. If the police get hold of the stones how shall we be able to ransom the girls? Philbeach will never let them go, if we can't hand over the plunder. At least, not until he has mutilated them first.'

Michael groaned and passed a hand over his tumbled, curly hair. 'I *can't* believe he'd actually do that.'

Cornelius's face softened as he saw the boy's distress. 'I'm afraid you don't know what these toughs are like.'

'I suppose you're right. Yet I wish we could have the police with us in this job because we've no guarantee that Philbeach will give us a straight deal.'

'None; we've just got to chance his good faith, but I don't think you need worry. It is the diamonds that he's after, and if we hand over those everything will be all right.'

Ernest nodded gloomily. 'You've said a mouthful, my boy. The police must be kept out of this. If they get wise to the fact that we've got those stones they'll take them off us, and if we fail to hand them over poor Sarie and young Pat will be properly sunk.'

Sandy rejoined them a few minutes later, with the information that he had secured a fast, open car, which would be
delivered to them in about twenty minutes, so they set about
making preparations for their departure. In case Philbeach
might try to trick them they thought it best to take their
pistols, but put them in a basket so that they would not
excite undue comment at places where they would have to
halt for petrol and a snack of food.

The car was duly delivered and handed over by the garage
man who had driven it out, then the four friends climbed in
and, with Sandy at the wheel, headed for Pretoria, Cornelius
having said, that, although it would involve a slight detour
on the first stage of their journey, this route should be quicker
on account of better roads.

The thirty odd miles of broad, metalled highway to the
capital of the Transvaal was covered in almost as many
minutes. The way was straight with an open view, traffic was
almost non-existent, and Sandy drove most of the time at
nearly eighty miles an hour.

As they flashed past the Military College at the entrance of
the city, Ernest leant over to Sandy. 'I say, you're not going
to drive like this all the way, are you? You're getting me
properly scared and I'm in a muck-sweat already.'

Sandy grinned back at him. 'No, don't worry. The road
gets absolutely filthy later on so I was taking advantage of
the only decent stretch you'll see to-day to get our average
up a little.'

Twenty minutes later Ernest saw that Sandy was right. A
few miles north of Pretoria the metalled road ended, giving
place to an equally broad stretch of reddish grit; but this, in
turn, came to an abrupt termination after another quarter of
an hour's driving, and the great highway to the north-east
dissolved into a narrow, rutted, stony track, which would
have disgraced a rural council even in a remote village of the
English shires.

Despite this, however, Sandy kept the car going at nearly
forty miles an hour—slithering over loose shale and dry-
skidding the corners by driving completely on his brakes in a

manner that alarmed Michael, who was beside him, and really terrified Ernest, who was in the back.

At ten o'clock they passed round the great crater of the Premier Diamond Mine and by eleven-thirty were taking in a fresh supply of petrol at Witbank, where the black dumps from the coal mines gave the place the gloomy appearance of some small Welsh mining town.

They were still in the heart of the high veldt, many thousands of feet above sea level, so the scenery continued to be monotonous and uninteresting. Long sweeps of rolling grass, mealie patches, or Kaffir corn were only enlivened now and again by a few lonely native rondavels and square mud huts, or occasionally a solitary tin-roofed farmhouse.

Skidding, jolting, and bumping in an alarming fashion, the car raced on, passing over a little patch of good road at Middelburg to fresh ruts, sometimes half a foot deep, on the far side of the town. At one-thirty they pulled up at the Transvaal Hotel in Belfast for lunch.

By two o'clock they were on their way again, making good going over slightly better roads, which wound now through hilly country. Sandy had hardly spoken during their five-hour journey, so oppressed was he by the thought of Sarie somewhere to the north-eastward down on the low veldt— hidden perhaps in some obscure shack at the mercy of Philbeach and his crew—but now he turned to Michael.

'In a few moments we'll be in Machadodorp.'

'What sort of a place is it?' asked Michael mechanically.

'It was the last headquarters of the Republican Government in the Anglo-Boer War. Oom Paul Kruger lived there for some time with his staff in a train on the railway siding. It was there that the famous Kruger sovereigns were struck in a primitive mint from the gold secured by the Boers from the mines on the Rand. A large quantity of it, which is supposed to amount to several million, has never been properly accounted for and it is said that it was secretly buried somewhere round here to prevent it falling into the hands of the British, before Kruger finally sought refuge over the Portuguese Frontier.'

'There is good trout-fishing in the mountain streams round here, too,' Cornelius added, 'and a hydro with radio-active thermal springs, so the place has become quite a popular holiday resort in recent years.'

Michael smiled at them appreciatively, realising that they were doing their best to ease the strain.

Five minutes later they were running through the main street of the small town, when a policeman suddenly stepped off the side-walk outside the Eastern Hotel and held up his hand for them to halt.

They were not speeding at the time, so it was with a sharp feeling of apprehension that Sandy brought the car to a standstill a few yards from the man. Next moment his worst fears were realised. The officer turned and bellowed: 'Here they are,' and Captain Moorries came out from the porch of the hotel.

He rubbed his long nose for a second and looked at Sandy with a half-suppressed grin. 'Made a pretty quick lunch back there in Belfast, didn't you?'

'Yes,' said Sandy briefly. 'What about it?'

'Only that we've had hell trying to catch you up all morning and it was the first chance we had to pass you. You're a pretty useful driver, I will say.'

'Catch us up?' Sandy echoed, feigning surprise, but with a sick realisation that his bluffing was useless. 'Why did you want to do that and what are you doing in this part of the world, anyhow?'

'Poor chap!' The Captain's grin broadened. 'You can't even guess, eh? Well, I'll dot the "i's" and cross the "t's"! You didn't think I was quite so slow as to let you get clear away like this—did you? It wasn't much trouble to follow you up to Johannesburg and sit on your tail until you thought you'd have a cut at running those diamonds out of the Union over the Portuguese border. Pull that car into the side of the road. Come on, now! I'm going to search the lot of you.'

27

The Road to Portuguese East

Michael's heart was pounding in his chest. This, then, was the end of the adventure. He had the diamonds round his body in a neat canvas belt that Patricia had made for him, and it was far too bulky for him to have any hope of concealing it. The police would take it from him now, and the lot of them would be escorted back to Johannesburg under arrest, while God only knew what awful fate would overtake Patricia and Sarie. Cornelius's words about Philbeach's threat to mutilate the girls had been ringing in his ears all the morning. While they had raced and bumped along those awful rutted tracks he had constantly forced his thoughts away from a picture he had once seen of a woman who had had her nose slit by Chinese bandits when her friends had failed to ransom her. If he had had his pistol handy the chances are that he would have shot the Captain in a desperate attempt to escape and ended his days on a South African scaffold, rather than leave Patricia to be the victim of Philbeach's horrible threat. He half rose but was suddenly jerked backwards into his seat; Sandy had been visualising his Sarie undergoing similar horrors and, with a quick resolve not to surrender without a struggle, he slipped in his clutch and the car shot forward.

The policeman, who was standing by the near front wheel, leapt backwards. Captain Moorries yelled something after them which they did not hear, and the next moment they were racing out of the town down into the dip, past the thermal springs, and up the other rise.

Cornelius leant over and bellowed in Sandy's ear: 'They've got a car, so they'll be after us in a moment. Our only chance is to take by-roads.'

'Is there one soon?' Sandy shouted back.

'Yes—I know this country well—you'd better let me drive.'

'Right.' Sandy brought the car to a stop on a level stretch and less than half a minute was occupied in changing seats. Then the car leapt forward again.

Two miles further on, Cornelius took the right-hand turn at a fork, and in a few moments their dust-cloud was hidden by the winding road and rocky hillsides from the police car which they felt certain must now be following.

The track which they had taken was worse, if possible, than the so-called main road. Every mile or so they came to a sudden steep gully which cut across it—the dry beds of narrow streams which would be filled with water in the rainy season. Each time they crossed one the car bumped with such violence that Michael feared the springs would break, although Cornelius slowed down to ten miles an hour whenever he saw one ahead and yelled a warning to Ernest and Sandy in the back. The latter was clinging desperately to the side of the car, but was constantly jerked bodily six inches from his seat.

Their speed was necessarily much reduced by this difficult driving, but they had at least the satisfaction of knowing that the police car could not be gaining ground upon them even if its occupants had spotted their tyre marks in the dust where they had left the main road. But Cornelius was hoping that Captain Moorries believed them to have taken the road towards Barberton—which was the highway to the frontier, or else going round by Schoemans Kloof and Nelspruit.

Half-an-hour after he had taken the wheel they passed the little village of Waterval Boven and flashed into a tunnel through which the road disappeared into a solid mass of mountainous rock.

The roar of the engine reverberated like thunder and the lights of the car showed ghostly on the rocky walls as they wound through the pitchy darkness of the curving tunnel until they sped out into sudden daylight at the further end.

'Coo!' exclaimed Ernest, wriggling his neck above the open collar of his shirt. 'We'd have been properly for it if we'd met anything coming the other way in there.'

No one replied to him, for the others were all too busy wondering if they had thrown the police off their trail but, even in that desperate situation, Michael could not help marvelling at the amazing panorama which was now spread before them.

As the car came out of the heat of the mountain he saw that the road wound away for miles in the distance, curving in and out on the hillside like the Corniche above the Mediterranean. The same sheer wall of rock rose on one side but instead of a blue sea upon the other there was a steep valley overhung by great rocky *krantzes,* at the bottom of which—parallel with the winding road—rushed the white waters of a foaming river.

The way shelved steeply as it curved round the rocky bends, and for mile after mile the car raced on down a seemingly endless slope until, in the short space of twenty miles, they had dropped no less than four thousand feet.

It had been sufficiently warm for them to remove their coats during the morning when they were running through the grassy uplands, but now in this low veldt it was stiflingly hot, so that even the breeze made by the passage of the car failed to cool them. The scenery was very different from that which they had passed earlier in the day. Great patches of cactus, aloes, and centry-plant lined the road, and for the first time Michael and Ernest saw something of the real African bush. Low, straggling, flat-topped thorn trees mixed with a dozen species of acacia and wattle, hemmed them in on every side and occasionally they passed a weird-looking tree which Sandy said was called Euphobia. It had a smooth, round trunk, from the top of which masses of prickly arms stretched up, giving it the appearance of a gigantic cactus on one leg.

At times the track almost disappeared in patches of giant grass standing ten or twelve feet high, which rustled on the coachwork as the car forced its way between them. Every now and again they had to duck their heads in order to avoid the branches of some tree which hung low over the track, and the infuriating runnels which crossed the road became more frequent, many of them now, on this low level, having a foot or more of rushing water flowing through them.

At half-past four they bumped their way to a halt outside a native trading station near Elandshoek, as Cornelius was now a little uncertain of his way and felt it best to inquire there before going any farther. The English owner of the store received them most hospitably and offered to take them up to his house behind the store to give them tea, but they dared not linger, and after he had given them full directions they pushed on immediately.

For another half-hour they jolted and bumped along by ways that curved in and out through patches of thorny shrub and dense grass, above which myriads of butterflies hovered. Twice they crossed a bend in the Crocodile river, then at last they regained the main road, which twisted now like a snake in and out of the sweltering, oppressive valleys. They passed Nelspruit and, rising to the higher ground again, at last pulled up outside the hotel at White River.

It was a pleasant, one-storied building. Several groups of smart-looking people in semi-tropical kit sat drinking at little tables in the long stone stoep which overlooked a semi-circular drive where a number of cars were parked.

Michael and Ernest were astonished to find so civilised a hostelry out here in the wilds after their experience of the little inns at Postmasburg and Zwart Modder, but, Philbeach not having put in an appearance, Cornelius explained the reason while they sat down to a round of badly-needed drinks.

'This is the jumping-off place for the Kruger Park,' he said, 'so lots of wealthy people come up here to stay while they see our national beauty spot.'

'Park, eh?' Ernest raised his eyebrows. 'Seems a queer kettle of fish to have a park out here to me. Plenty of open spaces without going to that expense.'

'Oh, it's not the sort of park that you're thinking of.' Cornelius laughed for the first time that day. 'It is the great game reserve, and there are eight thousand square miles of it. You could motor through it for a week without ever passing over the same track twice. It is bigger than the whole of Wales, you know.'

'Go on!' Ernest gasped. 'That's a park-and-a-half, and no mistake. What sort of game have they got in it?'

'Everything—lion, leopard, hippo, giraffe, wildebeeste, zebra, impala, baboon, sable, eland, kudu, and most of the other animals that went into the Ark.'

'It must cost them a pretty penny in iron bars,' remarked Ernest thoughtfully, 'if this place is the size you say.'

There aren't any. The animals live in their natural state and the lions make their kill each night. You see them standing right in the roadway sometimes when you're passing through it slowly in a car.'

'Lumme! I'd be scared to motor through a place like that.'

Cornelius smiled. 'They would never attack you unless you were fool enough to leave your car. They don't take any notice of strangers now because they've learnt that in this great area nobody is ever allowed to shoot them.'

Ernest nodded. 'I see. But eight thousand miles is a pretty fat chunk of country. I would like to have had the contract to do the fencing.'

'It's not fenced. They only have toll gates on the roads into it to collect a guinea a car from people who want to go in.'

'Well, you do surprise me. What happens if the wild beasts break out?'

'They do at times. Just like human beings, they're fond of a change of diet, so, when the lions get tired of antelope and buck, they come down from the reserve on the look-out for an ox or a nigger, and sometimes half-a-dozen of them will roam a district outside it for two or three weeks until they're shot.'

Sandy glanced at his wrist-watch. 'I wonder what has happened to Philbeach? It's just on six.'

'Yes,' Michael nodded, and sank his voice to a whisper, 'we should look pretty silly if the police have been following us and they drove up and caught us sitting here.'

'Oh, there's no fear of that,' Sandy assured him. 'This place is virtually a dead-end which leads nowhere. We left the main road at Nelspruit, so I think we can fairly safely say that we have thrown them off the track.'

As he finished speaking, a large, closed car drove up, with Philbeach sitting in the driver's seat. He caught sight of them at once and beckoned for them to come down to him in the drive, so Sandy paid the white-coated Malay waiter for their drinks and the group walked down the steps towards him.

'Have you got them?' he shot gruffly at Michael.

'Yes.'

'All right, but it's wisest not to hand them over here. Jump in the car and we'll move off a quarter of a mile down the road.'

'Just as you wish,' Michael answered, climbing into the seat beside him.

Sandy pulled open the door at the back, upon which Philbeach threw over his shoulder: 'You coming too?'

'Yes—have you any objection?'

'No, I don't give a cuss. You're too scared about what might happen to your women to try and do me any harm. So you can all come, if you like.'

The others followed Sandy into the back of the car and then Philbeach drove the party half a mile down the slope, until they halted on the edge of one of the great citrus plantations which thrive all round the district.

'Now,' he said, 'Come on, hand them over.'

But Michael shook his head. 'Nothing doing. We want the girls first.'

'Don't worry your head about that, little Galahad,' Philbeach said, with a touch of sarcasm in his voice. 'You stay here at White River and the two love birds shall be delivered back to you safe and sound by this time to-morrow night.'

'That's no good,' Sandy cut in. 'You're not getting a single pebble of those lines. You've got to take us to the girls or else bring them here; then we'll hand over the stones to you —but not before.'

'Likely, isn't it?' Philbeach sneered. 'Then, when I've got the diamonds you'd call in the police before I was a hundred yards away. Have me pinched for running them, and charge me with kidnapping into the bargain, probably. You've got to hand the stuff over now. If you don't I'll leave you here, and follow a fine old Chinese custom of sending you two nice little pink ears in a box by post to-morrow morning.'

'You swine!' Michael half-rose from his seat but Cornelius grabbed him by the shoulder and pulled him back.

'Look here!' he said. 'It's obvious that we don't trust each other, but we've got to fix this business some way, and we're not giving up the stones unless we get the girls. We haven't got the police with us now and if we follow you in our car we shall have no chance of getting in touch with them, so why not lead us to the place where you've got them hidden and we'll make the exchange there.'

Philbeach considered for a moment, then he nodded. 'Yes, I don't see any objection to that. You've not to come armed, though. I'm not taking any chance on you holding me up.'

'We couldn't carry a gun in this kit without you seeing it —could we?' Sandy said sarcastically. 'But what about you?'

Philbeach's small eyes flashed over the shirts and breeches of the party. 'No, that's true—and I haven't got one. You can search me if you like.'

Cornelius took him at his word and patted him over but he was not carrying a weapon. 'Better drive back to the hotel for us to pick up our bus then,' he said, when he had done.

Ten minutes later the two cars were on the road again, heading back to Nelspruit. Yet for a long time they hardly seemed to increase their distance from the rugged outline of the Logogotu mountain, which, like a vast crouching lion, dominates the whole White River district for many miles around.

Outside Nelspruit, Philbeach pulled up and told the others that they must follow closely because he meant to take a cross-country track through the bush to Kaapmuiden which would save them going all the way round by Barberton. They entered another wild area of the low veldt, and experienced again the violent jolting in crossing the gullies which seemed to occur with even greater frequency than in the early after-noon. The scenery round them was wooded and mountainous.

Here and there a lonely farmstead or plantation was to be seen far below them in a fertile valley but in the next hour they passed another vehicle and only half a dozen niggers plodding along the dusty road.

By nine o'clock Sandy began to wonder if Philbeach had managed to take the girls over the Portuguese border, for they were now nearing the town of Komati Poort, but just outside it Philbeach left the main road again for another track. It sloped downhill at first through tangled, wooded country and then wound in and out along the west bank of the broad Komati river. The sun had set and the evening light made the scene of rock-strewn waters and wild bushland dim about them. After a couple of miles the track ended at a tumble-down shack which looked out on a bend in the river, and, driving up to within ten yards of it, Philbeach stopped his car and got out. The others followed suit and walked over to him.

'This is the place,' he said when they came up, 'so let's get it over without any more delay.'

'All right,' Michael agreed, pulling down the top of his trousers and untying the canvas belt that held the stones. 'Where are the girls?'

Philbeach was grinning as he leaned negligently up against the side of his car. 'I had a hunch you wouldn't trust me sufficiently to pass the stuff over at White River. That was only a try-on because I didn't want to give away this hide-out if I could avoid it.'

'Oh, never mind that!' said Sandy impatiently, but Philbeach seemed in no hurry now and went on quietly:

'Fine country round here, isn't it? I knew it well in the old days and why I stuck in London all those years I just can't think.'

Michael eyed him angrily. 'I could give a darn good guess but we're not interested in your record. We want to get this business done.'

'Mighty anxious to see young Pat again, aren't you, Galahad? And you've got taste—you have. I like that kid myself; I like Sarie, too; she's got something of the same look about her in a queer sort of way, but there isn't a woman living who's worth what you've got in that belt.'

'Come on,' Michael urged. 'Let's see them and you can have it.'

Philbeach jerked his head backwards in the direction of the hut. 'They're tied up in there. You can go in and see if you like.'

'Thank God!' The thought of Patricia dominated every other consideration in Michael's mind, and, still clutching the precious belt, he dashed towards the shack.

Sandy and Ernest followed, but the latter pulled up with a jerk as Cornelius, suddenly suspicious of a trap, cried:

'Wait!—let him bring them out.' Then, rounding on Philbeach: 'Where are Ginger and Darkie Rickhartz?'

'Pleased ter meet you, Mister Van Niekerk,' Darkie answered for himself, stepping out from a tangle of nearby bushes with his pistol at the ready. 'Stick 'em up or you're for it—you bloody judge's pup.'

Michael had already thrust open the rough door of rotting timbers and stood outlined against the lingering light, peering into the pitchy darkness of the hut. Almost as Darkie spoke, another voice came from the black interior. 'I got you covered an' if you raise a finger I'll drill you.' Then Ginger emerged, forcing him back towards the others with a levelled pistol.

They were trapped and helpless. For one wild moment Sandy thought of making a desperate attack on Philbeach, who was still lounging against the side of his car, but he knew that these men would shoot him down without the slightest cumpunction. In this wild region even his body might not be discovered for many days.

He cursed his folly for having trusted Philbeach even an inch, and for having been taken in by the man's blarney about neither party carrying arms. If they had not all been half-stupified by their long day and the terrible night of anxiety which had preceded it, they would have taken Darkie and Ginger into their calculations. The saliva running hot in his mouth with the desire to kill, yet retaining just enough sanity to prevent himself committing virtual suicide by hitting out, Sandy raised his arms slowly to the level of his shoulders. Then he watched Philbeach snatch the belt containing the stones out of Michael's hand.

'Damn it,' cried Michael, wrought to the pitch of utter desperation. 'Take the blasted things—I promised them to you, didn't I? But for God's sake keep your part of the bargain and lead us to the girls.'

'Not on your life,' Philbeach snarled with sudden savagery. Then, his mood changing in an instant, he laughed and added: 'But you needn't worry about their faces. They're much too pretty to spoil. I've had a crush on that little Patricia of yours for a long time now, and Ginger is so matey with Sarie that you just can't keep the two of them apart. Those little birds are in a special cage I've got and they're going to sing for *us* to-night.'

28

Night in the Fever Country

'Keep them covered, Darkie, while we see to the boat.' Philbeach gave a last contemptuous glance at the four friends and, with Ginger beside him, walked the thirty yards to the river's edge.

'How much will you take to change sides?' Sandy whispered, with the sudden inspiration of suborning Darkie immediately Philbeach was out of earshot.

'Nothing you could pay me!' Darkie retorted swiftly, and next moment a hail from the shadows where the bank sloped to the broad waters of the Komati told him that the others were ready to make the crossing.

'Move a foot and you'll get it—understand?' he said menacingly, then he began to back away.

When he had covered a third of the distance he flourished his gun in a final warning and, turning his back on them, broke into a trot.

With the same thought in their minds, Cornelius and Sandy instantly dashed for their car. Another moment and they had pulled their automatics from the basket and were blazing away at the running figure which was now within ten yards of the bank.

Darkie swung on his heel and his pistol cracked once— then with a sudden lurch, he fell.

'Fling yourselves flat,' Cornelius yelled to Michael and Ernest, who were still standing by the ruined shack.

The warning came none too soon; Philbeach and Ginger had opened fire from the river. A bullet thudded into the woodwork of the ramshackle building and two more pinged into the body of the car behind which Sandy and Cornelius were crouching.

Michael sprang up a moment later and ran to them, secured his gun, and joined in the action.

In the growing darkness it was difficult for any of the combatants to see each other. Darkie's huddled form showed vaguely on the bank where he had fallen. The canoe lay below it, hidden from sight. Vague patches of whiteness showed, where the swift river foamed and tumbled over the jagged rocks which broke its surface and beyond, the dark trees which fringed the Portuguese side.

'Hold your fire,' Cornelius ordered. 'They've either got to come ashore if they mean to take Darkie with them or push out into the river—we'll get them then.'

Philbeach and Ginger also ceased fire. They had no intention of risking their skins to save Darkie whether he was dead or only wounded. Both were busy pulling the canoe, hand over hand, farther down stream under shelter of the bank.

'I don't like it,' Sandy exclaimed after the tense silence had lasted for a few moments. 'They may have come ashore and be crawling round behind us.'

Cornelius gave a swift glance into the dark bush over his shoulder. 'Best run for the hut,' he muttered, 'then we'll have something to protect our backs.'

'Where's Ernest?' asked Michael suddenly.

'God knows! He funked it, I suppose—come on,' and the three of them left their cover in a quick dash for the shack.

Once they were inside it and had wedged the door behind them, Sandy struck a match. There was Ernest crouching in a corner, his face white and scared, his eyes nearly popping out of his head.

'It's all right, old man,' said Sandy kindly. 'Now we're in here together we've got the whip hand and they won't chance making an attack; we could pot them from the windows. Keep your head down, though, in case they try to snipe us.'

'I should think they're half-way across the river by now,' Cornelius said quietly. 'After all, they've got the diamonds and that's what they came for.'

'But what the devil shall we do now?' Michael's voice rang with all the bitter anguish that he was feeling. Patricia's face, desperately imploring him to help her, was before his mental eyes. Sandy suppressed a groan as he thought of Sarie somewhere in that trackless forest on the far side of the river, about to suffer unthinkable horrors at the hands of the semi-halfcaste, Ginger.

'If only we had our passports and proper visas we might at least cross into Portuguese East by Komati Poort, but without them we can't even do . . .'

'Got you,' snapped a voice, and they swung round to see a pale blob of white face above a pair of broad shoulders against the faint light in the empty square of window.

'Put your hands up and no nonsense,' the voice went on. 'We are the police,' and as the man ceased speaking they saw that a pistol barrel rested on the sill—holding them covered.

There was a sound of quick footsteps and the door was thrust roughly open. Three other officers entered and one flashed a torch over them. Suddenly it came to rest on Sandy's face.

'Well, I'll be damned,' exclaimed the man who held it. 'If it isn't McDiamid. This is a bit of luck.'

'Hello, Moorries! so you've turned up again,' said Sandy bitterly, 'but if you're hunting for diamonds you're still on the wrong track.'

'Diamonds, *and* other things,' the Captain laughed grimly. 'Come on outside, so that we can have a look at you.'

They followed him from the shack, where the police relieved them of their weapons and searched them. Then, with a disappointed grunt Moorries pointed to Philbeach's big closed car. 'That's what brought me here. It was stolen in Johannesburg last night and as I was up in this area, headquarters told me to keep a look-out for it. When I was making inquiries for you I heard that it had passed through Nelspruit an hour and a half ago then I managed to trace it down here. Where's the bird who was driving it?'

'Over the river by now,' Cornelius told him. 'He's been gone about ten minutes.'

The Captain grunted. '*Ach!* that's a pity. I'm not allowed to follow him into Portuguese East.'

'I wish to God you could,' exclaimed Michael. 'He's got those diamonds that . . .'

'You seem to think we've been handling,' Sandy cut in loudly. 'He's had them all the time. He actually showed them to us to-night and the charge he brought against me was only a put-up job to throw dust in your eyes.'

'It's that big guy, Philbeach, that you're talking of, then?' Moorries took him up quickly. 'Why the hell didn't you let me know before?'

'I wasn't certain of it, and the truth is I've got an old score against the man that I wanted to settle personally without bringing in the police.'

'If you want the diamonds, for God's sake why not go after him?' Michael urged. 'He's got them on him.'

'I can't.' The Captain shook his head. 'I've already told you that I'm not allowed to cross the border.'

'Listen, man,' Cornelius broke in, 'there's more to it than the diamonds. McDiamid has just told you that we've a long-standing quarrel with this man and he's had the best of it altogether. He kidnapped my sister and another girl in that car last night and he's got them somewhere over there in the bush. We're sick with fear as to what may be happening to them. You've simply got to help us.'

'Those would be the two women reported lost in Johannesburg last night,' Moories nodded. 'I only heard about that just before I left this morning. That's pretty tough on you, I must say, but even so my hands are tied. I can't work the far side of the frontier.'

'Oh, for God's sake!' Michael pleaded. 'We're half-crazy with anxiety. That swine told us before he pushed off in his boat that he'd got them in a nice little cage and he was going to make them both sing to-night. Can't you understand what *that* means?'

'What's that you say—cage?' The Captain's eyes brightened suddenly. Then he went on half-reminscently: 'Could it be the same man, I wonder—but no—it's ten years since we heard anything of him. Yet now I come to think of it the description fits this chap from what little I remember.'

'Are you thinking of the Gorilla?' one of the other policemen broke in.

'Yes. Remember that hide-out that he had up in a tree, somewhere down in the fever country, that all of us knew about but none of us could ever find? He used to have women down there, too, in his "cage", as he called it.'

'There's a warrant still out for him over the Brendon killing,' the other man went on.

'Yes,' murmured Moorries. 'I'd give a lot to get my hands on *him*.'

Together Sandy and Michael began to plead again with the Captain that he should take some action but he still shook his head.

'I'm not allowed out of the Union, I keep on telling you; and even if I were none of us have got the least idea where his hang-out is. We might search those swamps and forests for a year without coming on it.'

'There's just a chance that I might be able to produce somebody who could lead you there,' said Cornelius suddenly. Then he ran off at a quick limp to the place where Darkie lay and, seizing him by the shoulder, turned him over on his back.

'Oh, hell!' groaned the wounded man. 'For Christ's sake be careful of my leg.'

'Thank God you're alive, anyhow,' Cornelius muttered in a swift whisper, 'but you're not going to be for long unless you listen to me. The police are up there at the shack now, and you're going to lead us to Philbeach's hang-out on the other side of the river—understand? If you don't, I swear to you by my mother's grave that I will kill you, even if I swing for it afterwards.'

Darkie dragged himself painfully into a sitting position. 'So that's the ticket, eh? Anyhow, there's no need to imperil your immortal soul on my account. The Gorilla left me here, didn't he?—the skunk! and if you'd cleared off, the lions that come down here at nights out of the Reserve would have got me, like as not. I'll learn him to go back on a pal.'

The others had hastened after Cornelius and as they approached he looked up swiftly. 'Here's you man, Darkie Rickhartz—Philbeach *is* the Gorilla—and he's just promised to lead us to his cage. Surely you'll have a cut at getting him now.'

Moorries considered for a moment, then, with sudden determination in his voice, he said: 'All right. It's worth taking a chance of trouble with the powers that be to bring the Gorilla in. But where did *this* chap come from? And how did he get shot?'

'We'll tell you all about that in a moment,' said Sandy hastily, 'but let's get him to the car. Every moment counts now and I'm frantic with anxiety about the girls.'

Darkie was wounded in the thigh and bleeding badly, but they staunched the blood and bandaged him up as well as they could while he cursed them for their trouble. Then they carried him groaning to Sandy's car, where he was propped up between Ernest and one of the policemen in the back.

Moorries agreed to the three friends receiving back their

weapons and since Ernest was now the only unarmed member of the party Darkie's pistol was handed over to him. The Captain climbed in beside Sandy and the others piled into the police car, which had been left a hundred yards down the track.

During the short drive back to Komati Poort Sandy satisfied Moorries' inquiries for the moment, then the car halted on the road below the Emigration Officer's hut.

Moorries alighted and spoke for a few moments with a tall, thin young man in khaki shirt and riding breeches. The others could not hear what he was saying, but would have been interested to know that he had invented a little story on his way from the shack, to the effect that some dangerous characters were endeavouring to escape from the Union over the river a few miles lower down and that he wished to post his men on the Portuguese side to head them back. He had made up his mind that he was justified in being a little unorthodox now that he had a real chance to get the Gorilla.

The officer asked who the other people were in the two cars, and the Lieutenant declared them to be plain clothes police. He was a kind-hearted fellow and, having witnessed Sandy and Michael's cruel distress, had not the heart to make them wait for him in Komati Poort.

The frontier officer agreed that as far as he was concerned they might go through, but that the Captain must take his chance with the Portuguese authorities.

Agreeing with a quick nod, Moorries jumped back into his seat and the cars ran down a slope, across the river, and up the farther bank. A mile farther on they pulled up again, still on South African soil, before the Customs Officer's house. He passed them promptly and a native policeman jumped on the step of the leading car to pilot them through the actual frontier posts.

Running down the steep hill that constitutes the short natural zone they entered the little town of Ressano Garcia. Another five hundred yards and they halted again before a two-storied building. This time they all left the cars and filed into a bare, lofty room, furnished only with a couple of

241

tables and a collection of native weapons on the white-washed walls.

Here a swarthy but good-looking young man, clad in a magnificent suit of brightly-coloured silk pyjamas, received them. He was extremely courteous to the police but dubious about allowing the others to proceed until Michael, to everybody's surprise, suddenly addressed him in Portuguese and gave him a rapid outline of the true situation.

For a moment the young official hesitated between annoyance that the South African police should have attempted to fool him, and the innate chivalry of the Latin races when it is a case of beauty in distress.

Chivalry won, and pouring out a torrent of grandiloquent expressions of sympathy and goodwill towards Michael, he stamped cards for them and with a flourish sped them upon their way.

Under two minutes the cars were out of the little township set down in this sparsely inhabited portion of Africa, so different with its continental atmosphere from those on the Union side of the river. The road now lay straight and wide before them, an altogether superior highway to those frightful tracks over which they had been driving for so many hours during that long day.

The headlights cut a gleaming path through the dark, tree-lined road, and only the roar of the engines broke the hot stillness which, like the miasma which emanates from the malarial marshes, hung over the whole of that fever-stricken country.

Three miles out of Ressano Garcia, Darkie turned to the policeman who was supporting him on one side. 'Tell him to turn left a hundred yards after we've passed the big tulip tree that we'll be coming to in a minute,' he muttered; 'it's only a track so he'd best slow down or else he'll miss it.'

The policeman leant over and spoke to Sandy, and soon the cars were lurching from side to side through a narrow opening in the dense scrub. Alternately they wound along comparatively flat stretches and then dived headlong down short steep slopes to plough through water splashes at the bottom and shoot up the other sides. Between the fever trees thorn bushes and acacias they glimpsed patches of cloudless starlit sky, yet with the coming of night no cool breeze relieved the suffocating atmosphere. Their chins were already covered with the abnormal growth of bristly stubble which comes from a long day spent in torrid heat. Their shirts were sticking to their backs with the perspiration that still oozed from them, and as they were bucketed from their seats by the continuous jolting of the car their limbs were sore and aching from fatigue. After a couple of miles Darkie gave the word to halt and the Captain descended from the car.

'It's about half a mile from here,' Darkie muttered painfully, 'and the going's terrible. I don't see how I'm going to make it but you'll never find the place unless I do.'

'We must carry you,' said Sandy quickly. 'We'll make a sling out of the car rug for you to sit in.'

Darkie was still bleeding badly but they adjusted his bandages and, carried by two of Moorries' burly policemen, he gave them fresh directions. Then the whole party set off into the bush.

It was a nightmare journey. The Captain led, thrusting his way steadily between great creepers and tall grasses. Darkie was carried next and Michael and Sandy, despite their terrible impatience, were forced to bring up the rear with Cornelius, Ernest, and the fourth policeman. Everything they touched seemed imbued with some special malice against them. The thorny bushes tore their clothes, the grasses that they thrust aside cut their fingers and poisonous nettles stung them as they brushed them from their way.

Every now and again a quick rustle in the undergrowth told of the wild life which was all about them, and every hanging branch under which they had to stoop their heads seemed, as Moorries' torch flashed upon it, to bear a hanging snake. The dead weight of the stifling fever-laden air pressed upon them, and a cloud of malarial mosquitoes hovered, dancing in the little patch of light which stood out like some supernatural halo, where Moories led the way through the all-pervading blackness; and as though their present bodily and mental distress was not sufficient an occasional coughing roar from the far distance told them that lions were out.

The half-mile through that ghastly, pitch black bush seemed never ending, but at last Darkie told Moorries to put out his torch and they came to the edge of a wide clearing lit by the dim starlight. In its centre, a hundred yards from where they were standing, rose a solitary tree. It was a wild fig, centuries old and of immense dimensions.

From where they stood, concealed on the edge of the bush, they could see nothing at first to indicate that it held the cage of the Gorilla, but as they peered towards it they saw that a faint light showed at one spot about thirty feet up between the thick foliage of the branches. Cautiously moving out from their hiding-place they made a complete circuit of the clearing, seeking the best position to attack, but when they again reached the spot where they had started Moorries shrugged despondently.

'We'll never get him alive in a place like that and we'll be lucky if he and his friend Ginger don't kill half of us if we rush in. I'm scared, too, that the moment he knows we've found him he'll slit the throats of both the women.'

At that moment a thin, hesitant contralto came to them from the tree—clear in the silence of the night. The voice had melody but it was full of tears and after a few bars it choked upon a sob of heartrending distress.

Sandy, standing there with his nails biting into the palms of his hands and the sweat streaming down his face, recognised the voice instantly—and the song. It was Sarie being tortured into singing 'Sarie Marais'. Preparatory to carrying out his other threats, Philbeach was indeed making the caged birds sing.

29

The Caged Birds Sing

With a choking cry Sandy sprang forward, but Moorries tripped him and he pitched his length into the long grass. Another policeman grabbed Michael, who also tried to dash towards the tree, by the collar of his shirt.

'You fools!' the Captain muttered angrily. 'D'you both want to be shot out of hand?'

'We've got to risk it,' Michael panted. 'Listen!—that devil is torturing them up there.'

Again Sarie's voice came to them across the clearing and then another joined it, Patricia's, uneven—sobbing—and a little out of tune.

'Let me go. I can't bear this any longer,' Michael almost wailed. His hands were quivering, his lips white and his eyes nearly starting out of his head.

'God! If only I could think of a way to get him down from that tree,' muttered Moorries desperately.

'You'll be mighty clever if you do,' Darkie murmured, with impartial interest, but next moment Cornelius had swung upon him:

'By thunder, I've got it! and you're going to do it for us. We'll carry you out and leave you just underneath it—then you must call up to him. He'll think that you've managed to make your way back here in spite of your wound and they'll both come down to carry you up.'

'An' what about me?' said Darkie gruffly, 'he'll shoot me the second he finds out that I've double-crossed him.'

'I'll shoot you if you don't!' Sandy snapped.

'That's enough of that.' The Captain's voice was curt. 'But listen, Rickhartz, now we know that you're a member of this gang there are a lot of charges against you that I'll be able to hunt up if I take the trouble. You needn't be afraid of the others—we'll look after them directly they're on the ground. If you'll do what Van Niekerk suggests I won't put my nose into the old files at headquarters as far as you're concerned.'

Darkie considered for a moment. 'All right,' he said, 'but you must give me back my gun.'

'Here, take it,' said Ernest promptly, evidently much relieved to be rid of the weapon.

'That's fair,' Moorries agreed, as it was handed over. 'Then you'll have the drop on them if they start in on you before we've had a chance to get busy.'

The two policemen carried Darkie across the open space and left him near the vast round tree trunk that supported the reed and wattle dwelling which had been so cunningly devised in the centre of its great branches. The others followed to within thirty yards and, Moorries' men rejoining them, they all lay down flat on their stomachs in the coarse grass, to await events.

The hearts of all of them were pounding with sick distress as the shaking, uneven voices of the two girls continued to float out in that terrible melancholy serenade from the tree-tops. The last bars of the song quavered into silence, then the crack of a whip lash sounded like a pistol shot. There was an agonised scream while the waiting men gritted their teeth below. Then the sobbing voices started the song over again.

'Hallo above there—Phil!' On Darkie's hail the singing ceased. Then a surprised shout came from Philbeach.

Tense in the grass the watchers waited, and soon a dark form dropped from the lower branches of the tree.

'Steady!' breathed Moorries. 'We've got to wait till Ginger comes down too.'

Philbeach said something in a low voice to Darkie and disappeared up into the branches again. Then Sandy, easing his strained position for a moment, noticed that Ernest was gone from behind him.

'Where's Ernest?' he whispered to Cornelius who was next in the line.

'Funked it again, I expect,' Cornelius replied abruptly,

'though we can't blame him as he hasn't got a gun. Hush! —here they are.'

Philbeach had appeared again and beside him the tall figure of Ginger. They walked the few yards to where Darkie was sitting, propped up against a boulder, and spread out a sling by which they evidently intended to hoist him up.

'Now!' cried Moorries, and his whole party, leaping to their feet, dashed forward.

Before the shout ended Philbeach had whipped out his gun and was blazing away at the running figures. Sandy felt a shot zip through his jacket and loosed off his automatic. From a few yards to Philbeach's right another succession of flashes stabbed the blackness of the night. Ginger was in action. One of the policemen fired and they ceased suddenly. Moorries was yelling to them to surrender but, catching his foot in a low bush, fell—his weapon going off in his hand.

With incredible speed for one of his bulk Philbeach dodged behind the great bole of the tree, but Sandy had seen him and followed. While shots were crashing on the farther side he charged in and Philbeach's pistol went off within a few inches of his ear, almost deafening him.

Sandy pressed the trigger of his automatic but the magazine was empty; he had forgotten to put in a fresh clip after the fight at Komati River. Dropping his gun, he lashed out with his right fist. The blow caught Philbeach full in the mouth and he went sprawling backwards. Sandy was on him like a leopard, his thumbs pressing into his antagonist's fleshy throat; but Ginger, whom the others had lost in the darkness, had crawled to the far side of the tree. Now he leapt at Sandy and struck him a glancing blow in the back of the head with his gun. Blinding stars circled before Sandy's eyes for a second, then he passed out and Philbeach, rolling from underneath him, sprang to his feet again.

'Where's Darkie?' he snarled at Ginger. 'I'll get that swine if it's the last thing I do.' Then, thrusting Sandy's body aside, he groped on the ground and recovered his gun.

In those few moments, Moorries, with his men and Cornelius, had been mixed up on the far side of the tree, afraid now to shoot for fear of mistaking each other for their enemies in the darkness, but Michael, coming round the trunk, ran full tilt into Philbeach.

'Got you!' he yelled and, pressing the trigger of his pistol, poured its remaining contents into the crouching figure. With a snarl of pain Philbeach was upon him and struck him flat with one blow of his great fist, but the others had rushed up instantly and a new burst of shooting lit the darkness.

Ginger went down to the Captain's gun, but Philbeach had blundered round the tree again and dashed across to Darkie. They fired together, Philbeach crumpled up with a scream of pain, and Darkie collapsed sideways with a grunting gasp, the blood pouring from his mouth.

The fight seemed over. One of the policemen flashed his torch into Ginger's face and saw at once that he was dead. The other two were helping Sandy to his feet, for Ginger's blow had only momentarily deprived him of his senses. Michael was already scaling the tree on his way to the two girls, with Cornelius hard behind him, and the Captain stooped over Darkie Rickhartz.

Realising that there was nothing to be done for him, he lowered Darkie's head to the ground, and turned to the place where Philbeach had dropped. His gun ready in his hand, he walked forward cautiously, but could find no body, so, calling up his men, they slipped fresh clips into their automatics, and began to hunt for the wounded desperado.

'He can't have got far,' Moorries muttered, and then his eye caught a faint movement in the darkness. There was a sudden grunt and a figure seemed to rise from the ground; the Captain and one of his men fired together. A coughing gurgle came from the spot and at the same time a sharp cry. Then, running forward, they found two bodies huddled in a heap.

Philbeach lay underneath, blood streaming from him by half a dozen wounds—quite dead. The other lay limp across him. The Captain shone his torch and one of the men turned the body over.

'My God!' he exclaimed. 'It's the chap they call Ernest.'

'Phew!' The Captain whistled as he focused his light on the trickle of blood which ran down Ernest's forehead. 'He's had a narrow squeak and no mistake.' A bullet had grazed the top of Ernest's head, cutting its way through his hair and knocking him unconscious.

They left Ernest propped against the tree trunk and came round it just in time to find the others lowering the two girls.

Their clothers were in rags and tatters, their faces white and haggard, but they were so overjoyed at their unexpected release that they were now weeping from excess of emotion. Sarie clung to Sandy as though she would never let him go, while Patricia sobbed hysterically on Michael's shoulder.

The Captain went up with his men to the Gorilla's cage and for twenty minutes, while the others comforted the girls, they were busy there ransacking the place for the diamonds, but when they came down Moorries' face wore a disappointed frown.

'They're not up there,' he said. 'We've searched every nook and corner. He hadn't got them on him either. Let's have a look at Ginger.'

Ginger was searched but the diamonds were not forth-coming and so, reluctantly, Moorries was compelled to agree that they should start back to the cars and accept Sandy's suggestion that Philbeach had probably buried the stones in some secret cache for fear that Darkie or Ginger might rob him.

They were becoming anxious about Ernest. He had not come round, although the wound on careful examination seemed to be quite a small one. However, it was bleeding still and they had no means of ascertaining if it was only a scalp wound or if the bullet had fractured his skull.

Apart from the fact that they were free now of anxiety about the girls, the struggle back through the bush seemed more terrible than ever. Ernest—unconscious—was carried by the police in the rug that had supported Darkie on the outward journey, but Michael, Sandy, and Cornelius—the latter now dragging his leg wearily—staggered on, doing their best to help the girls. They all seemed to have reached the limit of endurance for none of the men had slept for more than thirty-six hours and the girls only fitfully, during their long drive gagged and bound, in Philbeach's car the night before and for a short time during his absence that afternoon.

When they at last reached the cars Ernest was placed carefully in Sandy's, then Cornelius turned to Moorries.

'We've got to get him to a doctor at the earliest possible moment.'

The Captain nodded. 'I should think there's one in Ressano Garcia.'

'If there is he wouldn't be up to much in a rotten little dorp like that,' Sandy cut in, 'and Komati Poort won't offer us anything much better. The nearest place of any size is Lourenço Marques.'

Moorries hesitated. 'You're not supposed to be in Portuguese territory at all, you know.'

'I can't help it,' said Sandy. 'If his skull is cracked it's essential that he should have the very best attention.'

'We needn't worry about the Portuguese,' added Michael. 'The nice lad in the sunshine pyjamas gave us cards, and we can put our position right by seeing the British Consul in Lourenço Marques to-morrow morning.'

'It's eighty miles, you know,' Moorries hazarded.

'Well, Barberton is all of that, if not more,' Sandy countered, 'and that's the nearest place that's any good to us on the other side. Besides the road to Lourenço is so much better than those in the Union. We'll be able to make it in half the time.'

'All right, as you've seen the Portuguese authorities I'll content myself with telling them at the frontier that you've gone on—since this whole business has been a bit unofficial. Good luck to you.' Moorries turned away to where his own men were already waiting in his car, then suddenly he halted and came back—just as the others had settled themselves.

'You're mighty keen to get to Lourenço, aren't you? I wonder now. Come on. Out you hop!'

'Why, what's the matter?' exclaimed Michael.

'The matter is that I believe you've got those diamonds after all. You were up in that tree-top before I was.'

Michael shrugged and stepped out again. 'I'm afraid you're barking up the wrong tree this time. We've always told you that we've never had them. You can search the lot of us if you like.'

Moorries beckoned over his men and together they thoroughly searched the whole party. The girls allowed themselves to be gone over rather than be hauled back to the frontier and even the unconscious Ernest was lifted out that his pockets might be turned out and his trouser-tops pulled down. Then the police turned their attention to the car, took out the seats, rummaged the tool box and opened up the bonnet, but at last the Captain had to confess his suspicions unjustified and made them a generous apology.

They piled back into their car, Cornelius relieving Sandy of the wheel again, and bumped their way to the place where the track joined the road. Here the two cars separated, and after a cheery farewell to Moorries and his men, who were now chortling over the fact that they had put and end to the desperate criminal, known as the Gorilla, who had caused the police such trouble in the Northern Transvaal ten years before, Cornelius turned east along the broad highway to Lourenço Marques.

The headlights threw long beams of wavering light on the bush and trees edging the road. Patricia was sitting on Michael's knee, her arm round his neck, her face buried in his shoulder. Little tremors shook her and Michael patted her gently—soothing her frayed nerves as the car swept on. Sarie sat, tense and rigid, next to Sandy. He stole a look at her face occasionally and was worried to see the fixed stare of her eyes. Suddenly a bird came into the short arc of light above the bonnet of the car—flying straight as an arrow for the screen in front of Sarie's face. Just as it seemed that it must smash itself and the glass it swerved up—swift as thought— and vanished into the darkness. The shock seemed to break her calm—she put her hands up to her eyes and shuddered— Sandy saw that she was crying silently.

After a little her weeping ceased and, to distract her thoughts, Sandy said suddenly:

'I bet Philbeach cached those stones either in the tree or somewhere near it. If I thought there were a hope in heaven of finding them we'd come out here again to-morrow but when a man like that starts hiding things there's devilish little chance of anyone ever finding them.'

'No—they've gone for good this time,' Michael agreed. 'So this is the end of my African adventure, and I'll never be able to keep up Harcourt Priory like my father did now, but it's been a marvellous experience and we ought to be mighty thankful that we're all here safe and alive.'

Sandy put his arms round Sarie's shoulders and drew her to him. 'I'm thankful for more than that,' he murmured. 'If it hadn't been for old Uncle John's will I might never have met Sarie.'

Patricia pressed closer to her cousin, but at Sandy's words a sudden spasm of pain crossed his face in the darkness.

After that last exhausting trudge through the bush a new spurt of energy seemed to have come to Cornelius and, at the top of his form, he drove at a fine speed along the straight deserted road, until at one o'clock in the morning, they entered the capital of Portuguese East Africa. As they hummed through the fine tree-lined boulevards of the town and passed up the hill out of it again, Michael leaned forward: 'Where the deuce are you taking us now, Cornelius?'

'The Polana,' Cornelius told him. 'The best hotel in Africa, south of Cairo.' And a few moments later they pulled up at the porch of the great cream building perched on the cliff above the broad sweep of Delagoa Bay.

The night porter was amazed to see this strange dishevelled crew of belated visitors, but he recognised Cornelius at once as a frequent patron of the hotel, and promised that rooms and a first-class supper should be available immediately.

As Cornelius limped back to the car he saw with sudden surprise that Ernest was getting out unaided, for he had never even stirred during the two hours of their journey.

'I'm all right,' Ernest assured him in answer to his inquiries. 'Bit of a headache, that's all. Where have we got to now?'

'Lourenço Marques, in Portuguese East,' Sandy told him, as they paused at the office to sign the visitor's book.

Through a hatchway a portion of the manager's office could be seen and, as Ernest looked up from scrawling his signature, he suddenly exclaimed: 'Why, there's a caricature of Harry Preston. That makes this place just like an hotel at home.'

They laughed and moved towards the lift, but when they got upstairs they felt that there had been much in his casual statement as they revelled in the luxury of warm baths and well-furnished rooms.

Half an hour later they assembled for the supper that had been prepared in the great empty dining-room. Their tiredness had fallen from them, replaced by a wonderful feeling of security and well-being, as they were led to a round table in a corner of the room that had been re-lit for them.

'Champagne,' said Sandy, as Cornelius took the wine list from the waiter. 'We need it.'

'Why not?' Cornelius replied, giving a number, then, as the man moved off to execute the order, he added: 'We ought to celebrate our victory even if we haven't got the diamonds.'

'Who says so?' Ernest closed one of his small sharp eyes in a joyful wink. 'What do you think I took a chance on tackling Philbeach for?'

'Good God! you haven't got them!' Sandy exclaimed.

'Of course I have. I was only knocked out for a moment and it wasn't half a laugh making those coppers carry me back through the bush—I had a nice forty winks in the car on the way here, too.'

'You're joking. The police searched you,' Patricia protested.

Ernest lifted his left knee table-high and pulled up the leg of his trousers. Round his calf, putty fashion, was wound the belt that Michael had carried. 'That's an old trick,' he grinned. 'As luck would have it the coppers were so anxious to get up into the aviary that they gave yours truly time enough to fix it. All we've got to do now is to get my pal in

Hatton Garden to put them on the market. Then half goes to Michael and me—and you can split the rest between you.'

After that supper became an uproarious meal with magnums of champagne flowing. Ernest and Cornelius looked like staying there all night but Sandy was dying to talk to Sarie and Michael to Patricia. So the two couples left them and went towards the gauze swing-doors on to the terrace, beyond which Delagoa Bay spread below—beautiful in the moonlight.

'I suppose the time has come for us to congratulate each other,' Sandy said to Michael as they were about to turn in different directions, but Michael looked at Patricia with a sudden painful hesitation. Their double first cousinship and the thought of imbecile children still lay between them; then he looked back at Sandy.

'I congratulate you with all my heart, but I'm afraid Fate has been a bit unkind to Patricia and myself. We're both so keen to have children that we dare not marry.'

'Good God!' exclaimed Sandy, sweeping the wayward lock of hair out of his eye. 'Of course—I haven't seen you since you set off into the Kalahari from Zwart Modder, except when we picked you up half-delirious in the desert and during this ghastly time we've been through to-day. I've never had a chance to tell you about those letters of old Uncle John's that Sarie and I found in his derelict wagon.'

'What about them?' asked Michael listlessly.

'I went through the lot afterwards,' Sandy was almost stammering with excitement. 'Most of them were love letters but some of them were from Sarie's father, who it seems was a bit of a rip in his younger days. When he was over in England he had an affair with Patricia's mother, and he seemed to think it would amuse his old friend John to know that they had been having a most marvellous time together while Henry was in Ireland. In a later letter he made it quite clear that Patricia was on the way as a cuckoo in the nest; so she is Sarie's half-sister and half South African—but she's not related to you at all. I've got the letters upstairs. Shall I go up and bring them down?'

'No, let's leave it till the morning,' said Michael, with a new note in his voice. 'Oh, Sandy, this is wonderful!' Then he grabbed Patricia by the arm.

'Off you go,' laughed Sarie, 'even for you I won't spare Sandy another second of this moonlight.'

To be published in June 1972:

GATEWAY TO HELL

by Dennis Wheatley, price 35p

A new Black Magic story, appearing for the first time in paperback:

In Russia, in the Spanish Civil War, in Poland and Rumania, the Duke de Richleau and the 'Modern Musketeers' had adventured together. In England and the Caribbean they had faced Satanists and the Devil himself.

But now, one of them, Rex van Ryn, was accused of robbing a Buenos Aires bank of a million dollars, appeared to have as a friend an ex-SS Gruppenführer, was even claimed to be a murderer. Now he was missing.

The answer to the mystery seemed to lie in the heart of the desolate Bolivian Andes. And in the search, Rex's friends were to face once again the revolting orgiastic rites of the Satanists and to discover a Devil-inspired plan to bring open race war to every city in the world.